"A marvel. Cha finds new angles on a city that has been the focus of myriad stories and films. Unique and totally gripping."
—MICHAEL CONNELLY

"A mastery of form, Cha absolutely nails it. It is absolutely brilliant, and it keeps the pages turning."
—TODAY

"Elegant, suspenseful."
—NEW YORK TIMES BOOK REVIEW

"Steph Cha has taken a dark moment in Los Angeles's violent history and cracked it wide open, creating a prism of understanding. . . . A touching portrait of two families bound together by a split-second decision that tore a hole through an entire city."
—ATTICA LOCKE

"A propulsive, well-told, and, most important of all, well-researched journey of two families. . . . Cha's writing is memorable and often poetic."
—SAN FRANCISCO CHRONICLE

"Cha's prose is poignant and riveting. She writes with radiant clarity. . . . A tender story about pursuing justice and the Herculean task of finding forgiveness."
—BUZZFEED

"A gripping and deftly plotted story of two families, and two communities, set in the aftermath of a police shooting in Los Angeles. Steph Cha's *Your House Will Pay* is a sensitive portrait of racial tension, buried memory, and the difficulty of reconciliation." —Laila Lalami, author of *The Other Americans*

"In *Your House Will Pay,* Steph Cha fearlessly explores the duality of L.A.'s promise and betrayal, its vision of new beginnings and the brutal divisions that cut between race and class. Cha takes her place as one of the city's most eloquent storytellers in this soul-searching illumination of one of the tragedies at the heart of the 1992 L.A. riots." —Walter Mosley, Edgar Award-winning author of *Down the River unto the Sea*

"A haunting portrait of two lives—and a city—in turmoil, *Your House Will Pay* is both a crackling page-turner and a deeply felt work of eloquence, clarity, and devastating insight. With this riveting standalone mystery, Steph Cha firmly establishes herself as not just one of crime fiction's most exciting young voices, but one of its most exciting voices—period." —Elizabeth Little, author of *Dear Daughter*

"Steph Cha's *Your House Will Pay* is extraordinary, a deeply felt and sharply observed exploration of the ties that bind and divide family, community, and nation. It's moving, compelling, surprising, funny, explosive, and deeply human—an unforgettable novel." —Lou Berney, author of *November Road*

"A propulsive, lacerating novel about two families caught in the turmoil of a city and nation in crisis, and the tensions that drive history and fate, pit freedom against love, and lace our own best impulses to our worst. Fearless, insightful, and alight with a brutal compassion, *Your House Will Pay* is a devastating exploration of grief, shame, and deeply buried truths, and the hope that endures when all else seems lost." —Catherine Chung, author of *The Tenth Muse*

YOUR HOUSE WILL PAY

YOUR HOUSE WILL PAY

A NOVEL

STEPH CHA

ecco

An Imprint of HarperCollins*Publishers*

HarperCollins books may be purchased for educational, business, or sales pro-motional use. For information, please email the Special Markets Department at SPsales@harpercollins.com.

A hardcover edition of this book was published in 2019 by Ecco, an imprint of HarperCollins Publishers.

FIRST ECCO PAPERBACK EDITION PUBLISHED 2020

Designed by Michelle Crowe

Library of Congress Cataloging-in-Publication Data has been applied for.

ISBN 978-0-06-286884-8 (pbk.)

24 25 26 27 28 LBC 9 8 7 6 5

For Maria Joo

We ain't meant to survive, 'cause it's a setup.

—Tupac Shakur, *Keep Ya Head Up*,
dedicated to the memory of Latasha Harlins

Even to this day I can't believe something like this could happen to our family.

—letter from Soon Ja Du to Judge Joyce Karlin, October 25, 1991

YOUR HOUSE WILL PAY

I

Well, this is it," said Ava. "I don't know how we're supposed to find these fools."

Shawn gaped at the crowd gathered across the street. The movie wasn't supposed to start for another hour and a half, but there had to be hundreds of people waiting outside the theater. It was dark already, too, hard to make out faces even with the neat row of lamps lining the sidewalk. Ava said Westwood was white people territory, but almost everyone here was black, a lot of them high school kids. They'd have to get closer to pick out Ray and his friends.

Ava grabbed Shawn's hand as they crossed the street. He pulled back, thinking of all those older kids seeing him get dragged along by his sister. "Aw, Ave, I'm not a baby," he said.

"Who said you were a baby? I just don't want to lose you."

They walked slowly down the sidewalk, starting from the box office, where the marquee overhead announced the showtimes for *New Jack City*. Shawn smiled. He'd been looking forward to this night all week. Everyone at school was talking about this movie, and he was going on opening night. It didn't matter that Aunt Sheila had made Ray and Ava take him when they said they'd be watching *White Fang*. He was here now, sneaking into an R-rated movie, just like them.

"Ava! Shawn!"

He turned to see Ray coming toward them. Ray's best friend, Duncan, was with him, his face lit up with a big grin. Shawn let go of Ava's hand, hoping they hadn't seen.

"There you are," she said. "This is crazy. We gotta wait in that line? Don't tell me you gave up our spot."

"That's the line to get tickets," said Duncan. "We already got ours." He made a show of fanning them out with both hands while Ray whooped and danced behind him.

"You guys are stupid." Ava laughed. "See, Shawn, this is what happens when you cut school to go to a movie."

"Hey, show some gratitude. We been here for hours," said Ray. He balled his hand into a fist and shook it at Shawn. "And you remember what happens if you tell Mom."

"I ain't scared of *you*, Ray. But Aunt Sheila'd whup all three of us."

Ray laughed and put his fist down. He was just joking anyway. He knew Shawn would keep his mouth shut. He hadn't told on Ray or even Ava since he was too young to know better. And if he did want to get them in trouble, he had plenty of other ways. Hell, if Aunt Sheila wouldn't let them see a gang movie, what if she knew Ray was in a real gang?

She wouldn't understand it. Not like Shawn did. Aunt Sheila knew there were gangs, but she talked about them like they weren't her problem. She never warned her boys not to join. She just acted like she didn't have to, seeing as she didn't raise troublemakers and thugs. Her boys weren't like those bad ones. The ones who shot dogs for spite and disobeyed their mothers.

But it seemed like half the kids in the neighborhood were in gangs. A few of them were scary—the dude who shot his neighbor's dog, he was a legit bad dude—but not the ones Shawn knew. Duncan was intimidating but not in that way. He was just larger than life, funny and slick and popular with girls, the kind of guy Shawn hoped he might be when he turned sixteen. And there was no one in the world less scary than Ray. Shawn should know—they'd shared a room since Shawn was five. Ray wore Spider-Man boxers under all his slick blue gear. He sang songs from the radio in a girl voice to make Shawn laugh before they went to sleep. Ray and Ava were the same age, but Ava teased him like another younger brother, giving him crap for his goofy haircuts, his bad grades. If Ray was a Crip, anyone could be a Crip.

They walked over toward a closed electronics store, where Shawn recognized a bunch of kids from their neighborhood, all around Ray and Ava's age. Some of them were maybe even seventeen, old enough to get into the movie without pretending.

"Look who we found!" Duncan hollered, pointing at Ava.

Shawn watched as they all swarmed around his sister, greeting her with hugs and high fives. She'd gone to school with them until ninth grade, when she'd started at Westchester, and they must have been happy to see her.

One of the girls nodded at Shawn. He didn't know her name, but he remembered her face. She'd been in choir with Ava in middle school, and he could still picture the way her lips moved when she sang. She was even prettier now. He put his hands in his pockets and nodded back at her.

"You babysitting?" she asked Ava.

Shawn shriveled with embarrassment. He slouched, hoping it wouldn't show on his face. Ava smiled at him, and he knew she saw through him. She wrapped an arm around his shoulders and turned back to the group. "Y'all know my brother, Shawn," she said.

He stuck close to Ava as they joined the others. He stood quietly, watching the way they all goofed around together, so smooth and easy, spreading across the sidewalk like it was their own front lawn. Even Ray and Ava shone like strangers in this crew, looking older and cooler than they ever did at home. He hung back and listened, waiting for an opening. He wished he had something good to say, something funny or sharp, to show he wasn't just Ava's wack little brother.

Ava took her Walkman out of her backpack and put her head-phones crooked on her head, so they covered one ear. Shawn wished he had a Walkman. Ava had gotten hers for Christmas. He'd asked for one, too, but Aunt Sheila said he didn't need one, and anyway, he knew she wouldn't buy him any cassettes with swear words. Ava hit play and her eyes went dreamy. Her fingers tapped out a tune on her thighs.

"What you listening to?" asked Duncan.

Shawn thought of his aunt's strictness with new resentment. If he only had that Walkman, Duncan might ask him what kind of music he liked. He had a list of artists ready to go: Ice Cube, Tupac, A Tribe Called Quest, Michael Jackson. Maybe he'd leave off Michael Jackson.

"Nothing you ever heard of," said Ava, smiling.

Duncan snatched the headphones off her and put them on. "What's this?"

"Just some of the sickest tracks of the 1890s." She snatched the headphones back, and everyone laughed. They all caught her listening to classical music, and she wasn't even embarrassed.

"I heard of Chopin. Girl, we all heard of Chopin."

"This is Debussy. And y'all only know Chopin 'cause of me."

It was true, at least for Shawn and Ray. Ava played piano. She was good at it, too, going to competitions all around town. Aunt Sheila made them go watch her, even when they had to drive out to far, random places like Glendale and Irvine. Once, when she played in Inglewood, all her friends showed up, too—to make fun of her, they said, but he saw how they shut up and listened when she played.

They still bagged on her, though, just like they bagged on her for being a magnet school nerd. Like they didn't even think it was all that wack.

"You listen to this shit for fun?" asked Duncan.

"I don't even want to know what *you* do for fun," she said, putting her headphones back on.

Shawn couldn't believe it. While he just stood there, his sister—a girl—was making the whole crew, even Duncan, howl and slap their knees. She looked in the zone, all relaxed, her face in a half smile. Shawn crossed his arms and looked away.

There was plenty around to look at. Westwood was a nice place, like an outdoor mall: orderly streets and bright stores, palm trees taller than the buildings. It looked so much tidier than their neighborhood, nothing fading or falling apart. On the way over, Ava told him how everyone went nuts a few years ago because of one gang shooting, the only one anyone seemed to care about because it was here, and the victim was an Asian girl. Westwood was far, but not that far—less than forty-five minutes, even with Ava driving like an old lady, afraid of messing up Uncle Richard's car. But it felt like a different city. He watched the people in line for the box office, reading the impatience, the excitement, on their faces. He wondered if they all had come a long way to see this movie, too.

The line was still long, he noticed, and it looked even more disorganized than it had earlier. The movie was set to start in half an hour, and he worried it would sell out and all these people would have to go home. Then he saw that the crowd was shifting. It pushed forward, becoming less and less like a line, surging toward the box office. There was shouting, too, indistinct but building.

He looked at Ava, who was pulling her headphones down. When he caught her eye, he saw that she felt what he felt. There was something new and heavy in the air.

"Hey," she said. "Something's going on at the theater."

Ray stood on his toes to take in the scene. "Maybe they opened the doors. It's about that time."

Duncan clapped a hand on Shawn's shoulder. "How 'bout you help us out? Go run and see what's happening."

"Me?" Shawn's eyes widened, and then he straightened up, ready to prove himself useful. "Yeah, no prob."

"I'll go with you," said Ava, shoving her Walkman in her backpack.

"Nah, Ave, it's okay. I'll be right back." He jogged off before his sister could follow.

He dashed across the street and pushed forward into the heart of the crowd, navigating the gaps until they narrowed, then disappeared, still a good twenty feet from the box office. He couldn't go any farther; he was trapped, lodged like a scrap of meat in a row of teeth. It was loud now, everything pounding and close. Someone's body odor hit him right in the throat.

He looked up as the man to his left raised his hands and cupped them to his mouth. The man shouted, "I'll bet y'all praying this is the last time we show up in Westwood."

Shawn tapped his shoulder, and the man turned to him with fire in his eyes. "What's happening?" asked Shawn.

"They saying they sold too many tickets and we gotta leave."

"What if we already got tickets?"

"Don't matter. The show's canceled." He raised his voice again. "'Cause they scared of us. They see ten black people and they think we bring the hood."

"We got our tickets already. We paid for them and everything."

"That don't mean shit."

"But that ain't fair."

The man laughed. He wasn't much older than Ray and them, but his laugh was old and bitter. "What's fair mean to them? Didn't you hear about Rodney King?"

Shawn nodded like he knew all about it. Rodney King—he did know the name. A black guy the cops beat on last week or something. Aunt Sheila said it wasn't right, but that the guy should've known better than to run from the cops and that he wouldn't have been in that situation if he hadn't been a felon in the first place. She and Ava almost got in a fight about it over dinner.

"So there's no movie?" Shawn asked one last time.

He turned to go back to his group, but the path had closed behind him. He couldn't even see his way out. If only he were taller.

He felt like a little kid again, stranded and anxious and low to the rumbling ground.

Everyone was talking all at once, and the voices rose higher and higher, stacking and morphing into a giant mass of sound. He could almost see it, like a picture in a comic book: a fireball building and building until it was ready to blow.

His heart hopped and his palms prickled with sweat. This wasn't right. He could feel it coming—something destructive, something big, something permanent. There was a while, after his mom died, when he used to get nightmares. They took place in a dark old house he'd never seen before, where he knew he was alone. The details always evaporated when he woke up, but even now he remembered the gasping terror of those nights, the relief of escape from the depths of something he didn't understand. There must have been a time when he woke up looking for his mother, but the ritual he adopted—the only one that calmed him—was finding Ava the moment he opened his eyes. He needed the solidity of her body, the sound of her breath, to locate himself in his room, his house. It was why he slept in her bed, burrowed next to her, long after he knew he'd get made fun of if anyone at school found out.

That was years ago, a phase of his childhood, so distant he wasn't sure how long it lasted. Yet there were still times he'd wake up in the middle of the night, and at the cusp of consciousness, when the dream world lingered, scan his room in a panic before remembering—he was thirteen now, and Ava was there, just in the next room.

Where was she now? He had to find her. Hold her in his sights. He moved through the crowd, getting jostled, his jaw open, eyes wide, alone and afraid and searching for her.

Then the crowd loosened, expanded into the streets, a spread of nerves and sweat and energy. Shawn felt the excitement jolt through him, and with it, something new—a fever in his blood.

Someone knocked over a trash can. In the weak light of city nighttime, the spill of garbage seemed to glow.

A boy rushed past him carrying a rock the size of a soda can, and Shawn wondered where it could've come from, this rough chunk of nature in a village trimmed with locked doors and polished glass. Then he noticed three wide-shouldered men surrounding a tree, breaking off branches. They looked almost calm—the fire in their eyes was not wildfire, but a controlled, channeled anger.

He followed them. He wasn't alone—the crowd seemed to converge behind them. From the corner of one eye, he saw a flash of movement, a boy jumping to land on a parked car, but he stayed behind the three men with their branches, trailing them with a sense of wonder. Fists flew up all around him, and voices rose in exuberance and fury, their words swarming together until they morphed into chants. "Black power!" "Fight the power!"

And the men swung their branches, shattering a wall of glass.

He'd seen glass break plenty of times before, but never a pane so large and clean, so invisibly solid. This was a breach between worlds, a pried-open passage to another dimension. The crowd shouted again, this time with a clamor of triumph, and rushed over the broken glass. Shawn saw that he was back in front of the electronics store. There was no sign of Ava or Ray or their friends—they'd been in the way of the horde and scattered. He didn't know where to go, so he pressed forward, his whole body thrumming as he crossed the jagged threshold.

He found a blank stretch of wall where he could make himself small, where he could stand alone and look for someone he knew in this chaos. He watched as people he'd never seen before acted in ways he'd never seen either. The men with the branches were swallowed in the crowd, as was their proud, purposeful aura, replaced by a buzzing frenzy. The store was stocked full of fragile, expensive things that were laid out for the taking, their surfaces glinting in the low light. The crowd was going nuts, grabbing what they could, and the noise was so loud that he barely noticed the high fruitless whine of the alarm. He gazed at the scene, and he thought that all these people would get in trouble, that he should get far away from them.

It took him a good five minutes to weave his way out of the store and into the street. The crowd was wild, but there was a direction to its flow like there was to a roaring river. Shawn stepped in, joining in its movement, pressing forward, away from where they'd all come.

He heard someone shout, "Move!" and he jumped out of the way in time to watch a giant man swerve by, perched on a brand-new bicycle that looked meant for a child. He watched him ride off, wondering if he'd fall and knock people over, cause a fight.

Then Shawn heard his name. His sister's voice. He snapped his head in what he thought was the right direction, but he didn't see her, and he wondered if he was just being hopeful.

"Shawn! Up here!"

Ava stood on the edge of a planter, elevated two feet above the rest of the crowd. Making herself a tower so he could find her.

She stayed there, grinning, until he scrambled over. When he got closer, he saw Ray and Duncan were waiting, too.

"There you are," she said, hopping down to the ground. He had to stop himself from hugging her and was glad and embarrassed when she hugged him instead.

Duncan whistled. "Alright, let's roll."

He was holding a boom box over one shoulder. It was big, black, and shiny, with a tape deck and a CD player. Two speakers that bugged out like a fly's eyes.

"Where did you get that?" Shawn asked dumbly.

"I had it the whole time. Didn't you notice?" Duncan laughed and pointed to the electronics store. "You want one, you better act quick."

"I'm cool," Shawn said, as if he might nab a boom box next time, just wasn't feeling it today.

The truth was he'd never stolen anything before, not even a candy bar. The first year he and Ava lived with Aunt Sheila, Ray got caught stealing from Frank's Liquor, their old corner store. Nothing big, just a magazine—it had boobs on the cover; Shawn could picture it exactly—but Frank the Crank made Ray call Aunt Sheila, saying it was either her or the police. He was a huge jerk, an old Korean dude with cigarette breath and broken English who was always eyeing Ray like he was up to no good, but they had to do what he said.

Aunt Sheila showed up crying and shouting about God and prison. It was enough of a scene that they switched corner stores after that, and Shawn learned forever that stealing meant wrath from God, life in prison, and a volcanic eruption of grief from Aunt Sheila.

"Suit yourself." Duncan nodded at Ray and Ava. "But you know these hoods getting theirs. Show him what you got."

"Shut up, Duncan," said Ray. "None of this is happening, okay, Shawn? It's all a dream." He waved his fingers in front of Shawn's face, as if that could make this all any more dreamlike, this night like no other he'd ever lived.

Ava rolled her eyes, but then she produced a cassette tape from her back pocket. "I know it's kind of old, but I saw it and thought you might want it," she said. "You can borrow my Walkman. Just don't tell Aunt Sheila."

Shawn took it, not knowing what to say. Michael Jackson looked up at him, unsmiling in tight black pants and a black leather jacket. The word "BAD" splashed over his head, spelled out in red letters. He ran his thumb across the cover, bunching up the plastic wrap.

"Thanks," he said. Ava mussed his hair.

Duncan clapped his hands over the boom box. "Alright, smooth criminals. Let's move."

He marched ahead of them, and Shawn noticed he was wearing a new jacket, his old windbreaker tied around his waist, his pockets bulging with God knew what stolen junk.

"He looks like the Grinch who stole Westwood," said Shawn.

Ray and Ava burst out laughing.

The village was spattered with glass and trash, as if all the storefronts had retched out their guts. The air smelled like smoke and piss, and in every direction, people ran like wild children, hollering and thrashing.

But Shawn wasn't scared anymore.

A metal clothing rack stood in the middle of the street, most of its hangers bare, like bones picked clean on a slab of ribs. Shawn stuck his foot out as they passed, sent it rolling until it wobbled and fell over with a rattling crash.

"Shawn!" Ava shouted. But there was delight in her voice.

The night and the mob and the violent roar—he knew, with instinctive clarity, that these things wouldn't hurt them. If this was fire, they were flame. They were part of it, safe within the blaze.

ONE

SATURDAY, JUNE 15, 2019

It took Grace twenty minutes to find parking. She passed a seven-dollar lot, thinking there must be cheaper options, and wound up driving farther and farther away, gaping at the prices, before turning around and deciding the first lot would do just fine. Downtown was a maze of one-way streets, and they seemed to guide her away from where she was going. Two wrong turns and she was in a sketchy area, both sides of the street lined with tents. She glanced at her door, made sure it was locked.

By the time she parked—in a nine-dollar lot a good deal farther than she wanted—she was flustered and slightly sweaty, with the bad feeling that always clung to her when she was running late. It would take another ten minutes for her to walk to the courthouse, where she'd have to find Miriam and Blake in the crowd. She texted her sister.

Sorry, just parked. Where are you?

She was almost there, preparing her apology, when Miriam responded.

We're on our way! Ubering.

It was 6:13, almost fifteen minutes after when Miriam had told Grace to show up. Grace was relieved, but she felt like a sucker for even trying to come on time. She should've known better—Miriam ran on what she called "Korean time," though she was the only one in their family who wasn't fastidiously punctual. But this was a memorial for Alfonso Curiel, someone Miriam claimed to care about; Grace would've thought she'd make an exception, maybe start getting ready before it was time to leave the house.

She reminded herself that she hadn't seen Miriam in over three weeks. It wouldn't do any good to start the night mad at her, even if she had managed to turn their hangout into a whole stupid thing at the last minute, with Grace third-wheeling when all she'd wanted was to get some Thai food with her sister. Tonight was supposed to be Park girls only, but then this memorial had popped up, and Miriam got Grace to agree to go with her before dinner.

It was the kind of thing Miriam was always inviting her to on Facebook; Grace never went, and once in a while Miriam would scold her for her inattention, her indifference, her laziness, like it didn't matter that Grace actually worked a full-time job, or that her job was in Northridge. This time, Grace had no excuse not to go. She had the day off from the pharmacy, and she was already planning to see Miriam in L.A. When Blake invited himself along, she couldn't even argue—it wasn't like she could stop him from attending a public gathering. She wished he'd had the sense to make his own dinner plans, but he made a reservation for three instead, at some new downtown spot Miriam wanted to check out. His treat, of course. Grace was low-key dreading the next several hours, and Miriam had already left her hanging.

The memorial was in front of the federal courthouse, a huge shining cube of a building that looked like an evil Apple Store. There was a crowd gathered, maybe a hundred people, listening in silence to a large black man in the middle of what seemed like an impassioned speech. Grace stood back, wondering where she was supposed to wait for her sister.

She lingered on the sidewalk until she noticed another group a few yards away. There were about ten of them loitering, white men in their twenties and thirties, all of them in red hats and black polo shirts, like an aged-out frat or marching band. One held a sign that said COME GET SOME OF THIS, ANTIFA. She couldn't remember who Antifa was, but she wanted to get away from this crew. They gave her the same creepy feeling as the white dudes who took Korean in college, just to stare silently at the girls.

She joined the back row of the crowd and faced the way everyone else was facing, hoping to blend in. She was here; she might as well pay attention.

It wasn't like she didn't care. She understood that there was a lot of tragedy in the world, and it bothered her, for sure, that people were racist and horrible, and that black people kept dying.

And this was a terrible story, even as these things went. Alfonso Curiel was just a kid, a high school student who lived with his parents in Bakersfield. Two nights ago, a police officer shot him dead in his own backyard. One of his friends posted on Facebook, saying he'd been with Alfonso at a movie just an hour earlier. He said the boy was always forgetting his keys and that he was probably trying to get in through the back, and some neighbor had called the police on him.

He was totally innocent, from the sounds of it. It was an awful shame.

The man up front spoke loudly, though the noise of downtown swallowed some of his volume. He stood tall in a black suit with a black shirt and a black tie—he had to be a pastor. Grace recognized the stance of holy authority, the rich boom of his words, before she even started listening.

She heard the name of the dead boy, and she leaned forward, bowing her head, to hear what the pastor was saying.

"He was just trying to get into his home," he said. "His own house, where he lived with his mommy and daddy. See, it don't matter what you do if you're black in America. You can stay in your neighborhood, on your street, and still, some cop can find you in your own backyard. You can be an unarmed black boy, and someone can just come in and kill you with the full blessing of the law. And that goes for our women and girls, too. Remember our sisters. Remember Sandra Bland, remember Rekia Boyd."

He turned to an elderly woman standing next to him and placed a large hand on her shoulder before speaking again.

"Remember Ava Matthews, right here in L.A."

Grace listened to the pastor, yielding to the power of his voice. There was a murmur and a snapping of fingers—she'd never seen that before, but she recognized it as an amen.

"Alfonso Curiel's mother gave an interview last night. Said he was a good kid, never any trouble. Got good grades. Wanted to be a doctor. That's the kind of kid he was—a kid who did everything right. He's in heaven now, no doubt about it. But here, he didn't get a chance to live his dreams. Here, we lost another one. Only thing we can get for him here is justice."

Grace looked at the woman at the pastor's side, holding a homemade sign, a piece of poster board taped to what looked like a yardstick. She wiped tears from her eyes with her free hand, and for a second, Grace thought she must be the mother. But no, she was too old. In her sixties at least, with a crown of tight gray curls and deep grooves running under soft, round cheeks. The grandmother, maybe. She stood with such sadness even the sign listed forward, limp with grief. JUSTICE FOR ALFONSO CURIEL, it said, and under the words, a black-and-white picture. A handsome, round-faced boy, serious but bright-eyed in a collared shirt. A school portrait. He was supposed to go to college. He was supposed to be a doctor.

Grace felt dizzy and closed her eyes. When she opened them again, she was tearing up, too.

Miriam was right. It was wrong of Grace, selfish of her, to look away when there was so much injustice in the world. It had been too easy for her to feel nothing for Alfonso Curiel, to do nothing to honor his death. She had let herself luxuriate in apathy, her world separate from the real world.

Her heart swelled with wretched humility and righteous, motivated passion. It was a familiar feeling, one she knew from her church days, the feeling of Christian revival. She was full of love, abundant and pure and impersonal, enough to reach every fallen soul, to take part in the sorrow of all.

She was paying such close attention that she didn't notice her sister until she was by her side, Blake looming behind her. "You came," Miriam whispered in her ear, her voice breaking Grace's concentration. She gave Grace a quick hug, then drew back and looked her over. "You dressed up. Nice."

Grace felt herself flush. She'd put on makeup and real clothes tonight, something she didn't do often, as she spent most of her life in a lab coat and orthopedic shoes, seeing old Korean patients. She was wearing a black cap-sleeved dress, a little high on the thigh, that she'd worn over opaque tights for a recent church halmoni's funeral. It seemed like a smart choice when she was riffling through her closet that afternoon—somber enough for a service, sufficiently cute for dinner—but looking around now, she felt both frumpy and overdressed. There were others in black, but they wore T-shirts, blazoned with phrases like I CAN'T BREATHE and BLACK GIRL MAGIC. She just wanted to blend in and be respectful, and she'd managed to show up looking like Wednesday Addams.

Miriam, for her part, was dressed for a music festival, wearing some kind of sexy kimono thing, all loose floral silk and breezy sleeves over a cropped top and torn-up denim shorts. It was a ridiculous outfit, even discounting where they were, but because this was Miriam, she looked fantastic. Grace had always been envious of her sister's sense of style, which she had never been able to imitate with any success, even when Miriam loaned her clothes or took her shopping. It didn't help that Miriam had always been an inch taller and ten pounds thinner than Grace, the gap as constant as their difference in age. There was nothing to stop Grace from stealing this exact outfit and wearing it tomorrow, except that she knew she'd look like a hair washer at a second-rate Korean salon.

"The fucking Nazi goon squad is here," said Blake, nodding at the group of milky frat boys Grace had noticed earlier.

"Ignore them," said Miriam. "They're dying for someone to start shit."

Blake made a face like he'd been put on time-out. "What kind of lowlifes protest a memorial?" he said, loud enough to carry. A few people turned to look at him. He had a point, though of course no one else was trying to agitate while the pastor was speaking.

Blake and Miriam had been together for almost two years now, and Grace still didn't really get what her sister saw in him, unless it was just that he paid the bills while she bummed around on Twitter and chipped away at a screenplay or her long-suffering novel. He could maybe pass for handsome—he was tall with blue eyes; that did most of the work—but he was fifteen years older than Miriam, with receding blond hair and a tendency to wear statement blazers with glossy sneakers. He was successful at least—a screenwriter who'd created a popular television show about Appalachian drug addicts. Grace found it interesting that Miriam railed against the white maleness of Hollywood when she was in love with the whitest male Hollywood had ever known. Even Grace noticed the stark whiteness of his show, and, as Miriam liked to point out, Grace hardly ever noticed stuff like that.

He compensated in the most annoying ways, like telling everyone he was a feminist and practically a communist and asking people on Facebook to recommend books by women of color, as if Miriam and Google couldn't do that for him. One time, Grace peeked at his Twitter and saw that he'd posted something like "Listen up, fellas, oral sex is a two-way street." Miriam had liked the tweet, and Grace would've paid good money to burn it out of her memory.

A wave of applause caught Grace off guard—the pastor had finished his speech, but she'd stopped listening to him minutes ago.

"Now we're gonna hear from our sister Sheila Holloway," he said, putting his hand back on the older woman's shoulder.

Miriam watched, her eyes intense and misty. She was all attention, now that she was finally here. Grace listened long enough to satisfy her curiosity—the speaker wasn't the grandmother, just a community member or something—but the woman was quieter than the pastor. It took an effort to make sense of her words over the noise of the crowd, and after a minute, Grace stopped trying. She couldn't find her way back to her rapture; she was already starting to forget the feeling. It was like trying to fall back asleep to dream the rest of a promising dream.

The restaurant wasn't even a restaurant. It was a bar with food in Little Tokyo, and everything they ordered was cute and tiny, like toy food in a Japanese gift shop. Grace got tipsy without meaning to, taking small but steady sips from her screwdriver. She wasn't much of a drinker, and the vodka hit her fast, her blood warming around it.

She was still working on the screwdriver—the second half more tolerable than the first—when Blake made a trip to the bar and returned with three tumblers of brown liquid. "They have a lot of great Japanese whiskeys here," he said. "I got us some Yamazaki Single Malt."

Grace eyed the three glasses while Blake offered one to Miriam. She could tell from Blake's insufferable connoisseur tone that the whiskey was probably expensive. Miriam took a sip and made a noise of appreciation. Blake looked pleased, and Grace returned to her screwdriver while he held forth on Japanese whiskey.

"You should try it," he said, pushing the third tumbler toward her. "It tastes like honey. Honest to God."

Grace sniffed it and almost gagged; she didn't like the taste of alcohol, and brown liquor was the worst.

"I don't think this is for me," she said, setting it down.

"Oh, come on. If you can drink that shit, you can drink anything." He gestured at her screwdriver—it was the second time he'd commented on it, the same condescending smile on his face. "This is the good stuff."

Grace blinked, waiting for her sister to tell him to leave her be.

"Just take a tiny sip," Miriam said instead. "If you don't like it, I'll drink the rest."

Grace picked the glass back up and stared at it, mentally preparing. "Well, I guess if it's the good stuff," she said.

She stopped breathing through her nose and threw back the whiskey in one shot. Her throat burned. She coughed and chased with the remainder of her screwdriver.

"Not quite like honey," she said, blinking hard and showing her tongue.

Blake looked at her like he'd caught her strangling a baby, but Miriam burst out laughing.

"That was a twenty-five-dollar shot," said Blake.

It was even more than Grace had guessed. "Oh, wow, I didn't know," she said innocently. Her chest felt aglow.

"Go get her another screwdriver, honey," said Miriam, still laughing. "She earned it."

Blake started to object, but Miriam met him with a patient smile, one that promised to turn sour if he refused her. Grace didn't even want another drink, but it was nice to see him storm off to the bar, knowing Miriam was on her side.

"Two is probably enough for me," said Grace. "I have to drive back to Granada."

Miriam rolled her eyes. "Can you please move out of the Valley? It's impossible to see you, and even when you come out you have to leave at like six o'clock."

"It's almost nine now."

Miriam lived in Silver Lake, a hipster yuppie neighborhood, and ever since she moved there, she'd developed a biting scorn for the Valley—Granada Hills in particular. She refused to believe Grace liked her living situation, that she had, in fact, chosen it with full knowledge that there were other options available and didn't need Miriam reminding her that she could rent an apartment with roommates if she wanted. She'd lived with roommates—in college, in pharm school—but why should she throw away money on rent when her job was ten minutes from home, when her parents wanted her around, her mother, Yvonne, genuinely excited—Grace would swear on the Holy Bible—to cook her meals and do her laundry? Miriam should have understood. She'd lived at home after college and again for a few months after she quit consulting to follow her dreams. Instead she talked about the Valley like Grace had heard some people talk about tiny rural hometowns in Alabama and Ohio—as a place she'd escaped on her way to her true life, some shameful primitive village, when it was really a cluster of suburbs within Los Angeles city limits, maybe a half-hour drive from where she lived now.

Miriam hadn't made that drive in two years. That was the problem, not that Grace lived in Granada Hills. They rarely saw each other because Miriam had stopped talking to their mother and refused to come home.

Before the fight—if you could even call it a fight—it was unusual for Grace to go a full week without spending time with Miriam. They were close even for sisters, growing up sharing a bedroom, keeping each other's secrets. But then Miriam had cut ties with Yvonne and started dating Blake, and more and more now, Grace found herself marveling at how little they had in common. They didn't get each other's choices, lifestyles, goals, jobs, or loved ones. There were times Grace felt this distance between them like a cold wet breath at the nape of her neck.

"Just stay out tonight," said Miriam. She arranged her face into an expression thick with sisterly concern. "You look kind of drunk already. Blake can drive your car back and you can sleep over."

"Okay," said Grace.

Miriam looked surprised that she'd given in so quickly and without objection, and then she smiled and squeezed Grace's hand. Grace didn't especially want to stay out late with Blake, or sleep in his guest bedroom with the industrial metal bed frame and the posters of his drug show, but she missed her sister.

Grace was texting her parents to let them know her plans when someone appeared beside their table. He was a tall middle-aged white man with round wire-rimmed glasses, dressed like a cool professor, wearing a flannel shirt and a beat-up leather messenger bag. He touched Miriam's shoulder with the tips of his fingers.

She straightened, noticing him for the first time. "Oh, hi," she said. "Jules." She seemed uncharacteristically flustered, getting halfway out of her chair to shake his hand, making him step back a foot or two from the table.

"I thought that was you," said the man. "I was just at the Alfonso Curiel memorial. Did you hear about that?"

"I was there," she said.

"*I*," not "*we*." Grace looked around and found Blake at the bar, talking to the bartender. Maybe that's why Miriam was acting so stiff. Blake had a jealous streak, and she might be trying to lose this guy before he got back.

"Then you saw the Western Boys showed up?"

Grace thought of the angry-looking white guys in polo shirts. That had to be them.

"I did," said Miriam.

"I'm writing about them, for a project about white supremacy and racial violence in California. Actually, I'm glad I ran into you. I know you have thoughts on this. Maybe—"

"Sure," said Miriam, cutting him off with an agreeable smile. "You have my email, right? I should be free to talk during the week."

"Great. I'll follow up." He stayed standing where he was, like he wasn't quite sure that Miriam had dismissed him. "How's your mom doing?" he asked.

Grace tried to catch her sister's eye—it was an odd question; there was no way this white man knew Yvonne—but Miriam didn't turn to look at her. Something moved across her face. A flash of panic, Grace was sure of it.

"Fine," she answered. "Listen, it was good seeing you."

"You, too." He smiled at Grace. "Is this your sister?"

Another strange question—they didn't even look that much alike. She felt drunk all of a sudden, the air seeming to shift around her.

Grace was about to introduce herself when Miriam answered for her. "Yeah," she said. There was something steely in her voice now, bordering on hostility.

The man picked up on it. "I'll email you." He looked at Grace again, his gaze lingering a couple seconds too long. "It was nice to meet you," he said, and walked away.

"What was that about?" Grace asked, watching the man sit down alone at a corner table and pull a red Moleskine notebook from his bag.

"Nothing. Sorry. I just didn't want him talking to you."

Grace hadn't gotten a creepy vibe from him, at least not in a sexual way. The man was even older than Blake.

"Who is he?"

"Just a writer I know."

Blake came back to the table with Grace's cocktail and more Japanese whiskey for him and Miriam. Grace thanked him and drank, this screwdriver going down like juice. She waited for Miriam to mention the writer, but she never did, so Grace didn't bring him up either. They drank instead, and Blake and Grace quizzed each other about their jobs—mostly for Miriam's benefit, but it was nice of Blake to pretend he was interested in the pharmacy. Grace bought a fourth round and started feeling a little euphoric. She was even warming up to Blake. It was obvious he worshipped her sister, and he was only actively annoying like 10 percent of the time. Maybe even 5 percent.

"You're fucking kidding me," he said, breaking Grace out of her buzzed trance.

She looked up, wondering if that writer guy was coming back. But he was still at his corner table, eyes on the entrance to the bar. He was seeing what Blake was seeing: a half dozen of those Western Boys, smirking as they filed in, their faces splotchy and pink and filmed with sweat, their uniforms more rumpled than they'd been at the memorial but still recognizable. This was a hipster habitat, and they stood out like penguins on a savanna—which had to be the point.

They looked around, sticking their chests out. The whole bar was watching them—Grace saw heads swivel, heard conversations drop—and they knew it. One of them stepped forward and walked over to the bar, the others following behind him like chicks. He was the leader of their troop, about thirty years old with a square, meaty head and thick biceps, the sleeves of his polo tight around them.

Miriam shook her head, reading something on her phone. "This is a meet-up," she said, tilting her screen to show them a Facebook page. "They're doing a 'libtard bar crawl.'"

Grace looked back at the weird writer, watching from his corner with a pen and notepad in hand. He'd known they were coming here. If Miriam hadn't spazzed out on him, he would've given them the low-down, not that there seemed to be much to it.

"I should punch them in the face," said Blake.

"All of them?" asked Grace.

"They have some fucking nerve."

"Who are they exactly?"

"Right-wing losers," Miriam answered. "They think Americans should be white, women should be in the kitchen—you get the picture."

"Why were they at the memorial?" Grace had barely wanted to go, and she thought the kid's death was a tragedy. She didn't understand how people could feel anything but sorrow over the killing of a teenage boy, and strongly enough to leave the house to go bother the mourners. They reminded her of those crazy GOD HATES FAGS people—angry, stupid white people picketing funerals.

"Because that's one of their loser things. They show up anywhere they think they can trigger the libs. That's an end in itself." Miriam finished her drink and stood up. "I'm gonna let the doorman know."

Grace watched her sister march toward the door with an uneasy feeling. "Wait," she said. "I'll come with you." She followed her, leaving Blake at the table to fume.

The doorman was a brown guy, Latino or maybe Filipino, so bloated with muscle that he almost looked fat. He lit up when he saw Miriam.

"What's up?" he asked, like they knew each other. Now that Grace thought of it, there'd been some banter when he carded Miriam. He was probably half in love with her.

"Hey," said Miriam. "Those guys who just came in—do you know who they are?"

"I saw the hats," he said, with a shrug. "But I can't bounce people for wearing hats."

"They're a hate group. Like the Southern Poverty Law Center has them on their list."

"The Southern what?"

Grace touched her sister's arm—Miriam wasn't going to convince this guy to throw out six paying customers because of some list no one had ever heard of.

She went on anyway. "They're not just here to drink, you know?

They came to cause trouble. I think this is the third bar on their list."

"All I see them doing is ordering drinks in silly uniforms." He was starting to sound annoyed. Miriam did that to people sometimes— she acted less cute than she looked, and the gap threw them off.

"Can I talk to the manager?"

"And tell him what?"

"I just think he should know there are Nazis at his bar. What he does with that information is up to him."

He sighed. "Look, just let them have their little club meeting."

"Their Nazi club meeting."

They kept their eyes locked, waiting each other out. Then the doorman's gaze shifted. "Go back to your friends," he said.

The club leader was behind Grace, so close his voice made her jump. "Is there a problem?" The hope on his face was disgusting.

Grace willed her sister to keep her mouth shut.

Miriam didn't even hesitate. "I didn't come here to drink with the Simi Valley Hitler Youth."

"We're not Nazis." The way he said it made Grace think he had to make the denial often.

"I've never had to clarify that I'm not a Nazi," said Miriam.

"Whatever you think we are, we're just having a drink. You're the one trying to get us kicked out." He shook his head and smiled. "Come on, it wasn't that long ago when businesses discriminated against people like you. No blacks, no Jews, no Chinese allowed."

She scoffed. "You can take off your hat; you can't take off your skin. What do you have, like a fourth-grade education?"

"I went to Berkeley," he said, crossing his arms.

Grace could tell that caught Miriam off guard. She had a great respect for pedigree.

The bouncer cut in. "That's enough flirting. You," he said to the troop leader. "Don't give me a reason."

"I'm just defending myself." He raised his hands and backed away with exaggerated deference.

"You're giving them what they want," said the doorman. "When else does a girl like you give a guy like him the time of day?"

She ignored the peace offering. "The manager should know. Trust me. That guy didn't come here to have a quiet drink."

Blake started talking as soon as they got back to the table. He practically rattled with manic energy as he showed them his phone. There was a tweet on the screen, with a grainy video of the Western Boys laughing at the bar: **At @TheCrookedTail with @MiriamMPark and who shows up but these fascists. They just got here. Come help us let them know they're not welcome in our LA. #WesternBoysNightOut.**

"I posted this five minutes ago, and it has over thirty retweets already." Blake had more than twenty thousand Twitter followers, a fact he'd managed to drop in front of Grace at least five times. "I guess they were at Bells & Whistles earlier. There's a hashtag going. They left before they could get chased out, but there was a group heading over to confront them. Now they're coming here."

Grace felt a bolt of fear flash through her drunkenness. "Are you serious? Who?"

Blake was grinning, unable to hide his excitement. "Whoever wants to come. DSA people, activists, probably a few gawkers who are just bored on a Saturday night. Some people from the memorial, too. We weren't the only ones who noticed those douchebags."

She pictured them gathering, not just thrill-seeking self-righteous white guys but pissed-off black people. If these Western Boys made Blake mad, who knew how bad it might get when people with real grievances showed up?

"Jesus, Blake," said Miriam. "I know they're pathetic, but pathetic white men tend to have guns. This could get really ugly."

Grace was relieved—her sister, at least, had a tiny bit of sense. "We should leave," Grace said.

"What?" Blake huffed. "We can't leave. We need to stand our ground here, guys."

They both looked at Miriam, and Grace felt the room spin around her as she willed her sister to take her side. Then Miriam grabbed Blake's hand. "These fuckers spent their Saturday protesting a murdered teenager's memory," she said. "I'm not letting them chase me out."

She'd made up her mind—Grace could see it, and she knew that once Miriam made up her mind, Grace could exhaust herself fighting, and never gain an inch.

"Well, I'm going home," she said.

"You said you'd stay over tonight," Miriam protested.

"That was before you guys started a Wild West showdown."

"Can you even drive?"

"I'm fine. I'll sober up."

"Are you sure? You're not mad at me, are you?"

Miriam squeezed her hand, and Grace thought of all the reasons she should be mad at her sister. She was letting Grace leave the bar alone drunk, to get mugged or raped or crash and die on the 5, all so she could take part in some moronic turf war. She'd let Blake take over their first night together in weeks, their precious sister time sullied with his whiskey and smarm. She'd cut off their mother and severed the family, and Grace still didn't understand why. Grace caught a crashing wave of confused, inebriated emotion. She had to steady herself against Miriam to keep standing, to stop herself from weeping.

"I just want to go home," she said, hugging her sister. "Please try not to get yourself shot."

She had a hell of a time finding her car, and as soon as she got behind the wheel, she knew there was no way she could drive back to the Valley.

It was after midnight, but when she called home, Yvonne picked up immediately. She asked what was the matter, and when she heard

Grace slurring, she woke up Paul and said they were coming to get her. She didn't scold or complain—if anything, she seemed relieved that the problem was so simple, that something could be done. Forty minutes later, Grace sat next to her mother, drooling onto her seat belt, while Paul drove her car home behind them. Her head hurt, pounding with shame and gratitude, bitterness and love.

TWO

TUESDAY, JUNE 25, 2019

They waited for Ray in the parking lot, standing in a row on the asphalt, exposed to the pouring sun. It had been an hour already, but they held their formation, not wanting to be found in the car, sitting casual with the AC on. Ray would come out searching for them, and it seemed important that they be ready the moment he looked their way.

It was a nice day for a shaded picnic or a neighborhood stroll, but Shawn was suffering in the settled warmth, and he could see the sweat beading on Nisha's lip. Even the kids, so upbeat on the drive over, were quiet now, their excitement dampened by the anticlimax of a long hot wait in a dreary parking lot. It was a good thing Aunt Sheila agreed to stay home and get dinner ready. All this welcome party needed was a fainting grandma.

Dasha held a balloon the size of her torso. It shone in the sunlight, rainbow letters spelling WELCOME HOME on a background of silvery blue. She'd picked and paid for it herself, out of her weekly allowance, and she'd insisted on bringing it to Lompoc instead of leaving it back at the house with the cake and the rest of the party. Shawn saw now why it was worth the trouble. With the balloon and her butter-yellow sundress, she'd be the first sight Ray would see as a free man.

Darryl stood next to her, his pits sweating in the button-down

shirt Aunt Sheila had forced him to wear. The tie he'd loosened on
the drive, then taken off altogether. Shawn would help him knot it
again later—or Ray, if he remembered how.

The boy plucked the balloon from the air and flapped it between
him and his sister, back and forth, like a folding fan. It squeaked
against his fingers, and she started to protest, clutching the slack
string ribbon. She gave up and leaned closer instead, on the off chance
it stirred up a breeze. They looked like praying angels, thought
Shawn, their heads together, watching for their father.

All around them was concrete and chain link, grim gray spruced
up with patches of dying grass. Beyond the parking lot lay the stark,
mute buildings that made up the federal prison, where Ray had
spent the last ten years.

Finally, a door opened in one of the fenced-off buildings, and a
man came out alone, carrying a cardboard box. His face turned up
and out.

"It's him," said Nisha, standing on her toes. "It's him!" She waved
her arms and shouted. "Ray!"

He saw them and smiled. Stood taller, walked faster. It was Ray,
all right, and for a moment, the sight of him stunned Shawn into
something like disbelief. His cousin was wearing a brand-new shirt
and smart dark jeans—Nisha had sent the dress-out clothes a month
ago. Ray had been vain about his clothes, once upon a time, and it
was strange to see him in normal gear again. He seemed to shimmer
like a mirage, diligently imagined.

But he was there in the flesh, and the flesh, Shawn saw, had aged.
Not since the last time he'd seen him, just a few months earlier, but
since the last time he'd seen him free. It was obvious, outside the
timeless space of the visiting room: Ray was a forty-four-year-old
man, the end scraps of his youth left behind in an overcrowded cell.
There was gray in his hair, and his body was lean, without its former
wiry hardness. The tattoos on his forearms had a soft, worn-in look,
the black ink washed to a smudgy green. DARRYL and DASHA in large

Gothic font, surrounded by patterns and symbols in a dense, thorny thicket.

Nisha got a spot on his chest, Shawn remembered. LANEISHA over Ray's heart before they were even married, a rash late-night decision that had panned out in spite of it all. And on his right biceps, another tribute: AVA. Shawn had the same name on the same place. They'd gotten it done together, their friend Tramell inking it in the year Shawn turned fourteen. He'd done their backs, too. The name of their set, BARING CROSS, laid out in a crucifix, crossing at the *R*. Shawn felt the words glow warm against his skin. It was surreal, seeing Ray free again. Exhilarating and joyful. Yet it came with a heightened awareness of all that had brought them here, the past clinging to them in thin, sticky layers.

The kids pulled him out of his daze, back into the dazzling present.

"Daddy!" Dasha leaped up, springing forward and running to meet him as he came out the fenced gate. Darryl and Nisha followed after her, their eyes shining as they waited their turns. Shawn hung back and took pictures on his cell phone, knowing they'd want them later.

Ray put the box down and hugged his daughter tight, sinking his face into her shoulder. Shawn could see his eyes close, his tears darkening the yellow fabric of her dress.

"Thank God," Ray said, nodding his head as he held her. "Thank you God for this day."

"Hey, Dad," said Darryl, with a shy little wave. He was sixteen, and Shawn knew that lately, he fancied himself a man.

Ray laughed and let go of Dasha. He mimicked the half-assed wave, scooped tears away from his eyes with his other hand. "What was that?" he said, opening his arms. "Come here."

Darryl allowed himself to be folded in by his father, his arms held straight by his sides. When Ray didn't let go, the boy raised an arm to pat his father's back, and Ray hugged him all the harder.

It struck Shawn that he couldn't tell who was taller, his nephew or his cousin. Darryl was in the midst of yet another growth spurt, his tender bones stretching longer by the week. It surprised Shawn, sometimes, how fast the kids could change, and he saw them every few days, for one reason or another.

"He drove," said Nisha, beaming. "He wanted to be the one to pick you up."

Darryl pulled away from Ray and shrugged. "It was good practice."

Ray stared at his son, still holding him by the shoulder. "You can drive?"

"I get my license next month."

"If you pass," said his mother. "Don't get cocky now."

Darryl had gotten his learner's permit in January. Shawn had taught him how to drive: cruising their neighborhood in Shawn's Grand Cherokee, doing loops around Mall Ring Road, where they could practice around other drivers at under twenty miles an hour. In the last couple of months, Darryl had started driving freeways. This trek to Lompoc was his longest trip yet, and the kid did great. Shawn was proud of him.

He was, in a lot of ways, as much of a father to these kids as Ray. It was taboo, but he suspected everyone but Ray felt more or less the same. Lompoc was a three-and-a-half-hour drive from Palmdale. When the kids were younger, Nisha had taken them whenever she got the chance, but she had a job, and as they grew up, Darryl and Dasha started having plans of their own. Their lives revolved less and less around their dad, locked away where he couldn't bid for their attention, far enough and long gone enough that whatever guilt they felt became easy to overcome. Sometimes Shawn took them, but he figured they only went as often as he did. Three, maybe four times a year. Ray had watched them grow up in time lapse.

Shawn had been incarcerated, but he still couldn't quite imagine what it meant to lose a decade inside, while the world barreled ahead. He'd never done federal time, but he spent his youth in and out of jail, with stints in Central Juvenile and Twin Towers, and finally a

three-year stretch in Lancaster. That part of his life had been dis-
jointed, sometimes hellish and always uneasy, the ground never quite
safe beneath him. Each release was disorienting, like waking up from
a coma, the time he might have had outside beyond recovery. He
remembered being jealous of other people's memories: their quiet days,
their friendships, their Christmas dinners. It was a mercy, maybe,
that Ray didn't know what he'd missed. Darryl's soccer games, his
Star Wars mania. The hubbub when Dasha got her first period, Aunt
Sheila's celebratory red velvet cupcakes. The hard nights when Nisha couldn't sleep. When she and Shawn stayed up talking in the
kitchen, their fear and loneliness bonding them into true family.

Ray let go of his son and gazed at his wife. She looked good,
Shawn thought. She'd done her hair and makeup, and her clothes
were smart. She'd even cleaned her wedding ring. The metal glinted
like new. Nisha was Ray's age, and she'd aged, of course, since Ray
went away. Today, though, she glowed like a pregnant woman.

"Big D, Little D," said Ray, his eyes fixed on Nisha. "Look away
a minute."

The kids looked right at him instead, puzzled by the order or
by the nicknames—if anyone called his nephew Big D, it was news to
Shawn. They were still looking when Ray planted a deep, wet kiss on
their mother, and Shawn laughed as their expressions quick-changed
from confusion to performative disgust. The irrepressible delight of
seeing their parents together.

Ray resurfaced, his arms around Nisha's waist. He nodded back
toward the prison. "That'd keep me going another six months in
there."

Nisha laughed, and her face shone with happy tears. "Don't even
say it, Ray Holloway."

Shawn took more pictures. It was the first time he'd seen the four
of them together in years—since Ray's fortieth birthday, when they
had all made the drive to Lompoc. They were a beautiful family.
Smiling. Complete.

"Look at me," he said, holding up his phone.

They all turned, and Ray nodded at Shawn, as if noticing him for the first time. "Who invited you?" he asked.

"I love you, too," said Shawn. He took their picture as Ray's face broke into a grin.

He'd thought about staying back. His girlfriend, Jazz, was at Aunt Sheila's, helping her get dinner ready, and he knew she would've been happy to have him there. There was a lot left to do—according to Aunt Sheila, anyway—and Monique needed tending. Jazz's daughter had just turned three, and she had the kind of energy and fearlessness that required unflagging vigilance.

But Darryl and Dasha asked Shawn to go with them, and Nisha said he would have to, since Darryl insisted on driving—she made Shawn promise not to let her son get them killed on the way up and to take the wheel for the drive back home. They all wanted him with them, so of course he would be there. And besides, Ray was as much his brother as his cousin. He and Aunt Sheila were the closest blood Shawn had left.

Shawn walked over to join the family huddle. He hugged Ray, and neither man let go until they were both sniffling and laughing. Shawn picked up Ray's box.

"Come on, man. It's time to get out of Lompoc."

They piled into Shawn's Jeep, Ray in the front seat, Nisha and the kids in the back. Shawn started the car.

"I'm starving," said Ray, when they were on the freeway. "Can we get something to eat?"

"You didn't eat lunch, Daddy?" asked Dasha, poking her head between the front seats.

"Baby Dash, I ain't had a good meal in ten years."

Shawn remembered the vile taste of stale prison meat, discolored and chewy and wet smelling. For years, food had brought him no pleasure, only sustenance. Powdered potatoes and canned beans. Endless slices of plain white bread turning to mush in his tired mouth.

"If you can wait till we get home, Mom's getting a feast ready," said Nisha. "I swear she's been cooking since last week."

Ray was silent for a few seconds, and Shawn knew he was thinking about a cheeseburger with bacon and French fries. "How long's the drive?"

"Three and a half hours," she said. "It's your day, honey. We'll do what you want."

He stroked his chin as he weighed his options, and Shawn could see the satisfaction he took in making a choice. "Alright, I can wait," he said. "I want to go home."

Home was the house on Ramona Road, off the 138 in Palmdale. It was nowhere Ray had ever been before, but it's where his family had landed. Shawn remembered the first time he saw the house—the day seven years earlier when he left prison, for good if he could help it.

Aunt Sheila had come to get him. Alone. Ray was in Lompoc, and Uncle Richard had died of prostate cancer while both of his boys were incarcerated, a fact that still filled Shawn with shame. With all the men gone, Aunt Sheila had moved in with Nisha, to help out with Darryl and Dasha. They bought the house in Palmdale after the recession, leaving Los Angeles for the Antelope Valley, dusty desert land at the far reaches of the county. Nisha worked at LAX, and the move kicked her commute from ten miles to seventy. But it was affordable and quiet, a long way from the gangs and bitter memories of South Central. It also put them within twenty miles of the California State Prison in Lancaster, where Aunt Sheila visited Shawn every chance she got.

Palmdale was a far cry from the old place. No hustle, no bustle. No corner stores, no helicopters, no laughing teens running wild. Just arid suburbia with a coarse, plain face. It was boring here, and Shawn had come to love the bland peace of it over the years. But he knew it was different, and he felt Ray shift as they passed the sign announcing the Palmdale city limit. There wasn't much around: a warehouse, a wire fence, scrubby bushes on hard yellow ground, power lines draped across an empty, burning sky.

"So this is it, huh?" Ray said, as they got off the interstate and drove down the Pearblossom Highway, tract houses blooming along the tapered road.

"It's not that bad," said Nisha. "It's only fifteen minutes to the mall, and they got a lot of the same things we got in L.A. There's even a Tommy's now."

Ray laughed, reaching into the back seat to take her hand. "Baby, you know where I been. This might as well be heaven."

The house was beige and boxy with a sloped clay roof, identical to three others on the block. Cookie-cutter, built quick and simple, but it was big enough for the kids to get their own bedrooms. For a sofa bed for Shawn.

Aunt Sheila came out the instant they pulled into the driveway. Shawn sensed she'd been waiting for them, watching from the window. Ray stepped out of the car into his mother's open arms. They embraced for a full minute, while everyone else watched, Nisha recording this time on her phone.

"My baby, you're home," said Aunt Sheila, pulling back just enough to cradle her son's face in both hands and shake it for emphasis. "Don't you ever. Leave. Again."

If it hadn't been for Aunt Sheila, Shawn might be back in prison by now. She convinced Nisha to let him stay until he got back on his feet; it would be good for the kids, she said, to have a man around, and if he managed to get into gangster nonsense this far from his old hood, she would boot him out herself. This house had become his home, a safe place that let him breathe while he found a new grip on a slippery world.

Monique trailed Aunt Sheila and broke into a run when she saw Shawn, her hair in dandelion puffs bouncing on her tiny head.

"Papa Shawn!" she shouted. "Up! Up!"

He scooped her up and she swung her legs from the seat in his arms. She had known Shawn since she was grown enough to make memories.

"Hey, Momo," he said. "I want you to meet Uncle Ray."

Her eyes widened, seeing Ray for the first time.

"You must be Monique. I like your hair." Ray's voice was sweet, and he wiggled his fingers at her. She smiled, showing gums and milk teeth, then buried her face in Shawn's neck.

"Monique, baby, say hi." Jazz appeared behind her daughter, laughing at the girl's bout of shyness. She put one hand around Shawn's waist and extended the other to Ray. "I'm Jazz," she said brightly.

Jazz had wanted to meet Ray. Had insisted on it, actually. One of their only fights in the nearly two years they'd been together was over Shawn's refusal to take Jazz along to Lompoc. It seemed to her that if she and Ray were both so important to him, Shawn should want the two of them to meet. But he knew what it was like to be in a visiting room, wearing a uniform and an invisible leash, under the eye and thumb of hawkish guards. He didn't want her to see Ray that way, not when she hadn't known him before.

"I've heard a lot about you," Ray said, taking her hand. He'd always been good with women, and he still had his old charm.

"From him?" Jazz looked up at Shawn with evident skepticism.

"Nah, you know Shawn." Ray made his face unexpressive and deepened his voice. "'Jazz is cool. She's a nurse. She has a kid.'"

Jazz cackled and pulled Shawn closer.

"But my mom and Nisha think the world of you. Don't dump him, unless you want to break all our hearts."

They went inside, where Aunt Sheila had cooked up enough food for forty people. The table sagged with mac and cheese and fresh buttermilk biscuits, potato salad and baked beans. There was a whole tray of pork ribs glistening with barbecue sauce, another of roast chicken. A large Domino's pizza, too, with pepperoni, jalapeño, and pineapple. That was Shawn's touch, about the only thing that wasn't homemade. It was their favorite pizza, ever since they were kids, and Shawn remembered how good it tasted after years of prison food. Ray ogled the spread, his tongue showing wet in his open mouth.

"Well, I'm ready to eat," he said. "Let's pray."

They held hands in a circle, bowed their heads down, and waited on Ray, as if he always led them in grace. The truth was Shawn couldn't think of another time. They grew up going to church—for years, Aunt Sheila and Uncle Richard didn't let them miss one Sunday—but his cousin came by his religious passion in Lompoc. It was annoying sometimes, getting lectured by Ray, but it seemed to do him good. There were worse things a man could find in prison than Jesus.

Ray started to pray. "We thank you, Heavenly Father, for bringing this household together. Thank you for my wife, for keeping her strong. Her steadfastness and her love have been my rock these long years. For my children, who are so good and beautiful—"

His voice caught, and Aunt Sheila and Nisha chimed in with soft amens. Shawn opened his eyes and saw Ray swiping at his tears. Nisha found his hand and held it again, stroking his wrist with her thumb. Darryl and Dasha were watching, too, their faces cracked open with awe.

Ray cleared his throat and began again, louder this time, nearly shouting the words. "And I thank you, Father God, for delivering me. For keeping me sane, for keeping me safe. For taking me out of the darkness and bringing me home, where no man can ever drag me back away."

Shawn closed his eyes. He could hear Nisha sniffling, Aunt Sheila murmuring more amens.

"And I pray for those we've lost. Watch over them, Father God."

Jazz squeezed Shawn's hand, and he squeezed back.

"Protect this house, oh Lord," Ray thundered. "Let nothing tear us apart again."

The kids were on cleanup duty while the adults shared a bottle of champagne in the living room. Ray got up to get more dessert, and Nisha caught Shawn's eye and nodded after him. Shawn had promised her he'd take care of the nagging tonight, and this was as alone as Ray was likely to get.

Shawn hopped over to the dining table and watched his cousin stack fresh chocolate chip cookies on his plate and carve out a generous scoop of vanilla ice cream.

"Take it easy, man," Shawn said, laughing. "You're gonna wreck your stomach."

Ray smiled at him. "I don't care if I spend the next three months on the toilet. I'm eating all of this." He ate half a cookie in one ferocious bite.

"It's all set up with Manny," said Shawn. "He wants to meet you, just to make sure you ain't crazy, but you can start right after."

Ray nodded while he chewed on his cookie.

"I'll pick you up Friday morning. We should leave by four thirty to be safe."

Ray laughed, spraying crumbs on the floor. "Damn, that's when you leave for work? You an industrious Negro."

"I'm a Negro with a commute, and so are you."

Shawn had been working for Manny's Movers for seven years now, since right after he got out of Lancaster. Manny Lopez was Shawn's parole officer's cousin. He was a generous man who believed in second chances, and he'd hired Shawn as a favor to his cousin, as he'd now hire Shawn's cousin as a favor to Shawn. It was a good job, especially now that Shawn was the most senior employee, tasked with leading and supervising his moves. The only downside was that

Manny's office was in Northridge, the moves spread out all over L.A. The bottom of the hill, as they said in Palmdale. Shawn's commute was almost as bad as Nisha's.

Ray swallowed. "Alright, four thirty it is then. You know I appreciate it, Shawn."

"I gotta warn you. The first week's gonna be rough. We get a lot of guys, like young buff guys, and they quit after a week."

"I ain't afraid to work. I'm afraid of falling back, know what I'm saying?"

There was a good chance the job wouldn't stick. Shawn knew it; Nisha knew it; Ray knew it. Sure, a fresh parolee could only be so picky. But there were other options, ones that paid better and didn't involve trucking across the county with other people's belongings. Most of these happened to be illegal.

Ray hadn't had a legit job since high school. Shawn hadn't either, until Manny decided to give him a shot. They'd spent all their time with the Baring Cross crew, messing around, getting in trouble, moving dope and running capers when they needed money. It made it hard to find work even when they wanted to go straight. The last time, Ray got so demoralized he held up a bank with a toy gun he'd bought for Darryl. He got caught three hours later, still carrying his $7,000 take in cash, stashed in a duffel bag with the fake gun. That was armed robbery. One dumb-ass federal crime that bought him a twelve-year prison sentence, reduced to ten for good time. Now here he was.

"Look at you, though. You got your shit together," said Ray, pointing a cookie at him. "I like Jasmine, by the way. She's good for you."

"I like her, too."

"Can't believe Mom hooked that up. They oughta give her a Nobel Prize for that hustle."

Shawn laughed. It was true. Aunt Sheila had gone to the hospital to check out a breast lump one day a couple years back. She made the most of her visit, chatting up the pretty black nurse with no ring on her finger. She found out the nurse was divorced, and by the time she was done with her appointment, Aunt Sheila had managed to sell Jazz on a blind date with the ex-con nephew who lived on her couch. The lump, it turned out, was benign.

"You should lock that down," said Ray. "Be the man of your own house."

Your own *house.* It was a jab, but Ray had just enough shame to pretend otherwise, stuffing his mouth with another cookie.

Shawn knew Ray loved him, but he also knew that his cousin would never forgive him for being there when he was gone. While Ray was in prison, Shawn fell back on *Ray's* mom, *Ray's* wife, hung out with *Ray's* kids. Didn't matter that they were Shawn's aunt, Shawn's friend, Shawn's niece and nephew; Ray had the stronger claim, and he let Shawn know it. It wasn't fair, he told Shawn once, in his fury. It was the same whining complaint he'd lobbed at Shawn all through their childhood, whenever Aunt Sheila took Shawn's side against him. She was Ray's mom—why should he have to vie for her attention?

The arrangement was supposed to be temporary, but after a few months, Nisha asked him to stay. The kids loved their uncle. Ray hated this. It put his whole identity through the wringer—as a husband, a father, a man. He accused Nisha of trying to replace him, Shawn of moving in on his wife. But Ray was in prison—he could give them nothing—and in the end, he gave in, settling for passive aggression, the occasional muttered gripe. It was better to let Shawn help her than risk her remembering she could always leave. So Ray shut up and Shawn stayed. He stayed for six years.

Darryl came in from the kitchen and helped himself to a cookie. He looked at his father and smiled awkwardly, wanting to be near him, chewing to hide that he didn't know what to say. Ray patted his shoulder, and the boy flushed with happiness. There were times these days when Darryl seemed so grown up it nearly broke Shawn's heart. But he saw it now, the unspoiled tenderness of this child.

"How's school?" asked Ray.

Darryl shrugged. "It's okay."

"Classes and all that—good?"

"Yeah, it's good."

"Good, good."

It struck Shawn all over how out of the loop Ray was after ten years away from his kids. He had teenagers now, not small children who would babble about anything if you gave them a second of silence to fill. Ray didn't know much about their day-to-day lives, so he couldn't ask them anything but the most generic questions. He'd have to get to know them now, and Shawn saw that it would take work, a kind of work Ray had never had to do before.

"You study hard? Get good grades?" Ray asked.

"I do alright."

"As long as you don't cut class," said Ray, satisfied.

Darryl sneaked a glance at Shawn and looked away when they made eye contact. Back in May, Nisha had gotten a call from Palmdale High. Darryl had missed three days since spring break, and each time, he'd shown up the next day with a note signed "Laneisha Holloway," indicating that her son had been sick and had to go see a doctor. The administrator didn't point out what Nisha already knew—that Darryl was the picture of health—and she didn't come out and accuse him of forging his mother's signature. Instead, she asked Nisha if Darryl was okay and whether he'd be needing more time off to see his doctor.

Later, when she recounted the conversation for Shawn, she marveled at how quickly and calmly she absorbed what she was hearing. She did what she thought any parent would have done: she covered for him—a bold, automatic lie about a newfound corn allergy—and vowed to let him have it at home.

She'd enlisted Shawn's help, and he'd taken the boy aside, given him a heart-to-heart. Told him to stay in school and listen to his mother, that if he did those two things, he could stay out of prison, and wouldn't that be nice. Ray had heard none of this, which meant Nisha hadn't brought him up to speed. Shawn had suspected as much.

"Not that I'm one to give advice. I was the worst student," said Ray. "I used to knock off school to do the stupidest shit."

"Like what?" Darryl asked, with a spark of real curiosity.

"Oh, you don't want to know." Ray smiled coyly, enjoying some private memory.

"Nothing good," said Shawn. It worried him, how Ray went sentimental when he talked about the past. Shawn had never enjoyed the good times, the goofing and partying that came before and between the bad. Ray's youth was different, his childhood longer. When he was Darryl's age, being in a gang was mostly posturing and hanging with his friends. Ray talked about those days like a washed-up athlete reminiscing about high school, his memories rounded out and partial, sepia toned.

"Your uncle, always so serious." Ray was smiling, but that didn't do much to hide his annoyance. Shawn had crossed him, cutting in on his sad attempt to impress his teenage son with his bad-boy past—the same past that had led him to a decade in federal prison.

Dasha shouted from the kitchen. "Mom! Uncle Shawn! Tell Darryl to get his butt back here."

Ray shouted back. "Darryl's fine right here. You come here, too, Little D. The dishes can wait."

The sink shut off, and Dasha came to the table.

"Give your daddy a hug," said Ray.

Ray was a jealous man, and he'd spent a stupid amount of energy worrying about Shawn and Nisha, as if either of them was capable of that kind of betrayal. But Shawn had to admit, there was a part of him—the deepest, meanest part of him—that saw his cousin with the smoldering resentment of a rival. For as long as he could remember, Shawn had battled a seasick feeling—one that came and went, but stayed for years at a time—that he was loosely held by the world, that he was one snap away from a total unmooring. If it weren't for his aunt and uncle, he would have grown up without parents; if it weren't for his cousin, he would have grown up without a brother. These tightenings and reinforcements had helped him survive. So it seemed fitting that Shawn would be a father to his cousin's children. These kids, Darryl and Dasha—they were his kids. But there was no avoiding that Ray was their dad.

Shawn left them and found Jazz and Nisha on his old sofa bed, sipping champagne while Aunt Sheila sat in an armchair, reading to Monique. Jazz smiled at him, and he looked at the mouth that he loved, the kind, clear eyes.

Nisha was looking at him, too, gesturing toward the dining table with a meaningful nod. He gave her a thumbs-up, and she put a hand over her heart. No, his feelings for Nisha were nothing like his feelings for Jazz. He loved her, but what was she to him? Not a wife, not a girlfriend. Not a mother, not quite. A sister, maybe.

THREE

THURSDAY, AUGUST 8, 2019

Woori Pharmacy was finally closed for the day. Grace's back hurt, and the bright lights were giving her a headache. There were about a hundred treatments for both those problems, most of them right in the pharmacy, but no way to prevent fatigue after ten hours on her feet. She hadn't had a minute to herself since leaving the house with Paul in the morning. It was Miriam's birthday and she hadn't even gotten a chance to call her.

Javi went home when his shift was up, but there was still work to do for Grace and Paul. Grace had to check the tech's work and fill the remaining scripts, or she'd start the day behind tomorrow morning. Paul sat on the stool by the register, plugging numbers into the huge calculator—the same one they'd had in the store when Grace was a teenager, doing tech work and shadowing Uncle Joseph. Grace left the accounting to Paul and Yvonne, but she was pretty sure most other pharmacies didn't stick to longhand. Her parents were good with numbers, and they refused to pay for accounting software after getting by without it for so many years.

Paul was almost sixty-five now, but he looked like he could man the register another twenty years if he felt like it. He had amazing posture, despite the thick varicose veins that made it painful for him to stand, and he projected an air of competence and pride that

Grace had failed to inherit. Immigrant grit, maybe that's what it was. Miriam didn't get it either.

Grace had always known, on some level, that her parents were hard workers. They'd worked together before they had children—those years mostly vague and unimaginable to Grace—and then Paul had put in every hour he could to make money while Yvonne raised their daughters. She'd been a tireless mother while they grew up, approaching parenthood with the sort of dedication and zeal that won prizes in other fields. Now that Grace helped run the store, she saw that unflappable first-generation work ethic up close, in a way that she understood better. Her parents showed her up every day.

Lucky for Grace, she had the education. Woori was the Park family business, but Grace was the only licensed pharmacist among them. Uncle Joseph was a pharmacist, but he wasn't her real uncle, though she'd known him since she was a baby. He was Paul's best friend and business partner—they'd bought Woori together when Grace was in high school, after Paul had spent fifteen years managing Uncle Joseph's old store. Both men hoped their kids would take up the business, but only Grace had obliged. Uncle Joseph's kids didn't talk to him, and Miriam had never shown interest, even when she was still a participating member of the family. Only Grace had been a good girl, doing her studies and coming back home. Uncle Joseph was in semiretirement now, making Grace the primary pharmacist at Woori. Her parents needed her.

It wasn't especially fair, though they never thought to complain about it. They'd made enormous sacrifices so their children could grow up in the States. Korea was still poor when they emigrated in the '80s, but they would've had easier lives there. Paul was a college graduate with a good job at Hyundai. They could've ridden that out, set up in white-collar comfort, their friends and family nearby. Instead, they'd come to Los Angeles, where they knew no one and didn't speak the language. Paul's degree and experience meant nothing here. He'd had to start over, learn to count and read and write. It must have been even worse for Yvonne. She was only nineteen when she married Paul, an upwardly mobile man ten years her senior. She was twenty-one when he dragged her across an ocean, and Grace suspected she hadn't had much say in the matter.

Day by day, dollar by dollar, they built new lives in this foreign place, all so she and Miriam could grow up free and clear, American. She wondered sometimes if they regretted it all. Miriam was so American she renounced her own mother—a capital crime, pretty much, in a Confucian culture. Grace was the filial daughter, and here she was at twenty-seven, still just taking and taking and taking. In Korea, she'd be married by now, hassling her husband to let her parents retire and move in with them. Here, they let her live at home rent-free and wanted nothing more than to have her take over the pharmacy, the culmination of their decades of labor.

What sharpened her guilt was that she saw their pride in the store without quite sharing it. She was grateful, and she had a lot of affection for the place, but she saw it for what it was: a two-hundred-square-foot glass box adjoining a Korean food court and supermarket in an ugly deep Valley strip mall. The walls were glass, see-through where they weren't covered with vitamins and ointments and print-out ads for shampoos and Powerball tickets, but none of them faced the outside world. They got no sun, only the artificial light of the Hanin Market, a complex they shared with a Korean bank, a Korean bakery, a Korean cosmetics shop, even a fully Koreanized branch of the U.S. Post Office. All so Valley Koreans didn't have to drive to Koreatown to run errands in their own language. It was a nice setup, but it wasn't exactly the American dream.

For one thing, the work was exhausting. She just couldn't imagine doing it for the next thirty years. The physical demands alone were almost unbelievable, something years of higher education had never prepared her to face. She wore compression socks and massive, hideous sneakers, but still went home aching almost every day.

On the other hand, she didn't know what else she was supposed to do. She'd been raised for this, and the work was so tiring that she hardly had time to think about other options. She wasn't like Miriam, who majored in English and left Grace with their parents' hopes on her back. She couldn't be like Miriam—one of them had to think of the family.

She finished the last of the scripts and stretched her arms out. One more day's work done.

Paul called over to her from the register, in Korean. "All finished?" He stood up from the stool, ready to go home.

Grace had to call Miriam before they left. Home was only ten minutes away, and once she was there, Grace had no intention of reminding her mother that it was Miriam's birthday—not that there was any chance Yvonne had forgotten.

"I have to call Unni," said Grace.

He nodded, understanding. He'd remembered then, though he hadn't mentioned it all day. "You'd better call now," he said. "I'll wait in the car."

"Should I tell her you say happy birthday?"

"If you want."

"Do you want to talk to her?"

"She can call home," he said, and left.

Technically, Miriam had no fight with Paul, but as far as Grace knew, they hadn't been in contact either. It might've been solidarity on Paul's part—he'd been furious that Miriam could be so callous to Yvonne—but there was at least an equal chance that he just couldn't maintain a functional relationship with his daughter without his wife as a bridge. When Grace was in college, she never spoke to Paul unless she was talking to Yvonne and she put him on the phone, and there was no reason to believe he was any better with Miriam. Their dad was just weird like that. There was no way he'd call Miriam on his own, let alone make plans to see her.

The phone rang, and Grace found herself hoping it would go to voice mail. She hadn't seen Miriam since that awful night downtown.

Apparently something like thirty people had shown up after Grace left, and there was shouting and shoving and eventually someone called the cops, which of course pissed everyone off. Two people got arrested: one of the protesters, for punching a Western Boy, and one of the Western Boys, for punching a protester. The Western Boy had a bowie knife strapped to his ankle. It was probably something he saw in a movie, but it was still terrifying—in the movies, a knife like that cut throats.

Miriam acted like it was no big deal, like Grace had freaked out for no good reason. But over the last month and a half, there had been more blowups, street confrontations and internet wars, protests and counterprotests that built to a righteous fever. Then, yesterday, a Bakersfield grand jury declined to indict Officer Trevor Warren for the shooting of Alfonso Curiel.

Grace had been following the story since the rally, though if she was being honest, her feelings of personal outrage and sorrow had died down. She felt guilty about it, but she couldn't force herself to keep caring about this boy she'd never met, not with any passion, not when it seemed like the rest of the world was moving on.

It also turned out the Curiel kid wasn't exactly a college-bound Boy Scout. This wasn't his first encounter with the police—he was actually running from them when they tracked him to his parents' backyard. It wasn't a racist neighbor calling him in for no reason. Someone had seen him walking around after midnight, going up to people's doorsteps and stealing packages. A lot of gangs were into package theft these days, and there was speculation that Curiel was part of an organized ring.

That didn't make it right to kill him, of course, but coincidentally or not, the news coverage had gone quiet since that revelation, and Grace had found herself less distressed by the tragedy. Still, the grand jury decision felt like a punch in the stomach. There'd be no trial, no chance for even the bare minimum of justice for this poor teenage boy.

There was an immediate response. Crowds gathered in protest up and down California. The largest one was in downtown L.A., and the police had been waiting in riot gear, ready to nip any trouble in the bud. Miriam was there when the cops let loose with pepper spray, when they started making arrests.

She posted pictures from the scene on social media. Grace knew she had to be on her phone, counting retweets, liking comments. But when Grace called, Miriam didn't answer.

She wasn't answering now either. It was after 7:30—she was probably out to dinner, having a wonderful time. She would see that Grace had called, and that would be enough.

The house smelled like miyeok—it hit her as soon as she walked in, the briny scent clogging the air. Yvonne was in the kitchen, taking things off the stove. Grace stood and watched her, the scene straining her heart. Her mother looked so small and tired, her shoulders hunched, her eyes losing their light.

"I'm home," said Grace.

"Eung," Yvonne acknowledged weakly. She bobbed her head in Grace's direction without looking up. "Dinner's ready. Can you set the table?"

Grace grabbed plates, spoons, and chopsticks and set them down while Yvonne transferred the miyeok-guk, eundaegu-jolim, banchan, and rice to the table. Paul had gone to his room to change or watch TV or whatever he did every night while the women of the house set up for dinner. He came out with unerring instinct the minute everything was ready. Grace closed her eyes while he said the prayer. She remembered what Miriam used to say: *Umma cooks the food, we set the table, and Appa sits down just in time to thank God.*

He made no allusion to Miriam or her birthday, not that he ever did in Yvonne's presence. It didn't matter. The house was heavy with her absence.

Grace sat in her chair—the one next to her mother, across from her father, who sat next to the one that was always empty—and surveyed the bounty on the table. So this was what Yvonne had done all day. It was a massive amount of food, a meal with a sense of occasion, built around a platter of black cod and radish braised in a sauce hot with gochujang. Grace loved eundaegu-jolim—it was one of her favorite things her mother made. It was also Miriam's pronounced favorite, the dish Yvonne used to cook whenever her elder daughter came home.

But the miyeok-guk was the real clincher, the seaweed soup Yvonne made on every family birthday but her own. She'd told Grace once that it was the soup eaten by a new mother right after a birth, the nutrients targeted for postnatal recovery; that when she had Miriam and Grace, her own mother had brought it to the hospital by the bucket. It was like a traditional Korean culinary umbilical cord, eaten every year to celebrate the connection with mother and birth and body. And there it was, right in the middle of the table, challenging them not to turn it into a conversation piece.

Grace was stupefied by her mother's sheer masochism. All that labor, all that mortified love—God, it was just too much. It felt like a tribute to a dead person, an offering placed on a shrine with an attitude of unresolved guilt and self-punishment.

Paul started eating, and Grace followed dutifully, though she felt no hunger. Yvonne made no move to join them. Her hands were in her lap, her eyes distant.

"Yeobo," said Paul, lowering his chopsticks. "Eat. It's good."

This, from Paul, was a gentle, generous concession, almost painful in its naked recognition of her need.

They ate, Yvonne picking somberly at her own cooking. The food was great—it was always great—but they were all so aware of one another that the kitchen felt close and humid and the miyeok-guk took on a fetid, sweaty flavor that canceled out Grace's appetite.

The silence grew excruciating, and Grace was grateful when Paul switched on the TV. It was turned to one of the two Korean channels. Grace had tried to get her parents into Netflix; she'd even bought a smart TV for the house, replacing the twenty-seven-inch box they'd had since her childhood, which no one would take from them even when she listed it as free on Craigslist. But her parents said they were too old to learn. Yvonne had a few dramas that she watched as they aired; if she missed an episode, she went to the Korean video store in the Hanin Market and rented the DVD.

One of her shows was on now, a new historical drama, starring an actor Grace had last seen falling in love with his adoptive sister as she died beautifully of cancer. Grace wasn't exactly sure what this one was about—it seemed like her parents had been watching some variation on the same palace intrigue drama for the last twenty years. Men and women in flowing hanbok, with wide sleeves and tall headdresses, whispering behind sliding paper doors. Warring princes, scheming concubines. Grace liked Korean dramas fine, but the historical ones were tricky. The Korean was formal and hard to follow, and she could never get the eras straight. There'd been a time travel one she'd gotten into for a while, but for the most part, she lost interest as soon as the folding fans and horses came out. What did she care what her ancestors were doing in another country hundreds of years ago?

The king threw a teacup at a cowering servant, and the show went to commercial. Paul changed the channel to the other Korean station—he never rested on commercials; it was like he thought he was winning something by avoiding them. The news was on, and Grace zoned out as the anchor's melodious Korean commentary played over images of the president boarding an airplane. She could follow along if she needed to—her Korean was just good enough that she could understand it as long as she paid attention—but it didn't seem worth the effort.

Then Alfonso Curiel's face came on the screen. She recognized his photo—it wasn't the school portrait from the rally, but another one that had been going around, of Curiel in a hoodie, arms crossed and staring down the camera. She was still trying to make sense of the headline—she read slowly in Korean—when the channel changed with what seemed like an audible blip, back to the other channel. A commercial was on for a local Korean appliance store, advertising special prices on rice cookers and washing machines. Grace looked at her parents. Their faces were taut. Held still. At attention.

"It's still commercial," she said, taking the remote from her father.

She changed the channel back. They were playing a shaky video. Grace knew what she was watching right away: bodycam footage of Curiel's shooting. There he was, waving empty hands at Trevor Warren, then slowly moving one of them to his back pocket—to retrieve his wallet, as it turned out. The anchor narrated the scene in fast, solemn Korean, as five shots popped in quick succession. A tearful black woman came on the screen. "Remember his name," she said, pointing at the camera. Korean subtitles ran beneath her.

The video must have just been released, though Grace couldn't understand why. There was probably some legal explanation, but the timing seemed inflammatory, not to mention downright stupid. The grand jury decision was still brand new, the insult raw and vivid. And now here was proof that the kid was unarmed, that he'd been killed in cold blood.

Paul took the remote and flipped back to the drama, which still hadn't come back from commercial. Grace moved her hand to take back the remote, but Paul stopped her with a warning look. She glanced at Yvonne, who was staring at her lap, practically catatonic. It was so pathetic it made Grace angry. They couldn't even watch the news? That was too much for them to handle?

Ever since Miriam stopped talking to Yvonne—and maybe, Grace wasn't sure anymore, for years before—the merest allusion to black people, to race or racism, brought a prickly charge to the Park home.

She wondered if it was like this in other families, if her friends and their parents avoided this theme in the way they might avoid talking about sex.

Two years ago, Miriam brought home a man named Kenechi, for the sole purpose—Grace was convinced—of trolling their mother. He was the perfect tester black boyfriend for Korean parents: a clean-cut, Ivy League–educated investment banker from a middle-class immigrant family. Otherwise, he was completely wrong for Miriam, almost a caricature of a fratty finance guy, with his pink polo shirt and his constant allusions to Wharton. If he'd been white, Grace was sure Miriam would have hated him. Instead, she introduced him to her parents after their third date. She didn't prepare them— Grace suspected, in fact, that their mother expected a Japanese man, which would've been trouble enough—and Yvonne acquitted herself horribly. The language barrier should've worked to her advantage, but she managed to ask how many parents he had, and poor English didn't excuse the look of open distaste on her face. The only redeeming quality of that excruciating dinner was its unexpected brevity. It was the only time Grace saw the guy and the last time Miriam saw her parents.

But as bad as that was, it didn't really account for this lasting breach. Kenechi was just some dude Miriam dated for a month. She ended up ghosting him when she noticed he followed dozens of twenty-year-old Asian girls on Instagram. She met Blake online a few weeks later and never mentioned Kenechi unless Grace brought him up. Whenever Grace pestered her about him—which she did, often at first, trying to understand what had happened—Miriam got annoyed and changed the subject.

No, there was something else there, something bigger, she was sure of it. She could feel it like a glass wall, real and dangerous, but only made visible in certain lights—by dirt or fingerprints, or the glint of things reflected. Alfonso Curiel flashed against it, throwing its contours into relief, and she wanted to reach out and touch it. To confirm it was there and feel its resistance. To learn its shape and size, so she might find a way to remove it without shatter.

"What an awful story," she said.

Yvonne reached for Paul's dirty dishes and stacked them with her own. She stood up and started clearing the table.

"I mean it's crazy they're not even indicting him," Grace pressed on, watching her mother. "You saw that, didn't you? He just shot him in cold blood."

They didn't answer, and Grace wondered if the three of them were even equipped to have this conversation. She and her parents spoke to each other in a hybrid of English and Korean, slipping back and forth between languages, sometimes several times in a single sentence, but none of them was perfectly bilingual. Korean was Grace's first language, but it faded fast once she went to school; she could still speak with a child's vocabulary, plus pharmacy Korean, but her tongue tripped on anything complicated. Paul and Yvonne knew some basic English, enough to deal with their non-Korean customers, but despite living in California for thirty years, they'd never learned to speak it fluently. Most of the time, Grace and her parents understood each other. They had enough words to communicate what was important, Grace thought—needs, fears, comfort, love. But she didn't know how to say "indict" in Korean, which meant her parents were unlikely to understand when she dropped the word in English.

Miriam said she and Grace had grown up sheltered and incurious because their parents only ever talked to them about their tiny universe—school and church, family and friends. She said it was a choice, that Paul and Yvonne had decided to box them in like hothouse orchids, so they'd need and obey them without thought. It was another of her unfair pronouncements, an attempt to spin Yvonne's dedicated parenting as selfish cunning, to justify Miriam's perpetual ingratitude.

She was about to drop the subject when Paul shook his head. "You don't know the whole story."

"No," she admitted. "But I know he was an unarmed kid and that he's dead now."

"People make mistakes. The police didn't know he was unarmed, and he was running from them." He picked his teeth with a jagged fingernail.

"You can't actually be saying it was his fault."

"Grace," he said sternly, and she realized she'd raised her voice. He cast his eyes toward Yvonne, who was at the kitchen counter, cutting a melon, pretending not to listen. "Geuman dwo."

Geuman dwo. Stop it. Drop it. That's enough. It was how her parents rebuked her when she was a child, a sharp command that pressed their authority, leaving no room for questions. Now it just pissed her off.

She spoke loud enough for Yvonne to hear. "It's been two years," she said, the exasperation of months of careful silence coming out in her voice. "Why won't anyone tell me what happened?"

Yvonne came back to the table with a bowl of honeydew, sliced into pale green wedges. There were tears in her eyes—she was quivering from the effort of holding them in, and still they spilled over, falling down her drawn yellow face. She set the plastic tray down one corner at a time, as if afraid to make a sound.

"I'm sorry, Umma," said Grace. Her anger was gone, replaced by a worse feeling, a tangle of frustration and dread and guilt. Yvonne sat down and dabbed at her eyes.

What was on TV, in her news feed, out in the world, happening to strangers in strange places—it mattered, certainly, but it wasn't part of her life. She couldn't let all that sour her on what she knew to be true, the fundamental goodness and value of the people she loved. If she did that, she was no better than Miriam.

Yvonne scooped one last tear, like a seed pearl, with the nail of her ring finger. She rubbed her nose with a small settling sigh, then stabbed a piece of melon with a tiny fork. She held it out to Grace, one hand cupped under the fruit to catch the drops of juice. "Try this," she said, putting on a fragile smile.

Grace felt the usual resistance—it embarrassed her, even at home, when Yvonne tried to feed her like a child. But maybe it was best, for tonight, to accept her mother's mothering. She opened her mouth and received the sweet bite.

FOUR

SUNDAY, AUGUST 11, 2019

The light turned red and Shawn rubbed at a sore spot under his right shoulder blade, testing the muscle for any unusual pain. The sun was setting on a long Sunday, no day of rest for a mover.

He wondered what Ray was doing, if he had any regrets about quitting so fast. He'd lasted all of three weeks with Manny, two of those weeks straight sandbagging, before the drive and the labor burned him out. It was too much too soon, and besides, he said, he had to go to church on Sundays. Duncan hired him part time at his bar, to give him something to do and keep his parole officer out of his ass, but it made Shawn nervous, not being able to keep an eye on him. That Ray might slip up, get bounced right back to prison.

Shawn knew the job was hard. It was exhausting—the heavy schedule, the heavy lifting. He'd been in good shape when he started—there wasn't much to do besides read and work out in the pen—but moving was a challenge, demanding things of his body that had never been needed before. It had taken a while to learn the technique. How to pivot backward through stairwells, how to lift loaded boxes and couches without straining his back.

He was forty-one now, not young anymore, but he was built solid enough and knew his way around a move. He figured he could do this at least ten more years if he wanted. Manny had been a mover until he was almost fifty, only quitting to start his own business.

But there were some parts of the job that never got easier. The suspicious looks, the bad tips. Most people assumed he was stupid, that his life was little and wasted, plainly inferior to theirs. There was one customer early on—a black doctor with a thin white wife, moving into a mansion with marble columns in Studio City—who clapped him on the back and asked if he didn't wish he'd gone to college. Shawn almost quit on the spot.

Still, most days, he was glad he stuck it out. He liked the money, for one, the slow but steady flow of income it provided, clean money to add to Jazz's salary and keep him out of trouble. The labor kept him physically fit. Mentally, it wasn't extraordinarily stimulating, but there was always some problem solving, and he was picking up Spanish, since some of the people he worked with didn't speak much English.

And he was grateful, if not without ambivalence, for his continued connection to Los Angeles, the place he was born and raised and had never meant to leave. Despite all the shit, the baggage and tragedy, he had memories here, and they weren't all bitter.

Six, sometimes seven days a week, he ran across the city, skimming its streets in a moving truck. Some days he saw more of Los Angeles than he had in his entire childhood. This morning, his team moved a white couple from Echo Park to Sherman Oaks; in the afternoon, they moved a Mexican family from Boyle Heights to Compton, taking him within five miles of his old place, his nostalgia faint enough to enjoy without pain.

It was past five o'clock by the time he got back to Manny's office in Northridge, and he was looking forward to going home. He just had to get to Mid-City to pick up Darryl, Dasha, and Aunt Sheila first. They'd ridden down with him yesterday morning to spend the weekend in L.A., staying with Uncle Richard's sister, Aunt Reggie, and Claudette, her roommate and—they all knew, though they'd never been told—longtime girlfriend, who'd moved in shortly after Aunt Reggie and Uncle Eli's divorce. Now that Jason and Crystal were grown, she liked having the kids over, playing the part of the cool young grandma in the big city. Shawn shuttled them back and forth at least once a month during the summer. Every now and then, they'd get together with Jason and Crystal, who lived in Fontana and San Bernardino.

He called Aunt Sheila from the freeway.

"I was just about to call you," she said.

"I'm on my way, Auntie."

"Change of plans. Jules is taking us to dinner."

Shawn kept his sigh as silent as he could manage. Aunt Sheila hadn't mentioned seeing Jules Searcey, and he suspected she'd planned to meet him well in advance.

"It's Sunday," he said. "Don't we need to get home?"

"I already said we'd go, Shawn. Besides, it's what the kids want to do. They don't want to leave L.A. yet. We'll have our Sunday dinner here. Ray and Nisha'll be glad to have more time alone."

Sunday dinner was one of the cornerstones of their family life. It was practically sacred—had been so through all their shifts, their contractions and expansions; was probably precious because of them. Most weeks, they met at the Holloway house, where they'd cook or, on busy weekends like this one, pick up takeout. The important thing was that they were all together, or so said Aunt Sheila. If anyone else tried to change plans last minute, they'd be in for a sermon.

"Well, did you tell Jazz?" he asked.

"You know I did. She's gonna put Momo to bed early and watch Netflix. Sounded excited about it, too. I was almost offended."

"Alright, then. Go ahead. I'll pick you up later."

"What're you talking about? You're coming."

"Are Aunt Reggie and Claudette going?" He had a feeling they weren't—Searcey didn't know them, and Aunt Sheila wouldn't invite them along on his dollar. "I should catch up with them."

"Reggie's got an Al-Anon meeting." She paused. "She's not an alcoholic. I guess Crystal is, though." Her voice was lowered, trying to reel him in with some weak-ass family gossip everyone already knew.

"I don't know. I think I'll just hang for a bit, drive around or something."

"All you do is drive around. Come on, join us. The kids'll want you there."

He shook his head, knowing he didn't have a good excuse. "Alright. I'll pick y'all up in half an hour."

"Don't worry yourself. Jules is coming to get us in a minute. We're going to Roscoe's."

Of course Searcey was treating them to fried chicken. "The one on Pico?"

"Yeah, near Reggie's. We'll get in line. You get there when you get there."

They were all waiting for him when he walked in, seated at a booth surrounded by pink neon lights. Aunt Sheila waved him over, and Searcey stood to greet him, his knee popping as he rose, his long body extending like a ladder.

There was a time when Shawn stood in awe of Jules Searcey, when Shawn was a skittish teenage boy, and Searcey this tall white newspaperman who had Aunt Sheila in his thrall. Looking at him now, Shawn felt his own age. Searcey was well kept, his eyes still hawkishly bright behind his glasses, but he was starting toward bony where he had been lean, and his long, boyish flop of hair, once reddish brown, had turned a steel wool gray. It seemed incredible that he'd been in Shawn's life for so many years, when Shawn had done nothing to maintain their acquaintance. But he was stuck with him, loosely, at least, for as long as Aunt Sheila lived. She and Searcey would never let each other go.

He shook Shawn's hand and smiled. "For the record, Dasha's the one who picked Roscoe's," he said.

"I found it on Yelp," she said proudly, making room for her uncle. "Grandma says you used to come here."

"We've been coming here since your daddy and uncle were children, when there were no lines and no white people." She touched Searcey's shirtsleeve. "No offense, Jules."

Jules laughed. "None taken."

"I told Dad we were coming here, and he said him and his friends got in a fight in the parking lot once," said Darryl. He turned to Shawn. "Were you there?"

"Doesn't ring a bell," said Shawn.

"He said they were picking up food, and some guys jumped them when they came out. Dad and his crew won, but when the other guys ran off, they saw one of their friends was missing." Darryl grinned like he was getting to the good part of a favorite joke. "Turned out the poo butt ran away carrying the food bag. Said he had to protect the chicken."

Shawn recognized the story, but it was so distorted it might as well have been made up entirely. It had been at a McDonald's, not Roscoe's, and it wasn't some mischievous tussle. One of Ray's friends got shot in the arm, and that poo butt—Shawn had never heard Darryl use that phrase before; he must've picked it up from Ray— caught a beatdown so bad he had to go to the hospital.

"That's not a nice story," said Aunt Sheila, giving Darryl a stern look.

He shrugged with one shoulder. "I thought it was funny."

"Has your daddy been filling your head with this nonsense?"

"It's not nonsense, Grandma. I like hearing about how he grew up, that's all." He looked down, grumbling, and Shawn felt for the boy. He knew the kids were thrilled to have Ray back in their lives; he knew, too, that it wasn't all they'd hoped for, that there was an uncomfortable gap between the father they'd imagined and the father they had. It wasn't that Ray was neglectful, though he spent less time with the kids than Shawn expected. It was that the time they did spend together was subtly strained, plagued by an invisible sense of distance. The years away had worn on them all.

They ordered fried chicken livers, an Obama Special, and a Herb's Special with gravy and onions. Shawn had been hungry, and he was glad enough to keep his mouth full of chicken and waffles while the others talked around him.

"I ran into your aunt earlier in the summer," Searcey told Shawn, when there was a lull in the chatter. He glanced at Aunt Sheila, and Shawn swallowed, his guard pulled all the way up. He wiped his lips with a napkin and set it down, knowing this dinner was a setup.

Jules Searcey and Sheila Holloway didn't "run into" each other. Twenty-eight years after they first met, they lived in two different cities, with only a handful of acquaintances in common. They pretended at friendship—Shawn could even concede there was genuine affection between them—but what kind of friendship could there be between a man and his goose with the golden eggs? Searcey had been a junior reporter in 1991, fresh out of school, tireless and passionate, nothing to his name. He was looking for the story that would make his career. He found it in the death of a bright young black girl named Ava Matthews.

Searcey lived in Venice, last Shawn checked. "Did you meet up at the beach?" he asked.

"There was a rally for that poor boy, Alfonso Curiel, remember?" said Aunt Sheila. "Brother Vincent asked me to say a few words."

"She was amazing," cut in Dasha. "I didn't know Grandma could talk like that. She brought the house down."

"Oh, stop." Aunt Sheila waved away the compliment, looking mighty pleased.

Shawn looked at his sweet, cheerful, undamaged little niece. She had on the Black Lives Matter T-shirt she'd taken to wearing, and her face was fierce with pride. Shawn wondered if she understood what Aunt Sheila had lived through, what she had suffered and survived so she could "bring the house down." The kids knew the family history, but they hadn't been there when Ava died, when Aunt Sheila learned that she could trade their pain for attention, which at times felt almost like justice while being nothing like it at all. Darryl and Dasha were angry, sure, but their anger was inherited, abstract and bearable. They could indulge it without getting burned.

No one had told Shawn about any rally, and it was just as well. He loved his aunt, but he didn't need any part of her agitating, her relentless attempts to take Ava's death and put it to work. That was her right, and if it made her useful to Brother Vincent and Jules Searcey and all the others who could count on her to show her face and sing her song—well, it wasn't Shawn's place to take that away. He'd be damned, though, before he played along.

"I actually read *Farewell Waltz*," said Dasha, blushing a little as she looked at Searcey.

Shawn felt the chewed mash of meat and batter and gravy turn to a hot gluey knot in his stomach.

Farewell Waltz: The Life and Death of Ava Matthews. The definitive account of Ava's murder, her killer's trial, its impact on her community, on Los Angeles, on the '92 riots, built from Searcey's reporting at the *Los Angeles Times*. It was a bestseller, a prizewinner, widely praised as seminal and important. Shawn had read it, too, more than once, and he might've been on board if it were about someone else's sister.

"Thank you. That means a lot to me," said Searcey. "And I have to say, I'm impressed. It's not exactly light reading."

"I liked reading about my aunt," she said. "She lived such a short life, it's nice to know she was someone special."

"She was special."

Shawn watched Aunt Sheila close her eyes and nod. He felt nauseated.

"I mean I know that's not the important part," said Dasha. "It shouldn't matter. But I don't know, it's just so sad to think about what we all lost. Not that—I don't know what I'm saying." She bit her lip.

"I get what you're trying to say. I think we should celebrate her life, or she becomes nothing but a death. It's just a fine line to walk. We know Alfonso Curiel was a good student. It doesn't mean a bad student deserves to be killed. But it's worth noting that systemic racism is strangely indiscriminate. Unfortunately, many people are still willing to believe that only thugs get themselves killed."

Darryl spoke up. "People tried to act like our aunt was a thug, too. Like, she was the victim, but it was like she was on trial."

Shawn looked from his niece to his nephew. Together or on their own, they'd dug into Ava's story, deciding somehow that it was best to leave him out of it. It shouldn't have surprised him, but it did.

"It's inspiring to see young people engaged in this stuff," said Searcey. "There's a straight line between your aunt and Alfonso Curiel, and it's your generation that'll make sure that one day, kids like them aren't murdered with impunity."

"It's so fucked up," said Darryl.

"Darryl!" warned Aunt Sheila.

"Sorry, Grandma, but that's what it is. We're talking about kids my age getting killed for nothing. The same thing over and over. Been the same since before I was born." He clenched his fist while he talked, and Shawn thought for a second that he was about to pound the table.

"You're absolutely right," said Searcey.

This seemed to calm Darryl down. "Do you know what happened to her?" he asked.

"Who?"

Darryl glanced around the table, diffident all of a sudden. "You know who."

Searcey nodded. "She's off the grid. But as far as I know, she's still alive."

Shawn wondered, not for the first time, if he was telling the whole truth. Searcey was a tireless, thorough reporter—if anyone knew where to find Ava's killer, it was him. Shawn didn't know if it was pride or fear that kept him from pressing the issue.

"Jules is writing another book," said Aunt Sheila, changing the subject. "It's about antiblack violence in Southern California. Got a big book deal, too."

There was a murmur of congratulations, and Aunt Sheila beamed at him with actual pride.

"Oh, it's not about money, Sheila. I'm just glad I get to write it. People act like Southern California's this egalitarian wonderland, but there's so much violence and injustice right here that no one wants to talk about. Too many of us are getting by feeling good just because we're not Mississippi."

Shawn almost smiled. The way this man spoke, with a show of humility and magnanimity that was the gentle face of power.

"He's writing a whole section about Ava," said Aunt Sheila.

Shawn blinked. So this was why they were here.

It wasn't enough for him to use their family, to squeeze Ava for every last drop. He had to break bread with them. Required their blessing. Well, he wasn't gonna get it from Shawn.

"What's left to write?" He heard the acid in his voice and decided to let it stand.

Searcey's smooth face tightened. For the first time tonight, he looked uncertain of his welcome.

"Shawn." Aunt Sheila's tone would've put the fear in him when he was a child.

There was an uncomfortable silence before Dasha piped up, asking Aunt Sheila if they could make fried chicken and waffles together at home. It was a clever little subject change that let them get on with their dinner. But Shawn knew Aunt Sheila was upset with him, and when Searcey excused himself to make a phone call, she made sure to tell him.

"You're being rude to Jules," she said, talking fast, like she had a lot to say before Searcey came back.

"No, I'm not," countered Shawn. He heard a juvenile whine creep into his voice that he couldn't control with Aunt Sheila, no matter how old he got. He hoped the kids didn't notice. "You couldn't just talk to him another time? Why'd I have to be here for this?"

"It's my fault," said Dasha. "I wanted to talk to him."

Aunt Sheila looked at her granddaughter and sighed. Shawn suspected she might've offered the kids up as an excuse if they weren't sweet enough to volunteer. "He wanted to ask me some questions about Ava, about her legacy. I thought you might want to talk to him, too," she said. "You are Ava's brother."

"No. I'm not gonna do that."

"And why not?"

He took a deep breath and kept his voice low. "Because he didn't know Ava, and he's never been interested in who she was. Not ever."

Darryl's and Dasha's eyes widened in sync, and they glanced back and forth between their uncle and grandmother.

Aunt Sheila scoffed. "What a stupid thing to say, Shawn. He wrote the book on her."

Searcey had never met Ava, but with Aunt Sheila's help, he built up her lasting public image, first in his articles, then in *Farewell Waltz,* which came out two years after Ava's death. Most of the book was about the murder and its aftermath, but there was a thirty-page chapter about her brief, lamented life. Half of it was devoted to her musical genius, proven by her victory in a youth Chopin competition, where she played a nocturne and the Waltz in A-flat major, op. 69, no. 1, better known as the *Farewell Waltz.*

There was widespread agreement that piano was Ava's ticket to college, that it was her way of transcending whatever it was she was meant to transcend. Even in death, it made her extraordinary. Not just any tragic black girl, but one who was smart and talented, full of promise.

Shawn believed in his sister, and he'd spent plenty of time fantasizing about the life she might have had if she'd lived past sixteen.
But the piano, even that unforgettable day of triumph—it wasn't
what made Ava Ava, and it sure as hell wasn't what made her worth
mourning.

Searcey buried the real Ava, and no one but Shawn even seemed
to notice. They liked him, all of them. They were willing to let him
in. What would he take from them this time?

"That book." Shawn held his head. "That goddamn book."

"That book is the only reason people ever cared about Ava,"
snapped Aunt Sheila.

He forced himself to remember: this was the woman who spent
years phoning lawyers and politicians and reporters, anyone with
power who would pretend to listen, people who must have seen her
as a nuisance, the wailing black woman with the dead niece who
didn't understand her unimportance, who refused to move on and
leave them be.

"White people," he said softly.

"What?"

"It's the only reason *white* people cared about Ava."

Aunt Sheila snorted. "And who do you think runs the news?
Who do you think runs the courts?"

"And what happened in the courts?"

Her nostrils flared in anger, at Shawn or at history or both. She
took a long, simmering breath and glossed over his question. "Shawn,
honey. It's been twenty-eight years. People are forgetting her. I don't
want them to forget her. I want them to remember her and honor
her. Jules let everyone know Ava's name, so I really don't care what
you think of him. We can't let Ava be forgotten."

"I haven't forgotten her. But if you think Searcey honors her, maybe
you have."

For a second, he thought she would reach across the table and
smack him, and he winced in anticipation. When she didn't move,

he felt the unfairness of his accusation, hanging there, unretractable, brazen and unpunished.

"I didn't mean that," he said gently. When he moved to touch her arm, she stiffened, and he withdrew. "You do what you want, Auntie. But I want to be left alone."

FIVE

FRIDAY, AUGUST 23, 2019

Yvonne called over to Grace from the register. "Uncle Joseph's coming in tomorrow, isn't he?" She must have been finished with her accounting—they didn't chat much when there was still work to do.

"Yeah," said Grace, scanning a pill bottle to make sure its contents matched the script and the label.

"So you can relax and enjoy your date tonight."

There was a cloying solicitous hope in her mother's voice. This was something new, and it irritated Grace. Yvonne had spent an enormous amount of energy keeping her daughters sheltered and homebound growing up, away from boys and bad influences, to the point where Grace longed to go to church and SAT school just to be with people her own age on weekends. Grace had once heard Miriam describe her high school self as a "cloistered Korean freak show," and she knew that's how her sister still saw her, probably not all unfairly. Sure, she wasn't the most outgoing, but it annoyed her that Yvonne of all people worried about her social life now, just because she was suddenly too old to be single.

"You won't be late?" It was past seven o'clock.

"We're not meeting until nine," she said. "It's just for a drink, Umma."

Grace had made the mistake of telling her mother about this Coffee Meets Bagel date with a Korean American anesthesiologist. Yvonne was more excited for it than she was. Grace was exhausted, looking forward to her two-day weekend, and she'd spent the latter part of the day wondering how rude it would be to cancel. Too rude, she knew, when she was just feeling tired. And Yvonne would jansori her to death.

"What will you eat?" she asked.

"We have leftover kimchi jjigae, right?"

"Omona," said Yvonne, with genuine dismay. "You can't have kimchi jjigae before a date. I'll pick up some kimbap. You can eat it in the car."

Grace wrapped up at Woori while her mother went to the market. It was part of their routine, Yvonne shopping and feeding Paul and Grace dinner even after full days at the store. Radishes were on sale this week, and Yvonne was going to make a big batch of kkakdugi—that was the entirety of her weekend plans.

She came back just as Grace was getting ready to lock up. Grace noted that her mother had done her shopping in record time, probably worried about making her daughter late.

"Ready?" Yvonne asked.

Grace locked the door and relieved Yvonne of some of the grocery bags. When she looked up, her mother was staring at her. "What?" asked Grace.

"Aish." Yvonne shook her head. "You should do something about your hair."

The sun was low in the sky as they left the market and walked toward their car. It was quiet now, the parking lot less than half full. A car pulled out of its spot, and Grace watched idly as the driver lowered his window. He had a dark cap on, hiding his eyes, but he seemed to be looking in their direction. They were an awkward distance from the car—if he wanted to ask them a question, they'd have to get closer. There was something odd about his face, she thought. The color was off. The texture.

He was wearing a mask.

Yvonne shouted and shoved Grace so hard, she staggered and nearly fell down four feet away.

She never saw the gun, it happened that fast. One shot, cracking the world apart.

Her mother dropped to her knees and crumpled on the ground, her face white. She folded forward, holding her stomach, and Grace saw the blood there, dark and vital, dripping on the asphalt.

Grace was on the ground, holding her mother in her arms.

"Ga," Yvonne pleaded. *Go.* And Grace knew that even now, her mother was thinking of her.

But the shooter was gone. Grace hadn't even seen him drive away.

How much time had passed? Ten seconds? A minute, max? Just a few blinks ago, her mother was standing at this same spot, lugging groceries. The bags were on the ground now, their contents spilled on either side of her. Kimbap and tofu and sesame oil. Blue-skinned grapes and death-white radishes. Her body had been healthy and whole, all her blood hidden away. It was all over the place now. Grace felt it seeping into her shoes.

She saw herself holding her gutshot mother, crying and waiting for help, or for whatever was left to come. She heard the crash of an abandoned shopping cart, someone running in their direction. All at once, it seemed, they were surrounded by people, asking questions and offering things. Their faces were familiar but she knew none of their names. They were like a cast of minor actors, populating the background. And this was a scene in a movie—that's where it belonged, a slick suspense thriller, where people lived dangerously and violence was the rule.

Because how could this happen here? In this strip mall parking lot, in front of the place they went to work, where they rented their dramas and bought their groceries? This wasn't a war zone or some ghetto back alley. It was an ordinary place, too boring to belong anywhere but real life.

And people didn't get shot in real life. Not people like her mother.

Someone must have called 911, because the ambulance came, and Grace watched as the EMTs piled out, like so many extras with their rubber gloves, their monochrome jumpsuits. Yvonne was hanging on to consciousness, her eyelids fluttering, a whimper on her lips. Their arms came down, and they took her from Grace's lap, strapped her to a stretcher, and loaded her into the back of the ambulance. When Grace tried to climb in after her, they all but slammed the doors in her face. They were taking Yvonne to the Northridge Hospital Medical Center. Grace could meet them there, they said. They warned her not to try to tail the ambulance, then sped off, lights and sirens running.

Her mother was gone, and Grace was alone, filthy with her blood. The bystanders swarmed around her, talking at her, questioning her, as if she owed them an explanation. One of them even had his phone out, held up and pointed at her. She wanted them to leave. She needed to get out of this place. The car was right there. She closed her eyes and pictured the drive to the hospital, tried to breathe normally and steady her hands. She was still steeling herself when she realized Yvonne's purse was gone, her car key with it. She was stranded here, among strangers. She wondered if one of them might give her a ride to the hospital, if they cared enough to be kind when it cost them something, even if it was just bloodstains on a back seat.

She called her father, though as soon as she hung up, she couldn't remember what was said.

Sirens again—three police cars swept into the parking lot.

They were too late. Everything important had already happened.

The waiting room looked disturbingly grimy. She hadn't spent much time in hospitals and had always pictured them, thoughtlessly, as spotless, sterile places, as unpolluted temples of healing, helmed by handsome doctors in white coats. She was reminded now that they were full of the sick and the poor and the dirty. The waiting room was packed, some of the people in it clearly in need of medical attention. Others waited without visible injuries, and she wondered who they were waiting for. A young Latina woman sat with a little boy on her lap. She dozed lightly, but the child was awake, and he gazed at Grace, his wide eyes a watery brown. Were they waiting on a gunshot victim, too? The gangbanging baby daddy? This was racist, she knew. But this chola-looking woman, she was asleep in this terrible place; maybe a night in the ER was no big surprise. All these people, they looked like nothing if not friends of misfortune. What was Grace doing here with them? The boy blinked at her and she looked away.

The frame of things was changing, widening so fast that it hurt her head to even think about it.

She'd lived her whole life shielded from violence. No one had ever so much as smacked her, apart from her mother and Miriam, and they'd never caused damage that lasted beyond the hour. She'd never even seen a gun, let alone witnessed a shooting.

And this was not just violence, not just calamity, but an attempt made by another human being on her mother's life. Who would want to hurt Yvonne? She was just a harmless middle-aged woman. She didn't have enemies, unless she counted Miriam.

At least Miriam had come. Grace had managed to call her, doing what was necessary despite her shock. The past few hours were already blurred, improperly processed, but she remembered shouting at her sister, enraged by her initial hesitance to rush to Yvonne's side, as if her petty shit mattered when their mother might be dying. It was almost a relief, that extravagant anger, a bright feeling that beamed through her helplessness and fear.

Miriam showed up a half hour after Grace arrived with Paul. He and Miriam hadn't seen each other in two years, but there was no sense of reunion, only of family thrust into crisis together. Paul hardly said anything at all. He sat with them, face blank and posture rigid, getting up and wandering off every few minutes, it seemed, more frequently as the wait stretched and the suspense became unbearable.

Yvonne was alive, for now. She was in her third hour of surgery, and no one was telling them anything. Grace had googled gunshot survival statistics but couldn't bring herself to read the results. She put her phone away, and for the first time in ages, she bowed her head and prayed like she meant it, like she needed someone to listen. If God would deal with this, if He would just pull her mother through and make everything okay, Grace would do anything. She would go back to church. She would be kinder to strangers. She would be a better daughter, a better person.

She was still praying, rocking and whispering into her clasped hands, when she felt Miriam touch her back.

"Yes?" she heard her say.

Grace opened her eyes and looked up in time to see the detective sit down next to her and stretch his hand out to Miriam.

"Neil Maxwell," he said, as Miriam took it uncertainly. "I'm a detective with the LAPD. You must be Miriam. I met your sister earlier."

Maxwell, that was his name. He was a big, gruffly handsome white man, about forty years old, with wiry brown hair and a solid torso, a commanding figure in a gray suit that looked at odds with the rumpled, thrown-on clothes of the other occupants of the ER waiting room. He showed his badge, and it was just like on TV, this man the star of his own police show. Making Grace a bit character, victim's daughter #2, with two lines the whole episode.

He gave her a concerned but reassuring look, one that probably came in handy when dealing with families in shock. He'd been the one who found her in the parking lot, who'd spoken to her in mur-

murs until Paul arrived. She wondered if he'd been lurking the whole time, waiting to talk to her again.

"Miriam Park," said Miriam. In theory, she didn't like cops, but it looked like she might be willing to make an exception, now that her mother was the victim of a crime. "Have you found him?"

"Not yet." He spoke neutrally, hinting at neither apology nor promise. "We're still interviewing witnesses, though it seems no one saw much of anything. My understanding is that no one else was in the parking lot until after the assailant drove off. We have conflicting descriptions of the car."

Grace didn't check to see if he was looking at her. She stared at her lap, shamed by her uselessness.

She hadn't thought to study the car, remember the make and model and license plate. She wasn't even sure what color it was— silver, if she had to guess, but it could have been tiger striped for all she'd been paying attention. The detective had pressed her, gently, but she couldn't answer his questions with any certainty.

"How's your mother doing?" he asked.

"She's still in surgery," said Miriam. "We have no idea when she'll be out."

Grace's eyes filled again. They had no idea whether she'd come out at all.

Maxwell sat with them for a minute, silent and grave, as if he were in this with them. Grace waited, knowing he had more questions, hating her inability to give him basic answers.

"Do you know if your mother's gotten any threats lately?" he asked.

She turned to him and met his eyes, relieved to field an easy one. "No, nothing like that," she said, shaking her head.

She looked to her sister for agreement, but of course she wouldn't know. Miriam was biting the inside of her lip, her expression pensive and strange and alarming.

Maxwell picked up on it, too, and addressed her directly. "Is there anyone who might have reason to hurt her?"

"No, of course not," said Grace, a feeling of dread mounting inside her.

The detective kept his eyes focused on Miriam. "There's a rumor going around about your mother."

The whole room seemed to fall quiet, ready for Maxwell's next words. But he didn't elaborate, just watched Miriam, his silence probing, provocative. He wasn't comforting them anymore.

Paul rushed into the waiting room, out of breath and smelling like tobacco. That's where he'd been, smoking a cigarette for the first time in years.

Maxwell stood up to meet him, and Grace saw a worried glance pass between her father and sister. Two years they hadn't seen each other—what private concern could they possibly share?

The detective introduced himself, extending his hand. Paul ignored it. "What's going on?" he asked. "I told you to leave my daughters alone."

Grace was stunned. He was trying to hide it, but her father was angry at the detective in charge of his wife's case. A man he'd just met, who was here to help their family.

She touched his arm. "Appa?"

No one would meet her eyes.

Her mother had been shot. Her mother might not survive. And yet Grace knew in her bones that there was even more to come.

"Take her home," Paul ordered Miriam. "Now."

I t was understood, to Grace's relief, that they would spend the night together. Miriam invited her to sleep over in Silver Lake, but the distance from Northridge, the thought of Blake's concern—even Miriam understood it was the worse option. In the end they went to the only home they shared, the house in Granada Hills. Grace opened the door for her sister with an odd formality, like a Realtor giving a tour to a skeptical buyer. Anticipation in the turn of the key.

It was almost eleven, and the house was dark but hot, the air close and stifling. On any other night, both her parents would be home now, watching TV, getting ready for bed. She hated the thought of their empty room. It scared her, a cursed idea. She remembered when she and Miriam were children, how they would drag their blankets to that room and sleep on the floor, then climb on the bed to wake Paul and Yvonne.

Miriam took her hand. "Have you even eaten?" she asked. Her voice was soft, gentle and exhausted.

Grace realized she hadn't had anything since lunch. It had been such a terrible night, and Yvonne hadn't been there to remind her. She thought of the kimbap her mother had bought for her, spilled and wasted in the Hanin parking lot.

Miriam steered her to the kitchen and sat her down at the table before seeing about food. The fridge was tightly packed, and Grace watched as Miriam rummaged through it, pulling out containers of rice and banchan and leftover kimchi jjigae. "I definitely missed this," said Miriam.

She microwaved the rice and left the stew to boil on the stove. Grace hadn't thought she was hungry, but her stomach started to ache as the smell of kimchi rose, warm and pungent. She sat still as Miriam set the table, understanding that her sister was taking care of her, even though both of them had to be suffering.

While the jjigae cooled down, Miriam studied the small stash of liquor their parents kept on top of the fridge. She selected a bottle of Crown Royal and brought it over with two water glasses full of ice. "Good old KTown scotch," she said, sliding it over to Grace and presenting her glass. "Pour for me."

The bottle was dusty, a fuzz of grime coming off on Grace's fingers as she poured a drink for her sister. "I'm pretty sure no one's touched this since you've been gone," she said.

Miriam was the only real drinker in the family. Grace was a light-weight. She remembered the last time she'd been drunk, that lousy night with her sister, the flurry of bad feeling, the hangover that lasted through the next afternoon. But that was in another universe, one in which the people Grace loved were uninjured and everything else, in retrospect, seemed remarkably okay. After this day, maybe a drink was just what she needed.

She started to serve herself, but Miriam took the bottle away from her. "Come on. We don't pour our own drinks," she said, filling Grace's glass halfway. "That's seven years of bad sex."

"Shit," said Grace. She found her phone in her handbag, realized she hadn't checked it in hours. "I had a date tonight. I forgot to cancel."

"Oh, that's right." Miriam kept close tabs on Grace's love life, and Grace had so little going on that she reported whenever she had a date. Her sister and mother weren't all that different, when it came down to it. They both loved her enough to want things for her. It was only the things that were different. "You stood up the Korean doctor?"

Grace read through her messages—there were eight of them, and the last five were long and angry.

"I stood up the Korean doctor," she said, blinking at the profanity. "What?"

She gave Miriam the phone and watched her scowl. "'Frickin inconsiderate cunt'? Why 'frickin'?"

Grace shrugged and Miriam handed her phone back.

"God, I think you really—" She paused, her lips parted on the next word.

"You were gonna say I dodged a bullet," said Grace.

Miriam nodded, a grim smile on her face.

Grace sighed. "Well, that's two in one day."

"Jesus Christ, Gracious." Miriam laughed, and it made Grace laugh—so that was still possible, in this new world.

They drank whiskey with their kimchi jjigae, a funky, soothing meal. The alcohol hit Grace fast, a cool fog calming her mind. She was glad her sister was here. She knew Yvonne would be grateful.

Grace took another sip of Crown and asked, "You'll make up with her if she comes out of this, right?"

"I don't know," said Miriam. "I've been wondering the same thing."

"Someone tried to kill her, Unni."

"I know that, and I'm worried sick about her. But it doesn't change anything." Miriam shook her head. "She's not a good person, Grace."

"How can you say that? She's been nothing but a good mother to both of us." When Miriam said nothing, Grace pressed her again, gently, feeling a desperate kind of optimism. "Come on, you know she's a good mom."

"That's separate." But she didn't deny it.

"Is this seriously because she was racist against the surprise black guy you dated for a month?"

"You know it's not about him."

Grace sighed. "I really don't know why you think she's so horrible, but surely this is punishment enough."

Something rippled across Miriam's face, controlled but breaching the surface. A look of dark knowledge. Her mouth opened and closed. In the silence, the hum of the refrigerator sounded like waking hornets.

"What if she is being punished?" Miriam asked, her tone infuriatingly careful. She combed her fingers through her hair, which had picked up an oily shine over the last several hours.

"What the fuck, Unni? You think she deserved to be shot?" Grace snapped.

Miriam's face filled with pity, and Grace felt a new certainty click into place. The interview with the detective, the looks passed between her sister and her father, Grace the monkey in the middle. And before that, for months, for years, the sense of being left out, of missing some crucial thing: her failure to understand the breakdown in her own family. She had imagined none of it. There was something important Grace didn't know, and Miriam had hidden it from her.

"What aren't you telling me?" she asked.

Miriam swirled the liquid in her glass and took a long, slow swallow before setting it back down. Finally, she looked at Grace and nodded, biting her lip with grave determination. She asked her, "Does the name Ava Matthews mean anything to you?"

Grace cocked her head. She'd geared herself up for a gut punch, and she knew this had to be it. But Ava Matthews? Who on earth was that?

"No," she said. "Is it supposed to?"

Miriam grimaced. "Yes. It's a name everyone should know." She sighed again. "How about Rodney King, you know that one?"

"Yeah, of course." Grace blinked, wondering what Rodney King could have to do with her mother. "You're talking about the guy from the riots, right?"

"The L.A. Uprising, yeah. Do you know much about that?"

Grace thought about it. She was a newborn in April 1992, but growing up around Koreans, she'd heard plenty of stories. She remembered one conversation at a church retreat, Alan Chung—who she'd had a big crush on—talking about his family's dry cleaners in Koreatown, looted and burned to the ground. He said his dad went back and helped his friends protect their businesses, since the police were off holding down Beverly Hills. A few of the other kids chimed in with their own family lore: lost livelihoods and brushes with death, fathers and uncles and cousins lying on rooftops with guns. Grace had felt oddly left out. Her parents never even mentioned the riots, which must not have reached them in the deep Valley.

"I know it was bad for Koreans," she said.

Miriam nodded. "Koreans owned a lot of the businesses in South Central, and they didn't tend to get along with their customers, who were mostly black. When the Rodney King verdict broke, they were kind of a natural target."

Grace glared at Miriam—her sister was stalling. "What is this, Unni? I don't need a fucking history lesson right now."

"It's not *history*, Grace, it's—"

"Just get to the point," she said. "Who is Ava Matthews?"

Miriam took a long swallow of Crown before looking back at Grace. "Ava Matthews was a sixteen-year-old black girl from South Central. She's the other reason the rioters went after Koreans." She spoke rapidly now, the words tumbling out of her in a single breath. "One day, she walked into a convenience store, and the owner accused her of shoplifting a bottle of milk. They got in a fight, and the owner shot her in the back of the head. When the police came, they found her with two dollars in her hand."

Grace's heart was slamming against her chest—she knew this was it; Miriam had thrown open the door to the secret chamber, to show her the monster inside. Only she still couldn't see it. "And what?" she asked, her mouth dry. "The owner was some Korean dude?"

Miriam shook her head, sadly, and watched her sister. "She was a Korean woman."

SIX

FRIDAY, AUGUST 23, 2019

I t was a Friday night. That was a big thing when Shawn was younger—Friday night, make the most of it. When he was a kid, it meant school was over; Ava would get him from his classroom, there'd be no homework and two days of playtime ahead. It meant a trip to the movies, corn dogs at the mall, listening to music in a circle around a boom box. Later, there were parties and joy rides and curfews laughed into nothing. Friday night was the first taste of freedom—there was no need to savor it, to try and parcel out the fun to make it last. It was time for trouble and revelry, revelry and trouble.

But Shawn worked Saturday mornings, and besides, he thought, he was getting old. Not old old, but older than he thought he'd ever be in those days, when the only people he hung out with were boys shining with furious energy. Now he spent most of his time with a woman and a child. There were just about two things he wanted on a Friday night: peace and quiet.

These were hard to come by with a three-year-old in the house. Monique had run Shawn ragged tonight. She'd seen a rodeo in one of her cartoons—goddamn the son of a bitch who put a rodeo on a kids' show—and all she wanted to do was climb on Shawn's back and shoulders and demand that he giddyup. Jazz tried to stop her, but Shawn could tell she was torn by how cute it all was—her little daughter on his shoulders, screaming with glee as he bucked and huffed and neighed. There was laughter in Jazz's voice, and she had her phone out, recording, while she shouted at Monique that she'd had enough. What could a man do? He horsed around until the child was tired.

Now was his chance for a little sliver of peace and quiet. It was nine o'clock—he wanted to be asleep in an hour. He took a long, hot shower while Jazz put Monique to bed. His neck was tender, and it took a second for him to connect the pain with his evening spent as a rodeo horse. He smiled to himself, rubbing the base of his neck with his thumb.

He put on a T-shirt and boxers and got in bed to wait for Jazz, leaning back against a stack of pillows. She was still putting Monique to sleep, a process that could take an hour and a half when Monique was in a demanding mood. She'd made Shawn read her three books the other night, the last of them twice in a row. That girl ruled this house—Jazz was less of a pushover than Shawn, but she was still putty in Monique's pudgy little hands. They were powerless against her sweet pout, her gleaming brown saucer eyes. What that child needed was a sibling, someone to challenge her reign. Who knew what kind of tyrant she'd grow into unchecked?

He chuckled to himself as he thumbed through pictures Jazz had taken on his phone, the latest in a long wall of pictures of Monique. There she was pretending to lasso him—Jazz had stopped her from using a jump rope, even though Shawn said it was fine—there mounted on his shoulders, clinging to his head, her eyes half shut, squealing. And underneath her was Shawn, his face so giddy with joy he was almost embarrassed, looking at it. Papa Shawn was a silly, silly man.

He was still scrolling through pictures when his phone buzzed. It was a text from Tramell, who he was in touch with again now that Ray was out. He opened it up, smiling to himself.

Thas crazy bout jung-ja han

He sat up. He read the text three times, sure that his eyes deceived him. But there was her name: Jung-Ja Han.

Not counting the remember-when stories, the ones that always had fresh quotes from Aunt Sheila, Jung-Ja Han hadn't been in the news in over twenty-seven years. Hers was a name people associated with the violent '90s, like Rodney King, like Ava Matthews. For a year, she was everywhere, in papers, on TV, on flyers—Shawn couldn't avoid that tight, proud, fearful face, though he'd wanted to with all his heart. Then, after the trial, she disappeared. It was over—no longer in custody, she burrowed away from the media, into a private life far away from South Central. No one knew where she was, what she was doing.

He knew this because he'd looked. With the unthinking reflex of the wronged, he'd kept an ear to the ground for news. He couldn't imagine how she lived, and part of him had always wanted to know, had wanted to feel the smart of it. When the internet came along, her name was the second one he plugged into a search engine. The only hits were the ones he'd seen when he'd looked for Ava. He tried again, now and then, over the years, but Jung-Ja Han had changed names or stayed laid low or both. She left no bread crumbs after '92.

But Tramell knew something. And Tramell wasn't the guy who always knew something—there had to be word going around. Jung-Ja Han was back.

Shawn googled her name. His shoulders slumped—there was no mention of her in any news outlets. And yet something had clearly happened.

His phone vibrated again—another text, this time from Duncan.

KARMAS A NASTY BITCH

He got out of bed and put on a pair of gym shorts. Jazz was still with Monique, but he didn't want to be on the phone when she came in, not about this. It didn't matter that it might be cold out—if anything, the desert night might calm him down. He stepped into his sandals and walked outside, the phone already at his ear. The motion sensor light turned on, bathing him in a wash of white.

He knew he must be desperate, calling Duncan for news. For the thirty years they'd known each other, Duncan had made Shawn consistently uncomfortable, for an impressive variety of reasons. When Shawn was small and eager, trying to hang with Ray and his friends, Duncan mocked him and ribbed him, took obvious pleasure in dominating him for sport. When Shawn started banging, Duncan egged him on every chance he got. When Duncan stopped banging, he counseled Shawn with sudden saintly condescension.

To his credit, Duncan had made a good life for himself. He never went to jail—he decided that wasn't for him the one time he got picked up for questioning. He kept things cool with the Baring Cross crew, but as far as Shawn knew, he quit all criminal activity when he enrolled in community college. He transferred to Cal State LA and funneled his smart-ass initiative into something legal and lucrative. Now he was a legit small-business owner, running a bar off the 14, where he made solid money off a regular rotation of drunks. He was good at talking to people, even the right-wing white folk who populated the Antelope Valley. They trusted him for some reason. Maybe because he was light skinned and green eyed with a fluorescent, charlatan smile. Shawn knew better, but he also knew Duncan was stuck in his orbit for good. He was Ray's best friend, and life had brought them all to Palmdale. And there were pros to having him around—Duncan was the biggest gossip in Greater Los Angeles, yet people still told him everything.

"You celebrating tonight or what?" Duncan asked. Shawn could hear the grin in his voice.

"What're you talking about?"

"I'm talking about Jung-Ja Han." He laughed.

"What about her?"

Duncan took his time, delighted to have him in suspense, and Shawn wanted to knock the news out of him.

"She got capped!" he finally answered. "In her own store and everything."

Shawn walked to the curb and sat down, planting his feet on the dark asphalt of the street. The night sky, brushed with faint stars, took on a precarious tilt. It was cold outside his body, and the warmth inside him was dizzying. He felt his heart pump heavily, the blood crying out.

"Yo, Shawn, you there?"

"Where'd you hear this?"

"It's going around, man. It's all over Twitter."

"You sure it was her?"

"I'm just telling you what I heard, but it sounds legit. There's some Koreans on here spilling all kinds of tea. She changed her name, but she stuck around. There's one girl swears her dad's been friends with this woman since the eighties. Started going by Yvonne Park in the nineties."

"Yvonne Park," Shawn echoed.

There was a week, about fifteen years ago, when a rumor went around that Jung-Ja Han was back in South Central, running another liquor store. There were flyers taped onto telephone poles, telling folks to get down to King Market and smoke her out. When Shawn went to see for himself, there were two people in front, telling anyone who went by that the rumor wasn't true. They were a black woman and her teenage daughter, and they said the store owner was a woman named Sa-Eun Ahn, who hired neighborhood help and was forgiving with credit.

Shawn went in anyway. He bought a bottle of milk and looked her in the eye. When she looked back at him, he saw fear—she saw him see it and looked away. The change was on the counter, waiting for him to pick it up and walk out. Instead he stood there, in silence, studying her. She was just about forty, the right age, her short black hair straight and thin, a third of it gray, but in the same limp, blunt-cut style Jung-Ja Han wore in '91.

But by '92, Han's hair was different—longer, softer, a more feminine look to go with the ripe protrusion of her pregnant belly. A year after the shooting, she'd no longer looked like the woman in the video; she was already planning to give that woman the slip. Shawn took his change and walked out. He didn't know what he would've done if it had really been her.

"Who did it?" he asked.

"I don't know," said Duncan. "Probably don't want to be advertising his name. You know police are gonna be looking for whoever shot a poor defenseless Korean lady." His voice grew mocking and babyish in a way that sounded jarring coming from a man in his forties, but Duncan had a point.

Nothing Jung-Ja Han could ever do would neutralize the shield of her fragile little Asian lady persona. She had the stamp of a victim, someone in need of heroism and protection. This was true when she murdered Ava and sobbed and blubbered as the police arrived. This was true when she sold her story of self-defense, testifying in tearful, shaky English, her dome of a stomach on full display. Unless she murdered a white girl, it would always be true.

"Where was she?" Shawn asked.

"A drugstore. In Northridge."

The chill got him now. That was where she'd been hiding out all these years? Northridge—where he went to work every day, commuting in from the Antelope Valley at the crack of dawn? How could he have been so near her and not have known?

And it was so close to the old neighborhood, not even thirty miles away from Figueroa Liquor Mart. He'd run farther than that.

Shawn pictured Northridge, the suburban streets, the bland, bloated houses. He remembered one move he did there, a Korean family moving into a flashy modern mansion in a gated community at the top of a hill. The mother, like most Korean women between thirty and sixty, made him think of Jung-Ja Han.

Was that where she lived? In a house on a hill with armoires and custom cabinets, a grand piano Ava would've wept with joy just to play, without a dream of owning?

He knew Jung-Ja Han never saw a day in prison, and yet he had always told himself she couldn't possibly live well. She had to be an outcast, an exile, doomed to a life sentence of dullness and hatred, success and happiness forever out of reach.

She deserved so little. Ava died at sixteen. All that time she should've had, the experience, the happiness—it had all turned to nothing in the flash of a gunshot. It wasn't fair for Jung-Ja Han to have more than that.

Until now, Shawn had been able to think of her—as he did often, in spite of himself—as a fugitive and a vagabond, marked for life in an unknown hell. But now he knew where she'd been—a bullet put her back on the map, running another store within the borders of Los Angeles. All these years, she'd lived in Shawn's city, free while he was imprisoned, prosperous while he struggled.

"Feels good, don't it?" Duncan asked, probing against Shawn's silence.

The light turned off, leaving Shawn in thick darkness.

"I don't know, man. This is too weird," he said. "I feel like I'm dreaming."

"You ain't dreaming, cuz. Somebody got Jung-Ja Han. Served some justice cold."

Justice—was that what this was, after all this time? He closed his eyes and waited for the feeling of satisfaction to rise.

Instead, he saw a courtroom, a podium, a face—all of it flashed brightly from a ready corner of his mind, the images crisp and vivid. The judge, a long white face jutting out from a heap of black robe, perched behind her bench, looking down at the rest of the room, where Shawn sat, small as a pill bug, looking up, up, up. He still remembered exactly what she looked like, handing down her decision with the power of God. When, years after the trial, he saw her picture in a book, he was surprised that it didn't match his memory. It didn't change what he saw.

He opened his eyes with a start. "Is she—?"

"Dead?" Duncan provided. "Don't know that, but from what I heard, it ain't no scratch. She's in bad shape. Why"—his tone teasing—"you want her dead?"

The question buzzed in Shawn's ear. "I gotta go, man," he said, and hung up. This was not a conversation he was about to have with Duncan.

He wasn't sure how long he sat there before he heard the door open. "Shawn?"

He turned his head without getting up. Jazz stood behind him, arms crossed against the cold, her brows knit with concern.

"Monique's knocked out now. What're you doing out here?"

The motion sensor kicked in as she approached, and the light came back on, pouring on Jazz, on the house behind her.

This was his life now: this place, this woman, that child. He stared at Jazz; she was worth staring at, always, no less astounding than she was when they first met. She was beautiful, there was that—satin skin, sultry eyes, and lips that looked heavy with sweetness—but his marvel rose from a deeper recognition. Shawn had gotten used to the idea that if he wanted something, he had to chase it down, and chase it down, and keep on chasing it down. Not women, or not just women—nothing in Shawn's life had ever been fixed; the rules had always been changed on him, the goalposts dug up and moved. And then Jazz showed up, and after the first months of fumbling lust, he discovered her body—that tall, sturdy woman's body—was not just a body but a pillar. He relied on her dependable warmth, her unwavering promise of home. She was, without question, the best thing that had ever happened to him.

And yet he hadn't surrendered himself to her, not in the way he knew she wanted.

"Baby?" she asked, when he didn't answer her. "Did something happen? Are you okay?"

She hurried over to him. Her slippers slapped the ground.

When she stood next to him, he reached for her and hugged her, his arms around her knees, his head dropped against her thighs.

Jung-Ja Han might be dead or alive, but either way, she was back. He'd locked it all away—the woman, the murder, his sister—and now, against his will, the seal had been broken. Shawn felt Jazz's hand on his head, and he trembled.

The doorbell rang just before midnight, when they were finally in bed. Shawn was still awake, and the sound jolted him upright. He felt Jazz rise to attention beside him.

"Baby, was someone coming over?" she asked.

He shook his head and shifted his feet to the ground. "Stay here."

It would've creeped him out most nights, hearing the doorbell when he wasn't expecting anyone. Shawn didn't like late-night surprises—no one did, not where he was from. But tonight, it felt extra ominous. Jung-Ja Han was back—who knew what else was at the door?

He didn't keep a gun anymore. Couldn't, legally at least, but he had no desire to either. He remembered too well what it felt like to run around packing. The thrill of knowing how little it would take for him to shoot it.

He glanced around for some other weapon to hold while he answered the door, but he gave that up—he wasn't really afraid of a burglar.

The doorbell rang again, followed by loud knocking.

"Shawn!"

Shawn relaxed—it was just Ray. He rushed to the door and opened it.

"You'll wake Monique up," he said quietly, hoping to set the tone.

Ray didn't take his cue. He spoke high and fast and exasperated, almost out of breath, as if he'd run the two miles from his house. "You weren't picking up your phone."

"Sorry," Shawn said, letting Ray inside. "I was talking to Jazz, and my phone kept buzzing. I turned it off."

"She wasn't picking up either."

"We were talking." Shawn warmed, thinking of the last two hours. She'd known his history, of course, so why had he spent all this time avoiding it? Jazz's quiet patience, her undivided attention—it had been good medicine.

"About Ava."

Shawn nodded. "So you heard, too."

"Course I heard. What, you think no one's blowing up *my* phone?" He sounded offended, possessive, like Shawn was trying to fence him out.

"That why you're here? You know I gotta work tomorrow."

Ray frowned at him. "I'm here 'cause I thought something happened to you, you ingrate. But as long as I came all the way over, how 'bout a drink?"

Shawn thought about objecting, but Ray was already entering the kitchen, and he followed. "I thought you might be police," he said. The admission gave him a light-headed feeling, and he sat down while Ray opened up the fridge. "There's beers in there. Grab me one."

"Jazz asleep?"

Ray handed him a cold beer and Shawn took a swig. "No," he said. He knew she could hear them in the kitchen and that she'd pretend to sleep until Ray was gone. "She's just giving us a minute."

Shawn thought about going to get her, but he was grateful to her and suddenly relieved that Ray had come, that they could share this strange hour. Other than Aunt Sheila, they were all the blood left that ever cared for Ava. It was extraordinary, in its way—their cousin and sister, who'd be over forty now, finally avenged.

"So you thought I was a cop, huh?" said Ray. "And I thought your ass got arrested. Let's knock on some wood."

They chuckled, half-heartedly, and rapped the linoleum counter—close enough.

"So where were you tonight?" Ray asked.

Shawn shrugged. "Here."

"Let's try it this way. Mr. Matthews, where were you on the night of the twenty-third, between seven and eight P.M.?"

"Like I said, I was here."

"With Jazz and Monique?"

Shawn nodded.

"Your woman and her toddler. I guess it could be worse."

"I wasn't in Northridge, that's for sure."

"Better be ready to prove it," said Ray. "When they figure out who she is, they gonna wonder why some sweet old Korean lady got herself shot. They gonna ask if she got enemies. And here we are, two black-ass felons with a blood grudge."

Shawn almost smiled. "What's your alibi then?"

"I don't have one."

"You weren't at home?"

"I was out."

"Where?"

"Just driving."

Shawn's heart sank. Ever since Ray started working for Duncan, his reformed-church-boy act had slipped and he'd become hard to pin down. His hours were vague and irregular, but he was out of the house a lot more than forty hours a week. Seemed like he barely even saw the kids. There were a few times Nisha had called Shawn, worried that her husband was unaccounted for. Shawn was too busy to keep an eye on him, and besides, Ray was a grown man—a father, too, with no desire to land back in prison—but he couldn't help but worry. Palmdale was full of ex-bangers from the old hood, and plenty of them got tired of commuting into L.A. for bullshit pay. Some of them found other ways to make ends meet. Put their heads together with old friends or friends of old friends. There was mischief around, if that's what Ray wanted.

"Shit, Ray," Shawn said, tacking on a laugh. "Was it you?"

"No. And you're sure it wasn't you?"

For a moment, Shawn remembered the weight of a gun, the resistance of a trigger against his squeezing finger. He tried to picture Jung-Ja Han now—not in the bloom of pregnancy, but graying, wrinkling, a woman in her fifties with terror in her eyes, the knowledge that her sins had caught her at last.

"No," he answered. "I been right here the whole time."

There would be no more sleep for Shawn today. First, the rattling sound of pulled blinds, the flush of morning light, and then Ava was sitting on his arm, poking his forehead with a wet finger.

"Wake up, Shawn," she said, singsong. "Wake up, baby brother."

Shawn groaned. It was a Saturday morning, and he'd been up late reading comic books until his eyes wouldn't stay open anymore, waiting for Ray to come back from wherever he was. He glanced at Ray's bed: still empty.

He pulled the covers over his head and mumbled through them, wishing his sister would go away. "What time is it?"

"It's almost ten, sleepyhead. Aunt Sheila said to go get milk."

"She said for who to go get milk?"

"She didn't say, 'Ava, go get some milk.' She said we need it. For breakfast. And she's making breakfast, so that leaves you and me, I guess." She paused, and Shawn lowered the covers to see her frowning at Ray's side of the room. Getting milk was a Ray chore—he let Ava boss him and never thought Shawn could do much of anything, and until like a month ago, he was all about helping his mom.

"Do you know where he is?" Shawn asked.

"He said he was hanging with Duncan and them, didn't he? Probably stayed out late doing whatever and crashed with him." She shrugged, but Shawn knew she was just trying to keep him from worrying. The first time Ray didn't come home, Shawn had wandered over to Ava's room in the middle of the night and slept curled at the foot of her bed.

He didn't remember their mother too well. He'd been too young when she died to retain any memories he couldn't question. The short halo of hair, the narrow, gleaming eyes—he knew her features, but they matched her photographs too perfectly, her smile always the same smile, the one that went with her green cardigan, with the two children bundled in her arms. When he was three, he'd gotten lost at the supermarket and wandered out to the parking lot, where his mother found him playing with a grimy stray dog. Shawn remembered that dog, its perked-up ears and long whip of a tail, and he remembered his mother's shout of horror and relief—"Shawn Matthews! Get away from that rat!" But it was a story Ava had told him before that was maybe more vivid to him now than it had been when he was younger.

What he did know about his mom was that she'd left home one day like any other, and a drunk driver rammed her car into a building and sped away. It was that quick and that random, and it had changed everything.

Maybe it wouldn't be a drunk driver who got Ray, but Shawn knew something could get him. Anything could happen, and Ray was putting himself in anything's way.

Ava snatched the covers out of Shawn's grip and tossed them away where he'd have to sit up to reach them. "Up, up," she said. "You can go like that. Just brush your teeth."

When he came back from the bathroom, Ava was wearing a Dodgers cap—Ray's Dodgers cap, the new one he'd left out on their desk.

"That's Ray's hat," said Shawn.

"He won't mind."

"You took the tag off."

She'd given Ray crap for leaving the tag on last time he wore it. "I did the dum-dum a favor. He looked like a fool with the tag hanging off the back of his head." She clicked her tongue against her teeth, shaping her mouth into a grin.

It was early enough that the streets were quiet. Shawn's friends would all be sleeping, taking advantage of their one day to stay in bed with no school and no church. No Crips out either—whatever they'd gotten up to the night before, it was over now; the score would get counted later. Ava was right. Ray probably got high and crashed at Duncan's, like last time and the time before that.

They walked past Frank's Liquor, their old corner store, where Aunt Sheila and Uncle Richard still got their butter and eggs. Frank had probably forgotten about the magazine incident by now, and even if he hadn't, all three of them looked different—Frank wasn't from the neighborhood, so they never saw him around—but they were used to bypassing his store, and habit was habit.

"You know he gonna get it when he gets home," Ava said. "That's three nights this week."

Shawn nodded. "Aunt Sheila gonna whup his ass."

"Hey."

"His butt."

Ava rubbed his head in approval and Shawn glanced around instinctively, but no one took any notice. "He'll be lucky if he just gets his ass whupped," she said. "If Uncle Richard throws him out, that's game over for Ray Ray."

Their usual corner store was two blocks past Frank's. Figueroa Liquor Mart was also a liquor store—if they wanted a grocery, they all had to drive to the Food 4 Less on Western—but it had what they needed, more or less; milk, anyway. It even called itself a grocery—there it was right under the main sign, painted on the wall in blocky black letters: FIGUEROA GROCERY—MONEY ORDER—MEAT—PRODUCE.

An electronic bell sang out as they entered—two tones, ding-dong. A woman looked up from behind the counter, watching them come in with a strange expression that snagged Shawn's attention. He'd seen this woman a couple of times before. She was a Korean woman—he couldn't tell how old, maybe twenty, maybe forty—with bobbed hair and a thin, hard mouth. Probably she was Mr. Han's wife. She was there alone, where Mr. Han usually stood with his arms crossed, watching the happenings in his store. Shawn didn't mind Mr. Han. He wasn't friendly, but he wasn't rude, and he didn't look at Shawn like some Korean men looked at him, like he was nothing but trouble in a boy suit. He always nodded at him when he came in, a stern nod, but one that signaled recognition.

There was none of that in Mr. Han's wife. She was staring at them—no, Shawn realized, she was staring at Ava.

"What's up with her?" asked Ava. "She's looking at us like we're wearing ski masks."

Ava and Shawn were on the same page, picking up the same signs. It was a gift, this sibling connection, a joint intuition about as close to psychic power as anything Shawn had ever seen. Together, they ignored the bad vibes. What was another rude Korean cashier? They needed milk, and they were already there.

Ava held the door open and looked through the quart jugs. "Two percent, yeah?"

"Yeah." Shawn glanced back at the cashier. They were the only people in the store, and she was watching them closely.

"These are all about to go bad," said Ava. She pulled out jug after jug, setting them on the floor, going for the ones in the back. She frowned and picked one. "I guess next week is better than this week."

Shawn helped her put the rest of them back.

"That bitch still staring at me?" she asked.

"Yeah," he said. "Come on, Ave. Let's get home."

She made a show of looking at Mr. Han's wife with a wide smile, then she put the quart bottle in the kangaroo pocket of her sweatshirt and smiled a different smile for him.

By the time he walked away from the refrigerated wall, Ava was already at the counter, facing off with the cashier. The woman's face was red, and she was shouting at his sister: "I see you! That's my milk!"

Ava raised her hands and started backing away from the counter. The plastic jug was still in her sweatshirt, so large and obvious it might as well have been held in her hand. But it wasn't, and before Ava could take it out, the woman reached across the counter and grabbed her by the collar. She pulled her like she might drag her over the barrier between them, the wall of glass and plastic that was supposed to keep them safe, one from the other.

Shawn shouted something, he didn't know what. His fear mashed the words on his tongue. Ava would fight this woman. He was sure of it. His sister was not one to bear insults.

Her footing slipped as her legs slammed against the rows of gum and candy, knocking them loose. Shawn couldn't see her face, just the back of her head, Ray's cap gone now, fallen to the floor.

She struggled, trying to writhe out of this stranger's grip. The woman wouldn't let go; she was stronger than she looked. But Ava did not lose. If anyone asked him, he could have said so—he was her brother, and she had beaten him and shielded him. Ava did not yield and she did not lose.

Her feet scraped the dirty floor and then righted themselves as she held on to the counter and found her balance. He couldn't see her face, but he saw the change in the woman's, the rage mixing with a familiar curdle of fear.

Ava planted her feet, and with the woman's hands still on her sweatshirt, she punched her, swinging but swift, swift and true. Her fist landed on the woman's jaw, and she punched her again, and again, and again, four hits to the face, with all of her power.

He knew his sister could fight—Ray told him stories, things he'd seen and heard. She got suspended once, for fighting a junior after

school. The junior got it in her head that Ava was giving her attitude, and she stopped Ava by the buses, pushed her shoulder, and
said, "What you looking at, orphan bitch?" Ava socked her so hard it
knocked the wind out of her; she might've done worse if the junior's
friends hadn't gotten in the way.

But Shawn had never seen it. He'd seen her strength and her stubbornness, but never her violence, never what happened when someone tried to push her down.

The contorted cry rose again from his throat, but he didn't move.
He either couldn't or didn't want to. He was terrified—his sister
would get in huge trouble—but he knew, too, that she was there
blazing in front of him, sure of herself and winning.

The woman let go of Ava's sweatshirt. Her face was already
swelling, and she raised her hands to touch it, her eyes dry but enraged, crackling red. Ava stepped back, and Shawn stepped toward
her, numbed and vibrating with shock and relief. It was over. Ava
was gonna get it and get it soon, but right now, it was time to leave.

She turned around. She put her hand in her front pocket, grabbed
for the milk jug. That's what Shawn was watching—he wanted to
see what she'd do with it, whether she'd put it back in the refrigerator, or take it with her, or fling it to the floor—when Ava fell. She
dropped, and the jug dropped, and his sister was down.

And then Mr. Han was rushing into the store, shouting and shaking his wife. It was like Shawn wasn't there at all—Mr. Han barely
looked at him. He yelled at his wife in his strange language, and she
cried back at him, suddenly helpless now, a desperate woman choking with sobs.

Shawn couldn't move. He was on the floor by his sister—how had
he gotten there?—the knees of his pajama bottoms wet with blood
and milk. There was a hole in her forehead, raw and shining. That's
what this was—the woman had shot his sister.

Weren't there stories—he thought there were stories—of people
who got shot in the head and survived?

911, Shawn thought. He had to call 911. Would they let him use their phone to call 911?

Mr. Han was on the phone. Shawn wanted to be the one talking, but he couldn't move, and he couldn't talk.

"My wife. Rubber lady." That's what Mr. Han kept saying. "My wife shot the—"

Robber lady.

Ava still warm on the ground, and Shawn there, watching, listening, and already there were lies in the air.

I t happened so fast—that's what people said, and when he watched the video, he saw for himself, it was all over in a matter of seconds. But was there a moment when he could've stopped her? When he could've run to his sister, shouted and hugged her until she reabsorbed the poison of her pride?

How many times did he have to relive it? For the cops, for the lawyers, for the judge; for Aunt Sheila, for Uncle Richard, for Ray; and for himself, most often and never-ending. Yet what did he really remember? A hand tugging a quart of milk. The hand and the milk falling, and his sister on the floor. Later, he could call up Ava's face as a hole ripped through it, and the woman behind her, Jung-Ja Han, standing in awe with a smoking gun.

They told him he cried and fell to his knees, but he could have sworn he was silent, removed and catatonic. When he could speak again, he spoke, and he told the truth. The video backed him up. Ava wasn't armed, and Jung-Ja Han waited until her back was turned to shoot her in the head. It was a relief—even the cops believed him; they were nicer to him that day than they ever would be again, because he was still a boy then, for the hours before the shock wore off.

But even with the video, even after he testified—Mrs. Han's smooth-talking black lawyer in his face, urging him to remember Ava's threats to kill Jung-Ja Han, to kill her right there or come back and kill her later—even after a jury took four days to convict Ava's murderer of voluntary manslaughter; even then, the lie had sway, the young Korean wife in mortal fear of the black gangbanging robber. The white lady judge gave Jung-Ja Han five years probation, four hundred hours of community service, and a $500 fine. A week later, she sent a man to jail for thirty days. He had kicked and stomped a dog.

SEVEN

SATURDAY, AUGUST 24, 2019

Even with all the Crown Royal weighing down her blood, Grace couldn't imagine falling asleep. Miriam had given up looking after her at around four in the morning, going to sleep in Grace's bedroom, the one they'd shared for so many years. Grace was sober and miserable and wide awake, nothing but heartache and headache for her troubles. She felt *bad,* helpless against the torment clawing her from the inside out. She remembered her teenage years, before she went on the pill, curling up with merciless cramps every time she got her period. That desperate pain. Her mom bringing heated stones and stroking her hair to coax her to sleep.

There was something Yvonne said—that you missed your mother when you were sick, when you were suffering. Grace thought of her in the ICU, fighting for her life. She couldn't bear the thought that she might not make it out. How could Grace get through this without her?

She was alone in the kitchen. Before she knew what she was doing, she had her phone out, her browser open. Her thumb selected the search bar. The video—that's what summoned her. The twenty-eight-year-old security footage circulated around the world.

It didn't take her long to find it, linked from a retrospective about the L.A. Riots. She lingered over the link, wondering what good it would do to watch this thing. Grace was squeamish about violence; it fascinated her, but while she could spend hours reading about serial killers, she avoided horror movies and certainly had no interest in snuff films. And that's what this was, wasn't it? A snuff film, with her mother behind the gun.

But she had no choice. This was the video that had damned Yvonne, the one that was meant to show she was a villain, a cold-blooded murderer. All those people who watched it and judged her, they didn't know her like Grace did; they were biased going in, the mere idea of a dead teenager enough to rile up their sympathies, to make them side with the victim. As if teenagers were all so innocent. Grace owed it to Yvonne to watch the footage with an open mind; she owed it to her mother to try to understand her.

She clicked the link. The video played. It was only fifteen seconds long—it took almost the full loop for Grace's eyes to adjust, to locate the moving blobs on the screen. She blinked, hit replay and pause before YouTube could generate the next video. Incredible. She'd just watched her mother shoot and kill a stranger, and she'd missed the whole thing.

This was the video that got everyone all worked up? It was so short, so silent, so removed from anything grand or gory or even particularly human. The footage was blue and grainy—she squinted at the still image. It took some concentration to distinguish the human outlines from the fuzzy blues of their surroundings. They were just left of the center, their black hair the two darkest spots on the screen. Facial features were blurred, expressions unreadable.

She replayed it, and this time, she knew where their limbs were and followed their every motion. Five seconds in, she paused again—she'd just seen Ava Matthews, the victim, punch Jung-Ja Han.

What on earth? How was this not self-defense?

She rewound and watched it again, and this time she saw that Jung-Ja Han had grabbed the girl before she got punched, yanking her forward. But she didn't *punch* her. Grace had never been punched in her life, and she doubted Jung-Ja Han had either, at least not before this—people just didn't go around punching other people. This girl—she was obviously crazy. She wasn't some innocent little angel.

Grace hit play again. Her righteous anger gave her a tiny jolt of courage; she felt more equal now to what was still to come.

Jung-Ja Han dropped out of sight, behind the counter—was she ducking or did she faint?—and Ava Matthews turned around, ready to flee the scene.

Then Jung-Ja Han came back up, her black hair reappearing above the counter, and Ava Matthews dropped, disappearing behind the store's aisles. Grace had to watch again to catch the quick movement of Jung-Ja Han's hand, the glint of an object, otherwise invisible.

This much was undeniable: Jung-Ja Han shot Ava Matthews from behind.

Grace eyed the view count—64,771 since the video was posted on YouTube in 2015, by a user named lee woohyuk with the message, "I want to give my deepest condolences." The number made her heart jump. Tens of thousands of people had sought out this footage in less than five years? How many had seen it when it was playing on every news channel? Millions? Tens of millions? More?

She put her phone down, stood up, walked around, swinging her arms like she was warming up for a wrestling match. It didn't help. She stopped pacing and lay down on the couch, held a hand to her throat, willing her pulse to calm down. She closed her eyes and concentrated on breathing. There wasn't enough air in the room.

Less than a minute later, she was back on her phone—she'd started this, and now she couldn't stop. She scrolled down to see the comments; she had a sudden, rapacious need to read them all.

There were so many vacuous comments, poorly spelled and worded exclamations of sympathy, anger, and virulent racism. "korean bitch just wanted to kill a black teennager!!!!!!" "Ghetto tripe got what she desreved. good!" It didn't seem right that so many people chose this particular comment section for their fly-by N-bomb drop missions, but the attacks on Koreans hit her much harder. After all, people sided with this girl just because she was black, then turned around and said *Koreans* were racist.

A commenter with an American flag avatar pointed out, in several threads, that Ava Matthews's assault of Jung-Ja Han was "viscous and terrifying" and that the "Hard Truth" was that the shooting was therefore justified. Grace found herself huddling toward these posts—though she wished he could spell *vicious*—like they were the only candles in a dark, cold room. She clicked on his profile, curious about this voice of reason, and to her chagrin found that he commented on dozens of videos relating to black shooting victims, criticizing every one of them, even ones much more blameless than Ava Matthews. He had a blog about something called "racial realism," and Grace decided not to look that up, unsure she wanted to know anything more about Jung-Ja Han's great defender.

Jung-Ja Han—that was the name of the woman in this video, the woman who shot an unarmed teenager in the back of the head. It wasn't a name she'd heard before, so how could it belong to her mother? And the video—what, was she really supposed to turn on the woman who raised her because of *that*? Her mother didn't appear in that video. There was almost nothing to see; that blurry figure could have been anyone.

Except that it was her and only her. The girl's killer and Grace's mom.

The garage door rumbled open, startling Grace awake. She'd fallen asleep after all, her face in her folded arms on the tabletop, her phone, low on battery, clutched in one hand. For a second, she perked up, a Pavlovian response wired into her since childhood. The sound of the garage that meant Umma or Appa was home.

She checked the time—almost eight in the morning. Paul had spent the night at the hospital.

She heard him shove through the door to the house and take off his shoes.

"Appa?" she called.

He didn't hear her, or ignored her, and before she could gather the strength to get up and intercept him, he'd disappeared into his room.

There was so much she needed to ask Paul. She was almost to his door when she heard the shower running. She barged into the bedroom and stopped just short of barging into the bathroom. How could he shower before checking in with his daughters?

"Appa!" she shouted, knocking aggressively. "What's happening? Is Umma okay?"

Paul's voice came through the door, but his words were lost in the water.

"What?" Grace called back.

There was no answer, and she went back to the kitchen, fuming. When he came out of his room, dressed in clean clothes, making what looked like a beeline for the garage, Grace was ready to tackle him.

"Dad, wait," she said.

Paul looked at her, doing nothing to hide the exasperation on his face. "I have to get back to Mom. You come with Miriam when she wakes up."

"How is Mom? I haven't heard anything since you sent me home."

"They finished the surgery. She's still not awake. They say she hasn't gotten any worse."

"That's good news?"

"It's not news." He shrugged and turned away again.

"Dad."

"What is it?"

She looked at her father, her only parent in this crisis, treating her as an annoying distraction from the task at hand. "Miriam told me," she said, and started to cry.

His jaw tensed, his Adam's apple clutched high in his throat. "Told you what?"

"She *told* me."

She was full-on crying now, falling apart in a way she never allowed herself in front of her father. There was relief in the abandon, the burden thrown from her body for Paul to dive down and catch. He needed to help her this time. There was no one else.

"She shouldn't have done that," he said.

The cold anger in his voice cut off her sobs like a slap.

"She had to. You should have told me ages ago, instead of leaving me to think everything was fine and normal until—"

"Enough," he said, raising his voice. "I'm going back to the hospital. This is not the time."

"When is the time? Mom could be dying. There might not be another time."

"Don't even think about bringing this to Mom. The last thing she needs to do is worry about answering to you."

"But—"

"I said that's enough, Grace. You don't know anything. Neither of you girls do."

"Just help me, Dad. Please. I want to understand."

She waited for an explanation: the special circumstances, the debilitating fear. A plea for love and forgiveness. She felt a sudden wild tenderness for him, picturing him tapping his foot outside a courtroom, in line at the DMV, stumbling through clerical conversations in his rickety English, so he could change the family name. Grace was the only one who was born a Park—Miriam had been Miriam Han until she was four years old, not that she'd remembered. Grace was ready to be let in.

He sighed, his temper subsiding as he looked at her. "I know you do," he said gently. "But you can never understand."

EIGHT

SATURDAY, AUGUST 24, 2019

H is phone alarm went off at six and Shawn thought about calling in sick for the first time in years. He'd stayed up drinking with Ray until just over three hours earlier, when Ray had nodded off in the middle of his fifteenth toast to Ava and Jung-Ja Han's shooter. Instead of knocking Shawn out, the alcohol seemed to swarm in his veins and keep his body buzzing. He must have fallen asleep somewhere along the way, but he only knew it by the pain of waking up. He shouldn't have given in to Ray's goading. Ray could afford to indulge his sentimentality; he had nowhere to be in the morning.

Shawn turned his alarm off and rolled back deep into his bed, grabbing for another quarter hour of sleep. After a minute he gave up—his mind was too active, too glutted with old memories. When he opened his eyes, they were sore and parched but fully alert.

He checked his email, out of habit, and saw that his inbox was jammed with notes and inquiries from friends and strangers. The word had spread overnight. When he searched the internet for Jung-Ja Han, he found her name mentioned several times on Twitter but in no news stories since yesterday. One of the tweets linked to an *L.A. Times* story, posted late last night. It was light on details, but it reported an early-evening shooting outside the Hanin Market in Northridge, the victim in critical condition.

He put his phone away, got ready for work, and kissed Jazz and Monique goodbye. It was only as he entered Northridge, in his Manny's Movers T-shirt and basketball shorts, that he knew he'd been fooling himself about going in today.

The Hanin Market was only a mile and a half from Manny's. He knew she wouldn't be there and that the store would be closed—even without the shooting, it was still just after seven o'clock on a Saturday morning. But he had to see it for himself, the place where Jung-Ja Han had hidden in the open all these years.

He called Manny and left a message, said he had a family emergency and had to miss work today. Manny would cut him the slack. Shawn never pulled any bullshit, and his boss knew it. Even today, he would've gone in if he couldn't be spared, but Shawn had been heading a three-man team since Ray quit, and he trusted Ulises and Marco could handle a move on their own.

The streets were wide and empty this early, and Shawn decelerated as he came up on a stretch of strip malls studded with signs written in Korean script. He recognized the foreign alphabet, less crowded than Chinese, softer and loopier than Japanese, with those dangling Os. It had been a while since he'd seen it. There wasn't much need for it in Palmdale, where the only Koreans he even knew about ran the all-you-can-eat sushi joint—there weren't many Japanese people either. He'd probably driven through this area before but hadn't had reason to stop. He hadn't realized there was this suburban Koreatown just a five-minute drive from Manny's office.

He turned into an enormous strip mall, the vast lot mostly empty, the businesses closed. The Hanin Market sat at the center of a long row of storefronts, all facing out from the same sand-colored box of a building. It was a huge complex with a tired suburban feel, the businesses listed on a large grimy directory, its dull lettering visible from Shawn's car. A Starbucks, a Realtor, a Honeybaked Ham. A Korean school and several after-school programs—music and art and SAT prep. A small town's worth of services, all of it seeming to flow from the market. A food court and a nail salon, an optometrist and a dentist. A drugstore called Woori Pharmacy.

He parked the car and hesitated before turning off the engine and stepping out. Was this really it? There were no cops, no cameras, no crime scene tape. A few cars in the lot, people early to work, he assumed, none of them out here gawking. This didn't feel like a place where something big had just happened. Maybe twelve hours was all it took to clean up and start forgetting. Yet he felt a nagging need to be furtive, like he was returning to the scene of his own crime. He looked around—nothing alarming, but maybe this was a bad idea. What was he getting out of it, after all?

He walked to the entrance to the marketplace, a set of automatic glass sliding doors, locked firmly against him. It was a nice morning, the sky cheerful and open and gentle; a smiling kind of day. Day like today, he and Jazz might get out the lawn chairs and sit out front, watch Monique run around on the driveway. Day like today was made for restless children. He saw himself running up and down the sidewalk in front of his old house, chasing after Ray and Ava as they kicked a rubber handball down the street, shouting, "Marco! Polo!" What had they been doing? He couldn't remember. He hadn't thought of that day in years.

Woori Pharmacy was in the entryway arcade leading into the market, a glass box of a store, small, from what he could see, squished between a bakery and a cosmetics shop. It was undisturbed—the shooting had happened outside, not in her store this time. The closed market was too dark to let him see deep into the drugstore, but he could picture her sitting behind the counter, safe and hidden for years, until someone brought her into the light.

A car entered the lot, and Shawn stepped away from the doorway. The driver was a middle-aged Korean woman with a wide-brimmed hat perched on a head of short permed hair. She parked two aisles from Shawn's car and got out carrying a monogrammed purse close to her body. Shawn walked back toward his car, feeling conspicuous, with his brown skin and his tattoos, the confusion of emotion that must have rolled off of him, perfuming his sweat. She didn't meet his eye or even look in his direction. But she went in a long arc around him to get to the market's doors.

Jung-Ja Han had probably left work through those doors. Walked to her car the way Shawn was walking. Had she seen her attacker coming? Or had he come at her from behind, aiming for the back of her head?

His breath caught—he made a sound like a moan, a wordless prayer. There, on the asphalt, Shawn saw a washed-out blot showing dark red in the sun. Jung-Ja Han's lifeblood, spilled and scrubbed, but not scrubbed away. Proof that some justice, however messy, had found her at last.

Ava was buried in the Paradise Memorial Park in Santa Fe Springs, though where exactly, no one was sure anymore. Four years after her funeral, the cemetery closed shop when its owners got caught re-selling burial plots, stacking multiple bodies into single graves, most of the dead poor and black, with poor black families who were easy to ignore. They dug up corpses and coffins, dumped them in piles of dirt and remains to get scattered again, sharing the ground with the bones of strangers. Ava didn't have a gravestone anymore—where her grave used to be, there was a gravestone for someone named Cornelius Henderson, a World War II vet, dead since 1959. The bodies had been piled and shuffled, and there was no way to know if Ava was anywhere near where they laid her down.

It had been years since Shawn last came here. Aunt Sheila hated the place. When she found out what happened, she lost sleep for weeks, this last insult bringing back all the ones that had come before. There were memorials for Ava over the years, plenty of them, but none of them took place at the cemetery. They were always at church or, on the bigger anniversaries, when Aunt Sheila could get a crowd together, at the intersection of Ninety-First and Figueroa, outside the Numero Uno Market, built over the remains of the place where Ava died.

It had taken him more than an hour to make the drive from Northridge, stopping at a plant shop along the way. The park was quiet and neglected; the grass was brown and the weeds were tall. It pained him that this was where his sister was buried, that she couldn't have a neat grave, her name on a little stone on a watered lawn. That seemed like so little to ask, yet even that was denied her, stolen from her.

What she had instead was a share in a mass burial site, marked by a big granite tombstone engraved with the words:

WHOMEVER   FOREVER

WHEREVER

REST IN PEACE

This stone, at least, was in better shape than most of the others. It looked like it got cleaned once in a while, despite the mildew and bird shit; there were even a few remembrances at its base: an American flag, a cluster of plastic roses. Shawn leaned a tiny potted succulent against the stone and closed his eyes.

When he was little—between one and three years old, they never did quite nail it down—Ava made him high-five a cactus. She set it up with a series of high fives that had him chasing her hand like a cat chases a light. *Up high, down low, too slow!* For her finale, she extended her hand, palm out flat, over a potted cactus, and when he slammed down as fast and eager as he could, she whisked her hand away. Ava laughed until he started bawling; then she cried and confessed to their mother, who spanked her for the prank. This was his first memory, the spike of the cactus the jolt that brought him online.

He remembered the way he abhorred and adored her, the vicious way they fought, holding nothing back, trying every time to break each other's hearts, then making up without effort, the wounds they gave each other easily forgotten. She used to sucker him out of the best trading cards, the best Halloween candy; once, he called her an asshole, and she used that to blackmail him into servitude for what felt like several years. Yet he worshipped her. The first time she went on a sleepover, he sat in front of her picture and cried.

When she was murdered, their relationship was already changing, morphing into something less volatile, more affectionate, a preview of the stable, nurturing companionship they would provide each other into adulthood. And sometimes he missed this as much as he missed her, the broken promise of a lifelong friendship with the person who knew him better than anyone. This is what Jung-Ja Han took away from him: an ordinary girl who meant the world to him.

Ava was not a genius. She did well in school, but whether she would've graduated, let alone gone to college, there was no way to know. Shawn was smart, too, and he hadn't done either. She was a talented piano player, but there was a limit to her talents. It was plentifully apparent even in her brief career. She didn't have the resources to compete with the kids who practiced for hours each day, the ones who'd been playing since they were five, with professional teachers, with parents to prod them and pay for their lessons.

She was not a saint or an angel. Bad things had happened to her, and they didn't make her good; good things, too, and she took some of them for granted. She swore and talked back. Fought back, too. And Shawn knew it was gospel that she never stole, but she stole. He'd seen it firsthand, one night in Westwood, when a riot broke out under their feet.

She took a cassette tape—a gift for him—and a pair of jeans from a Guess store, a pair she'd coveted that Aunt Sheila wouldn't buy for her because they were tight and low-slung and expensive. It was nothing, in the scheme of things. That same night, Ray got a new pair of sneakers; Duncan got a leather jacket, a boom box, even a cell phone—the first Shawn had ever seen, a black plastic thing the size of his forearm. But it was more than a quart of milk. It was a violation to the tune of something like seventy dollars. It was, in the end, much more than some people thought her life was worth.

Shawn didn't know if Aunt Sheila remembered what Ava was actually like. She gave her aunt hell in her teen years. They fought constantly; Aunt Sheila had strict standards for her one baby girl, and Ava was always falling short of them.

One time, when he was in his twenties, running with the Baring Cross Crips, he told Aunt Sheila it was possible that Ava meant to steal that milk from Jung-Ja Han, that it wasn't out of character, and that she was plenty pissed enough to do it. He was tired of pretending Ava was a perfect child; he hated that perfection was what the world required to mourn her.

Aunt Sheila had slapped him across the face. "You know what happens to a girl like Ava, people start thinking she was a bad girl? She gets tossed in with the rest of them. The pile of black girls no one's ever heard of. It is a mass grave, Shawn. Baby, *we* don't even know their names, 'cause no one's talking about them or writing about them for any of us to hear. Is that what you want for your sister?"

Shawn had turned from her in anger, stunned that his aunt had hit him, a grown man with his own life, his own problems, his own way of solving them; he had turned away because he knew he had nothing to say.

NINE

MONDAY, AUGUST 26, 2019

She couldn't leave the bedroom without running into Blake. Blake in the den, watching TV, practicing yoga. Blake in the kitchen, drinking his disgusting kombucha. In all fairness, this was his house, and it was his right to hang around, even if it was a Monday afternoon when normal people were at work.

With Paul gone at all hours and speaking to her as little as he could get away with, Grace was guarding her sanity by staying with Miriam. She'd managed to show her face at the hospital every day, but she was spending most of her time in the spare bedroom, avoiding Blake while her sister ran around doing whatever she did. Going out for lunches and drinks and coffees, but also almost certainly spending more time at the hospital than Grace. It wouldn't be so bad if he'd just ignore her, as usual, but he'd stop what he was doing whenever she ventured out for a glass of water, asking her questions and following her around with that pitying good-guy gaze.

Part of her thought she'd be better off at work, where she could distract herself. But she'd asked Uncle Joseph to fill in for her so she could continue what she'd been doing since Saturday morning: holing up and obsessing about her mother.

Even if Miriam hadn't spilled Yvonne's history, Grace would've found out yesterday, when the *L.A. Times* ran a story on her mother's shooting, which outlined the facts of the Ava Matthews killing in plain, cold text. Grace didn't really read the news, but there was no way this would've escaped her attention. The story had blown up. There were trending hashtags on every social media platform, rampant with opinion and speculation, hot takes and ill will. There was even a new flurry of one-star reviews on Woori Pharmacy's formerly sparse Yelp page. Grace was getting carefully worded emails from a string of strangers claiming to be journalists, nudging her for fact and comment, offering her a chance to tell her side of the story—this story she wanted no part of and knew almost nothing about. There had even been calls, enough of them that she would've turned her phone off if she weren't standing by for life-or-death news.

These people were shameless, and no matter how much sympathy they pretended to offer, Grace knew they were not on her side. She responded to none of them, and she saw the way they twisted her family's silence, the sneering implication that a lack of comment was an admission of vice, when her mother was in a literal fucking coma. She recognized one of the reporters as the professorial man from that night at the bar. His name was Jules Searcey, and he emailed her no fewer than six times, acting like their glancing encounter made them pals. Then he wrote a long, damning *New Yorker* article linking Jung-Ja Han to Trevor Warren, Alfonso Curiel's killer, a comparison that struck Grace as breathtakingly unfair. He went on and on about the violence against black bodies in Southern California, about the failures of a justice system that treated black life as something less than human. He kept referring to the mounting unrest in Los Angeles, as if he weren't actively trying to add fuel to the flames.

Grace read everything she could find about Yvonne: dozens of articles, old and new, but also blog posts and comment threads, micro-histories, wikis. Now that she knew what to look for, it seemed remarkable and insulting that it had ever been hidden. The shooting was everywhere, the only thing that came up when she searched her mother's name. As far as most people were concerned, it was the only thing that defined her. This single act, the pull of a trigger, one moment eclipsing every other.

She just wanted some fucking air, to go for a walk, get away from Blake, maybe outpace the screaming anguish running through her head.

Miriam's place sat on a hill in Silver Lake, near some kind of ugly reservoir where Miriam loved to go running. She was always talking about how much she loved it, how running released endorphins and helped keep her calm and happy. Grace wasn't a runner—the few times a year she ventured cardio exercise, she had to tear her room apart looking for her one sports bra—but she wondered if a brisk walk would have the same effect. God knew she could use some endorphins about now. Grace looked up the reservoir and started walking in that direction.

Miriam's street was residential enough that there weren't many pedestrians. Grace was grateful for the quiet, she realized, and thought better of her plan to wander toward a greater concentration of people. She didn't know how she was supposed to arrange her face or how she was expected to behave. She kept her eyes trained on her feet, studying the ground. *Step on a crack and you'll break your mother's back.* She walked carefully, on smooth pavement only, avoiding even the nicks and pockmarks.

Then something—someone—poked her shoulder, startling her off her game, and she stepped on a big crack with the widest part of her right foot.

"Shit," she said, turning around.

The boy before her looked maybe old enough to drink, a thin, blond, emo-looking dude, wearing slim jeans and black plastic-framed glasses. She'd never seen him before, and her first thought was that he wanted directions. Grace didn't know east from west in Granada, let alone these confusing hills. She wished he'd bother someone else.

"Excuse me," he said, his tone insistent and demanding. "You're Grace Park, aren't you?"

She blinked and took a step back. She'd never been approached in person by a stranger who knew her name, and it left his mouth like an accusation, cornering her in her own skin. He had to be a reporter, one of the vultures circling her family for snatches of misery and death. What was she supposed to do when she couldn't just hit the spam button or hang up the phone? She felt her body go heavy with dread.

"Why?" she asked. "Who are you?"

"I'm Evan. Evan Harwood. I work for Action Now. Have you heard of it?"

She shook her head, getting ready to move.

"Well, I know your sister, Miriam," he said, not quite masking his disappointment. "I was hoping to talk to her, actually, but I wonder if I could just ask you a few questions."

She snapped back around and power walked away from him, stopping just short of breaking into a run. She made it to the end of the block before turning to see how she was doing. He was right behind her, his stride as urgent as hers.

"I'm not interested," she shouted. "Please don't follow me."

He kept apace with her, pressing after her. She could hear the even rhythm of his steps; she felt like the first victim in a slasher movie, stupid not to start running. She was gearing up to take off when her foot caught on the tall side of a broken-up slab of sidewalk. She lost her balance and lurched forward, careening toward the pavement. The fall was fast—she had a second, maybe, to decide whether to absorb it with her face or her hands. Hands, she chose hands. She shot her right hand out, too late, and knocked her chin against her wrist, which already felt good and shattered. She tasted blood and turned around to see Evan Harwood—now a respectful distance behind her—recording her on his phone.

"What do you think you're doing?" she spat.

The boy ignored her question, and without acknowledging his role in her fall, he pressed the advantage it gave him. He planted his feet, standing over her, and said, "I just have a few questions."

"How about 'Are you okay?'" She ran her tongue over her teeth, testing them for looseness. They held firm.

"Any updates on your mother's condition?"

Her bottom lip was split. She dabbed at the ragged cut with her uninjured hand and drew away blood.

"Have the police shared any theories about who might have done this?"

A thirtysomething couple approached from the opposite side of the street, the woman locking eyes with Grace in concern, the man a few steps behind her, guiding a white pit bull on a leash.

Grace spoke to the phone camera, loud enough for the pedestrians to hear. "Whoever's watching this, you should know that this dirtbag stalked me so hard he made me trip, and instead of helping, he's interrogating me."

The woman jogged up and extended her hand. "Are you okay?" she asked, casting the boy a sidelong dirty look.

Grace took the hand with righteous gratitude, and was about to tell off the boy, when he spoke again, his tone hurried with the frantic, fuck-all spirit of a half-court shot flung right at the buzzer.

"Could this be retaliation for the murder of Ava Matthews?" he blurted out.

She snapped upright, surprising the Good Samaritan, who almost lost her own balance when Grace yanked and let go. Under ordinary circumstances, Grace would have fallen over apologizing, but she had other things to say.

"Retaliation?" She set her teeth and felt her blood welling in the cut. "My mother is in the hospital, and you have the nerve to track me down and talk to me about *retaliation*?"

"But it's true that your mother, Yvonne Park, is the Jung-Ja Han who used to own Figueroa Liquor Mart?"

The couple was watching and listening closely now—even the dog was sitting at attention, her ears pointed and open. Grace couldn't tell if they were enthralled by the scene or if that was a look of recognition crossing the woman's face. She wanted to order them to mind their own business and leave.

"My mother is my mother."

"What would you say to people who think this is justifiable revenge? That your mother got away with murdering a teenage girl?"

Somewhere deep inside her head, a voice piped up and told her to ignore this stupid boy, to cut her losses, turn around, and walk away. But it was too small and timid to overcome the flood of furious indignation, the need to put this ignorant kid in his place.

"That *girl* hit her first. She beat her up. And you know what? She wasn't some skinny little kid, she was five-five and 135 pounds!"

She knew she was shouting. It felt good, intoxicatingly good, the release more pleasurable than anything she'd felt since before the shooting. She saw the boy pointing his phone at her and wanted to slap it down, but she would have to stop her flow, and she couldn't stop, it was like the clear water of truth gurgling up from the depths of her, the purest part, bright and exploding with love.

"I'm twenty-seven years old and I'm five-five now. I weigh 130 pounds, and I know I'm bigger than my mom. What if some savage six-foot fifteen-year-old boy started beating you up? Would you defend yourself? I bet you would. I bet if some high school Shaq punched you in the head, you'd forget he was supposed to be a kid."

The boy's eyes bugged and he coughed out a disbelieving laugh that infuriated Grace. "This wasn't a self-defense case. She was convicted of manslaughter—she was declared guilty in a court of law."

"She's suffered enough," she said.

"For killing a child?"

She cast her eyes down and turned, holding her swollen wrist, and sprinted away. This time, no one followed her.

TEN

MONDAY, AUGUST 26, 2019

Shawn had been dealing with cops since he was a child: talking to them, ignoring them, avoiding them when he could. They were never not part of his life. Palmdale wasn't like South Central back in the day, but even here, squad cars always patrolled the neighborhood, rolling down their windows to talk to anyone who looked worth talking to. Sometimes it felt like they were out fishing, putting out lines in active waters, just to see who they could reel in.

So far, though, the Palmdale cops hadn't given Shawn much trouble. Could be he'd aged out of the deepest part of the hood pool; it wasn't like it was when he was younger, when a cop would sooner put him against a wall than say hello. Maybe it was that he was rarely out without a woman or a baby these days. Made it harder to imagine him getting in trouble. And that's what it came down to, in a way—people were lazy, they reached for the first thing that came to mind and held on to it like it was true. These cops were white boys: healthy, clean-cut, beef-eating kids in starched uniforms who'd been taught to fear black boys with tattoos and baggy pants. They were the same kids who quoted Samuel L. Jackson and thought they'd like to have Morgan Freeman for an uncle.

Shawn could tell right away that Detective Maxwell wasn't one of those cops. He wasn't young, he wasn't in uniform, and he'd driven a long way to talk to Shawn.

"Nice place," he said, nodding his head as he scanned the kitchen, still cluttered from dinner. He was a man who commanded a room; there was something aggressive even in the way he looked around, as if he meant to see more than anyone wanted to show him.

Jazz set coffee down in front of him. Shawn almost smiled. She was playing the polite hostess, but she'd chosen the ugly mug she'd gotten in a white elephant exchange, the one shaped like a shaggy cat's paw. They never used that mug; Jazz would die before pulling it out in front of good company. Maxwell said his thanks and took a sip, showing Shawn the pink paw print painted across the bottom.

When Jazz sat down next to Shawn, Maxwell smiled indulgently, like he knew the game she was playing and had let it go on long enough. "Actually, Mr. Matthews," he said, "I was hoping we could have a word alone."

"I'd rather stay," said Jazz.

He kept his eyes locked on Shawn. "I'm asking nicely, aren't I?"

"Does he need a lawyer?"

"Don't see why he would. This is a casual conversation, in the comfort of his own home," Maxwell answered lightly. "Does your girlfriend always speak for you?"

It was a transparent play—get the black guy to talk by insulting his manhood. That told him something, at least: Maxwell thought he was stupid.

"I'm alright," he said to Jazz. "You should check on Monique anyway."

She kissed his head and went to her daughter's room, leaving the two men in silence. The detective finished his coffee before speaking again.

"Do you know why I'm here?"

"I have a pretty good guess," said Shawn.

"So it wouldn't surprise you to hear that Jung-Ja Han was shot Friday night." Maxwell watched him, pupils glinting.

Despite himself, he felt the nervous reactions of a guilty man—the lump in his throat, the sweat coming on under his skin. "I did hear that."

"Did you know she was still in L.A.? Crazy to think about, that she'd just stick around after getting away with murder." Murder, he called it. Not manslaughter. He was slick.

"I didn't know until Friday night."

"What time Friday night?"

"I found out by text. My phone's in my pocket if you want me to check the time stamp." There was only one gun in this house—under the detective's jacket, probably, which hung loose on the big man's frame—but Maxwell didn't know that, and Shawn knew better than to bank on the benefit of doubt. He moved only after Maxwell gave him the go-ahead and, even then, with demonstrative caution. He pulled his phone out and found Tramell's text. "Nine seventeen."

"Who told you?"

"Is that important?"

"Yvonne Park—that's what Jung-Ja Han goes by these days—Mrs. Park was shot just after seven P.M., when the store was closing up. I know it's all over the news now—did you see the *L.A. Times* story yesterday? Sunday edition, front page."

Shawn nodded. The victim's identity made it more than an average shooting, and after sparse initial coverage, the media had been all over the story. He'd spent hours tracking the coverage, reading greedily.

"Well, it's all over the news now, but Friday night? It was just starting to trend on social media. Maybe that's how it got around to you, maybe not. But yeah, I'd say it's important who told you about the shooting two hours after it happened. Give me a name."

He thought about Tramell, the former fat kid who'd flirted with gang life before marrying his girlfriend, who was seven years older and entirely unimpressed by thug posturing. These days, he was an X-ray tech with two daughters who drove for Uber on his off days. His one vice was that he smoked weed in his garage some nights after the girls were in bed. Tramell was about as likely a suspect as Ava herself, returned from the dead.

Even so, he hated the idea of bringing a detective down on his house, especially one who was so obviously grasping at straws. There was a time he would've been ashamed to consider it. When it came to police, to give an inch was to snitch; to drop a name for any reason was the basest kind of betrayal.

But he couldn't afford to think like that anymore. He was a man with a record and a family. "Tramell Thomas," he said, as if it cost him nothing. Tramell would have to go to bat on his own.

Maxwell wrote the name down.

"Where were you when you heard?"

"I was home. About to go to bed."

"At nine o'clock?"

"I'm an old man, Detective, and I wake up early."

"For work, right? You work for Manny's Movers, over in Northridge." He had a notepad in front of him, but he wasn't consulting it. "I talked to your boss this morning. He said you no-showed Saturday."

Manny had spoken to the police about him. There it was—the flash of heat between his ears. It passed quickly. Manny had his own self to worry about, too. "That's correct. I took the day off."

"First time in a few years." He flipped the pages of the notepad without looking down. "What, you don't get sick? Lucky guy."

Shawn didn't say anything. He wasn't meant to anyway.

"So. Shawn. What made you decide to take off this Saturday of all Saturdays, with no notice?"

"You think maybe I tried to kill this woman after over twenty years, but you don't see why the news might've shook me up?"

Maxwell let Shawn's question slide off with a smile. "If I were you, I would've been out celebrating. Is that what you were doing?"

"I was remembering." He left it at that.

"Is that what you were doing at the crime scene?" the cop asked. "Remembering?"

Shawn clenched his hands under the table, thinking about the Korean woman who wouldn't look at him. She'd really gone and called the police. And if not her, someone else had. "I was remembering my sister. I went to her grave after, too. Did no one call that in?"

The detective shook his head, all solemnity, his expression regretful, even a little chastised. It occurred to Shawn that a man like this needed all kinds of faces, and he was pulling up a soft one now, the manner reserved for mourners.

After an appropriate pause, he took up where he'd left off. "Listen," he said, his tone confiding. "Word on the street is the Baring Cross Crips are taking credit for the shooting."

Shawn's eyes widened; he couldn't help it. "Word on what street?" he asked. "Not this one."

"You know how these things work. People talk; word gets around. If you've heard it, you have to think maybe I have, too."

"I haven't heard anything about Baring Cross."

The detective looked at him without speaking for a while, riffling the pages of his notepad with his thumb. Somewhere in there, Shawn knew, Maxwell had come up with a story about him, the one based on public records, the connect-the-dots version of his forty-one years of life.

"I gotta tell you, this couldn't have come at a worse time. With the Curiel case ending the way it did, last thing we need is for people to be thinking about the early nineties. I think we would both be glad to find that this shooting had nothing to do with what happened to your sister. But that would be one hell of a coincidence, wouldn't it?" When Shawn didn't react, he continued. "You in touch with any of your old friends? Jaleel Prentiss, Kevin Price, Isaac—

whaddya call him—'Newt' Johnson?" He smiled, rattling off the names.

They were names Shawn hadn't heard in years, names that belonged to nerved-up, hard-eyed boys, not men his own age, dealing with families and consequences. Kids, that's what they were—he knew that now—riding around in Newt's dad's car, talking about girls, sports, music, giving each other shit, laughing. But they were serious kids, kids with short childhoods, the privilege of innocence behind them. They spoke the language of life and death because they knew death, and they acted like that made them unafraid.

Once upon a time, he'd known all their phone numbers by heart; now he wasn't sure where they all lived. Newt, he knew, was in prison for drug trafficking and attempted murder. He'd been his best friend when they were teenagers, and Shawn sometimes wondered if Newt might've gone a different way if only Shawn had been different. There was no use thinking about this shit—what if, what if—but there was also no avoiding it. So many mistakes, so many bad cards. He was a man who believed in his responsibility, his duty to do his best with what he had—but that didn't mean he didn't wonder about the caved-in channels, the cut-off roads. His mother had died, and then his sister; both had been taken from him, and he'd been left to survive. That was the life he was given. Had there been a better life waiting for all of them, on the other side of misfortune? What had that looked like, and when had it disappeared?

The detective was staring at him. Shawn shook his head. "It's been a long while," he said.

"How about Ray Holloway?"

Shawn suppressed a shudder. "Yeah, course I see Ray. He's not an 'old friend,' he's family."

"I thought all you bangers were supposed to be 'family.'" He paused long enough to let Shawn take the bait if he wanted to. "Must be why someone took it on himself to get Jung-Ja Han. When she killed your sister, she hurt the family, and the family never got its revenge. Sure, you all ran her out of South Central, and maybe you thought that was enough. But someone must've found out what she was up to. Her nice, quiet, free American life. You know that little Korean lady never wanted to be in the hood. You think she was devastated that her store burned down? My guess? She took that insurance check and used it to buy a clean start. I've seen bangers mow each other down over silly rumors and funny looks. The only thing that surprises me is that it took so long for the family to strike back."

"Ava wasn't a Crip," said Shawn.

"But Jung-Ja Han thought she was. She died wearing Crip colors."

"A Dodgers cap."

Maxwell shrugged. "A blue cap. But sure, let's say she wasn't involved; you and your cousin were. I know you're playing house now"—he waved vaguely at their surroundings, as if they were nothing more than a magic trick, something he could vanish by snapping his fingers—"but I've seen your rap sheet, Matthews. Slinging, fighting, shooting. And I know how this works. I know this is the tip of the iceberg."

Shawn looked him dead in the eye. The man wasn't wrong. Shawn had gotten away with plenty. But he'd never killed anyone, and he'd paid a lot more for his crimes than Jung-Ja Han.

"You're OG, the real deal, and you're angry."

Shawn took a long, audible breath that became an openmouthed sigh. "My sister was murdered, Detective. I was angry about it twenty-eight years ago, I was angry about it last Friday, and I'm angry about it today. You wasted your time coming out here. Any fool could've told you I was angry. If you'd just called ahead I would've told you myself. I know that's all you got 'cause that's all there is to get." He stood up. "And I think I've had enough."

ELEVEN

WEDNESDAY, AUGUST 28, 2019

It took Grace several seconds to remember where she was—in the guest bedroom of her sister's house, hiding like a fugitive from the judging gaze of the world. She had woken up, and she was back in the nightmare. She closed her eyes again tightly and burrowed deeper into the bed.

"Come on," said Miriam, shaking Grace. "I brought food. Have you even moved since I left the house? It's almost nine. You have to eat."

So the whole day had passed—she'd slept longer than she'd thought, four hours at least. She felt an odd sense of achievement, but her head still hurt, and she was no more prepared to get out of bed.

"We went to the new vegan place in the Junction," Miriam said, a slight eye roll in her voice, somehow Blake's veganism being the only quirk she held against him. "I got you a rice bowl with like teriyaki tofu. Come on! Just sit up! I made you a tray. This is full Umma-style service."

Grace opened her eyes again and saw the tray in her sister's lap. The take-out food had been transferred lovingly to a ceramic bowl, flanked by a Sriracha bottle, a side plate of kimchi, and a can of Diet Coke. She pulled herself up on her elbows. "Thanks, Unni," she mumbled.

Miriam watched her eat. "How is it?"

She shrugged. "The tofu's whatever. The kimchi's good, though. You got it there?"

"Are you kidding? I don't pay white people for kimchi. That's mine."

Grace looked up, incredulous. Where could Miriam have learned to make kimchi? Had their mother taught her? Grace had never learned to cook; what if the food she loved died with Yvonne?

"I mean it's mine, not the restaurant's. I got it at HK Market," Miriam said. She took Grace's chopsticks, stole a bite of her food, and shook her head. "This rice is trash. I thought the seitan was bad. Fucking vegans can't even get rice and tofu right." She squirted squiggly lines of Sriracha over the top of the bowl and mixed it in. "Here, this should help."

Grace ate; it was her first meal of the day, and she realized she'd been hungry. When she was finished, Miriam took the tray to the kitchen and Grace lay back down, wondering if she could fall asleep again.

Her sister came right back; she sat by her side stroking Grace's greasy hair. The gesture, Miriam's tender fingertips, made Grace choke up with new tears.

"Do you hate me, too, now?" she asked.

"Of course not."

"But you think I'm a racist."

"Grace, I think everyone's a racist."

For the first time in her twenty-seven years, Grace felt herself hated. Her whole body burned, her skin crawling with a hot itch she couldn't scratch away. Hers was a modest existence—her social circle had always been comfortably small, her opinions vague, her presentation inoffensive. She knew of only two people who'd ever disliked her, one girl in middle school, one boy in college, and she'd spent more time than was healthy obsessing over their opinions, probably long after they'd stopped thinking about her. It wasn't that people *liked* her—she knew she never got anywhere on her charisma—but it drove her crazy to think that anyone would take issue with her, when she never hurt anybody.

That was before, when she was just the second-generation daughter of two quiet, hardworking Korean immigrants who went to church, ran a store, and raised a family, their lives as contained as a tended garden. Now she knew—they'd built their house on sand, and the rain had come down and the waters risen, the cold swallow of the real world.

Yesterday morning, she'd opened her inbox to find more than a hundred new emails, about ten times the usual volume. At first she thought the reporters had gotten hungrier. Then she noticed one of the subject lines: **fuck u you gook bitch**.

She clicked on it—how could she not? The body of the email was filled with vile abuse, calling her a racist as well as a chink with a sideways cunt who deserved to be raped and shot.

No one had ever said anything like that to her before. It made her want to throw her cell phone out the window. Instead, she read the next email and the one after that. There were dozens of them, varying in coherency and vitriol, but they were all angry, even the more measured, formal messages. They were all from people she didn't know who despised her enough to track down her email address.

One of these helpful strangers included a link, and Grace opened it, her head hot and tight, as if her heart were in there, trying to pound its way out.

It was a Facebook post, titled in bold letters: **DAUGHTER OF AVA MAT-THEWS SHOOTER GOES ON RACIST RANT watch until the END!**

She clapped her hands over her mouth as she watched herself shouting at that dreadful boy. This wasn't happening. It couldn't be happening. It had to stop. There had to be a way to erase it.

When Miriam found her, she was nearly catatonic, her eyes dry from crying and staring at her phone, reading every abusive email, every angry comment. Miriam had taken the phone away from her, quietly deactivated Grace's Facebook account, and given her hot tea and Xanax. She felt no less miserable now, but she was grateful for her sister's attentions, her uncharacteristic withholding of judgment.

"How's my video doing? Am I fully viral now?" she asked.

"Grace, don't."

"Tell me, Unni. I need to know where I stand."

Miriam sighed. "It's not good."

"How many views?"

"It's hard to say. It's on too many places."

"But millions?"

"I don't know about millions . . ."

"So maybe millions."

Miriam was silent, and Grace shuddered; she'd expected her sister to deny it. Millions? She couldn't figure out what that meant, whether it might be standard cute animal video or footage seen around the world, like the grainy security tape of Jung-Ja Han. How many people were even in Los Angeles? One million? Ten million? Were they all watching her?

"Are people coming after you, too?" She didn't think to hide the note of hope in her voice.

Miriam smiled sympathetically, not holding it against her. "No. I mean people know I'm your sister, but they're not coming after me. I think you're probably keeping them busy."

"I'm getting eaten by the bear while you escape."

Miriam chuckled. "You made a joke."

"It's not funny," she said bitterly. "That Evan kid only got to me because he's supposedly your 'friend.' You should be getting eaten by the bear."

"I told you, I've met him like one time. He must've found your photo by stalking my Facebook. And honestly, Gracious, you should've known better than to talk to a site like Action Now, especially at a time like this."

"You know what sucks? I'll bet everyone I've ever known has seen this video by now. Like every friend I've ever had, from church, from school. This is grade A gossip—no way it hasn't gotten around."

A sob built up in her throat, and Miriam stroked her hair.

"And if they've seen this video, that means they must know about Mom, and that means they know all this stuff came out because she was shot. My *mom* was shot right in front of me. So where are they, Unni? Where are my friends?"

"You said Jeannie and Samaya called you."

"Yeah, I know. So did Melanie, and a few of my UCI friends have been texting me. But no one's defending me. People are saying whatever they want about me and not one of my friends is stepping in to say, 'I know Grace Park. She's not a racist. She was having a really bad day—in case you haven't heard, her mother is in a coma.'"

"This is why I told you to stay off social media. Just let that play out—the villagers are voracious, but they move on fast. It's better if you don't engage. Your friends, too. They should just stay out of it."

Grace sat halfway up, propping herself against the hard bed frame. "You could defend me," she said.

The look on Miriam's face—like Grace had asked her to give up her dog as a blood sacrifice.

"I can't defend what you said."

"Not what I said. *Me.*"

"You don't understand, Grace. I'm a writer who lives on the internet, and on the internet, you are what you say. It would be career suicide for me."

"To defend your sister? I don't believe it."

Miriam said nothing. She was no longer looking at her.

"Is that why you stopped talking to Mom? So if this ever broke wide open, you could point and say, 'Look, I behaved perfectly'?"

Grace lay down again and turned away from her sister, sniffling and wiping snot from her nose. Her hand was wet and glistening, and she rubbed it dry on the duvet. Miriam said nothing, and Grace wondered if she would leave.

Instead, she lay down next to her. She sighed, and Grace felt her forehead tap against her shoulder.

"I have this theory. It's something I've thought a lot about over the last couple years," said Miriam. "I think if you love someone well enough, their evil makes you evil."

Grace closed her eyes and saw a black girl dying. Five foot five, 135 pounds, and shot in the back of the head.

"I found out about Mom not long after the shit hit the fan for Bill Cosby. I know you live in your bubble, but you remember that, right?"

Grace nodded. She'd never watched *The Cosby Show,* but it had still been shocking, the warm goofy dad turning out to be a serial rapist.

"Did you ever read about Camille Cosby?"

"No," Grace mumbled. "His daughter?"

"His wife. They were married for over fifty years. Still are, I think, though I have to believe she hates him by now. Anyway, she made a statement, maybe a couple statements, where she said Bill was a good man and all those women had to be lying."

"Weren't there like a hundred of them?"

"Maybe not quite, but definitely dozens. Enough that you'd have to be pretty fucking motivated to believe they were all lying. Camille got a lot of shit for defending Bill, and rightly so. She was feeding into this very damaging myth that women go around crying rape just to make life difficult for men. Yet another score for rape culture."

Grace tried to picture Mrs. Cosby. A black grandma, probably, small and old, pissed off and pointing fingers.

"The thing is, I couldn't quite find it in me to blame her. She'd been married to him most of her life—I know marriage is complicated, and it's hard to believe she knew nothing, but she must've loved him. Certainly, after a while, you think you know someone better than a bunch of strangers do—strange women, strange people on the internet. If some rando accused Blake of rape, I'd spit in her face before I heard another word."

It was easy to picture Miriam going to the mat for her man. But then again, she'd cut her own mother out of her life; she wouldn't post a Facebook comment in defense of her sister.

"Did you spit in any faces when you heard about Mom?"

"No one told me about Mom or maybe I would've. I found out on my own, just reading about the ninety-two uprising. There was nothing to dispute, or I might've found a way to dispute it."

"There's plenty to dispute. I'm holed up here because of all my disputing."

"That's the thing. Look, Grace, I get why you went on that rant, but come on, you know it was racist as hell. It doesn't matter that Ava Matthews was taller than Mom. She was a kid. Mom shot a kid in the back of the head. You don't want to think Mom's a bad person, but to think otherwise, you have to contort yourself to justify a murder—and if you bend too much that way, you'll become a different person. A worse person."

Grace snapped. "And what, you're so great? Because you turned on the woman who raised you? Who sacrificed everything to come to a foreign country so her kids could have a better life? Why do you think you're so goddamned enlightened in the first place? It's because Mom and Dad busted their asses so you could go to a fancy Ivy League college. Have you ever worked in a convenience store in South Central? Have you ever even been *inside* a convenience store in South Central?"

Grace heard Miriam open her mouth and close it again, and Grace could tell that she'd been inside a convenience store in South Central but thought better of saying it. Probably research for an essay.

"That's what I thought," Grace powered on. "Just like they've never been in a poli-sci seminar. I don't expect them to know shit about organic chemistry. I don't know how you expect them to understand advanced theories in racism and justice or whatever. Mom didn't go to college, and she went to high school in Korea—they don't even teach MLK in Korea."

"We're talking about murder, Grace, not an insensitive comment." She sighed, and Grace felt it on her back. "But you're right, you know. I'm not so great. We all want people in our lives who if we killed someone, they'd help us bury the body. I think we all want to be that person for somebody, too, and I know that's not who I am, not for my own mother. So I'm a worse person because of what she did. Because I was cold enough to cut her off. Sometimes I wonder if I'm less human than I used to be."

"I don't think anyone ever asked you to help bury a body. Why can't you accept that she's your mom and that she did this one bad thing?"

"What, 'hate the sin, love the sinner'?"

"Yeah."

"I think the only way you can pull that off is to put your head in the sand and keep it there."

Miriam got up and Grace kept her back to her, refusing to move, sure that she couldn't look at her sister without dissolving into tears. The lights went out, and she struggled to fall back asleep, her breath hot, her mind a muddle.

When the lights snapped back on, there was drool on her pillow, but she wasn't sure if she'd been asleep or awake. Miriam had her phone to her ear, but she was staring at Grace.

"It's Dad," she said. "Mom woke up."

TWELVE

WEDNESDAY, AUGUST 28, 2019

Shawn was working with Ulises to get a king-sized mahogany bed frame up a winding marble staircase when his phone rang in his back pocket. By the time his hands were free to check it, he had three missed calls and several pleading texts from Nisha.

Please pick up
It's about Darryl
Call me as soon as you get this!

His first thought: Darryl was dead. Sixteen years old, tall and strong, his black boy body writhing with life. Big game for a banger, a cop, a storekeeper. Every day in danger.

He almost jumped when Ulises tapped his shoulder.

He was asking, "¿Está todo bien?"

Shawn swallowed and nodded vaguely. He pointed at his phone. "Tengo que usar el telefono. Un momento."

He went out to the yard and sat on the empty deck. No, Darryl wasn't dead. That would be ridiculous. There were other things Nisha might want to talk about. Shawn just couldn't think of any on the spot. He called Nisha, ready to be relieved. She picked up instantly.

"What's wrong?" Shawn asked.

"He's okay," said Nisha, and Shawn knew what she meant was "He's alive." "He's not even hurt. But he got in a car accident."

"When?"

"Just now."

Shawn pulled the phone from his face to check the time. It was just after 1:30.

"He cut school again," he said.

"Yup."

He remembered their talk, Darryl nodding, seemingly chastised, as Shawn told him how important it was that he stay in school. He thought he'd gotten through to him. Maybe he had, and it didn't stick. Maybe Darryl was just nodding to get the lecture over with. It wouldn't have been the first time a teenager put one over on an adult.

"Who was driving?"

Nisha sighed heavily, and Shawn could tell she'd been crying. "He was."

Darryl had gone for his license last month, the first day he was able. He was so excited about his driving test that he forgot to look both ways before making the left turn out of the parking lot. A reckless maneuver, an automatic fail. He was due to retake the exam next week. In the meantime, he was just a teenager without a license.

"The little punk," Shawn said. "Whose car? Don't tell me he stole it."

"Of course he stole it. But he stole it from Ray."

"Where's Ray?"

"Lord knows. I can't get in touch with him. I swear, Shawn, sometimes it's like I got three teenagers. It's too much."

Ray had been gone more and more with each week he was out of prison. None of them could pin him down—not with love or guilt or anything in between. Sometimes it felt like he was still in Lompoc, living his own life out of sight, letting spare parenting chores fall to Shawn by default. Nisha was patient with him, but Shawn wondered how long that could last. The kids pretended it was no big deal, but

Shawn knew it hurt them. They'd been so happy when Ray came back, and he was barely around. And now this. Darryl getting in trouble; his father off the radar.

"What happened?" Shawn asked.

"Just a minor accident, it sounds like—no one hurt, but there's damage on both cars."

"His fault?"

"Yeah. He says she's an old lady, probably a bad driver, but he also says he turned in front of her when she was going straight. I heard her shouting 'right of way' in the background. Not that it matters, what with him not having a license."

"He called you?"

"Yeah, he called me, not that he had any choice. It was either deal with me or deal with the police, and I guess I'm not that scary."

"At least he didn't try to run."

"We don't know he didn't try it." She laughed a little, and Shawn was glad to hear it. "But I hope I didn't raise him that stupid."

"How did he sound?"

"Oh, he sounded shook, Shawn. I think he was crying." She laughed again. "Serves him right, the little liar. I don't think I've ever been so mad at him."

"What you gonna do?"

"That's why I'm calling. I'm not off for another five hours, and even if I leave now, it'll take me two hours to get to P-dale. I can't get a hold of Ray. Where are you now?"

He ran through the game plan for the day's move in his head. With all three of them working, they'd be done in three hours; with just two of them, it'd be closer to four, maybe five. Ulises had a family, a wife and three little kids. Marco was a student, enrolled part-time at CSUN, so he had time to work while he studied accounting. They had their own lives; Shawn knew that. But he made a snap decision—Ulises and Marco were his guys, but Darryl was more important.

"I'm in Calabasas, but I can leave now. It'll take me about an hour and a half."

"That's fine," said Nisha. "Let the dumb fool cool his heels for a while."

Darryl waited for Shawn in a Burger King parking lot, right in front of the intersection where he'd had his crash. The other driver was still there when Shawn arrived, and to Darryl's credit, she looked like someone who had no business being on the road, about a hundred years old, shrunk to four foot ten with inch-thick bifocals and a shrubby little fro of black-and-white hair. When Shawn pulled in, she climbed out of her car—a fearsome Dodge Durango—to meet him as he parked.

They converged at Ray's Chevy Malibu, wedged between them, and Darryl slumped out of the driver's seat, his head hung, miserably contrite.

The old lady gestured at Darryl and said, "This is your son!" It was a question, maybe, but it sounded like an accusation.

"He's my nephew," he said, trying to exude calm. He spoke as slowly as he thought he could get away with—lay it on any thicker, and he risked insulting the old woman, and Shawn wasn't looking to displease her any further.

To his relief, the accident wasn't serious. Darryl wasn't hurt, and through some miracle—maybe the blessing of the monstrous SUV— all eighty-five pounds of old lady had come out unscathed. It had been a low-speed collision, Darryl turning in front of the Durango with what he thought was plenty of room, the woman hitting the brakes in time to slow down before smashing into the back wheel of Ray's sedan.

Darryl had told her he'd left his license at home, and the lady wasn't buying his bald-faced bullshit—said she didn't raise three boys to get lied to by some other mother's son. Shawn wasn't sure if she guessed he was an unlicensed driver ditching school to ride around town in his daddy's car, but she knew she had Darryl by the balls, and she wasn't looking to relinquish that power—it was hers to give up, and she was enjoying it like a dog enjoys a bone.

If Shawn were a different man, he could charm her grip loose. He thought about how Ray or Duncan might work it—ask her where she was headed, did her kids live around here, where did they all go to church. But Shawn wasn't smooth enough to talk sweet without letting on what he wanted, so he decided the best course was to come out with it and tell her. He begged her to let Darryl go—he promised he and Nisha would pay for the damage to her car and that the boy would get the whupping of his life from every adult in the family. But there was no need to call the police or involve insurance companies, who were sure to involve the police.

She took down Shawn's contact information, examined his driver's license, and made a show of photographing Ray's Chevy, with Darryl loitering by the door. But finally, with a huff and a grumble and a few choice admonishments, she got in her SUV and drove off, drifting proudly between two lanes.

"I told you she was a crap driver," said Darryl.

Shawn looked at his nephew, who glanced at him with a hopeful twitch at the corner of his mouth. Shawn did not smile, and Darryl's expression fell back into one of solemn remorse.

They went into the Burger King to get out of the sun. It was almost empty at this hour—past three o'clock now—and when Shawn pointed at a corner table, Darryl shuffled over and sat obediently while he got fries and drinks so they could sit down for a spell.

Darryl was nine years old and all of four and a half feet tall when Shawn moved into the Holloway house, but he was canny enough that Shawn had to work to win him over. He loved Shawn, who'd been in his life since about its sixth hour, but he knew, somehow, that his dad didn't like the situation, and he must've worried on some level that Ray wasn't coming back, that Shawn was there to replace him. He was moody, that nine-year-old, and Shawn approached him with the delicacy of an earnest stepfather, giving him room, then buttering him up with irresistible attentions. He read to him out loud—*A Wrinkle in Time; Roll of Thunder, Hear My Cry; Where the Red Fern Grows.* Books Shawn said were too scary, too sad, too advanced for six-year-old Dasha. He learned to cook the kids' favorite foods, and once in a while—Nisha insisted this was at most a once-a-week treat—he took them out for chicken nuggets and chocolate milkshakes. They'd been to this Burger King plenty of times before.

He set a chocolate milkshake in front of Darryl, this frowning, long-limbed teenager. He nodded thanks at his uncle, an incongruously manly gesture, and helped himself to a handful of fries.

"What were you thinking?" Shawn asked.

Darryl swallowed and took a gulp of his milkshake.

"You know you're lucky she was black. I don't think a white woman would've waited around for two hours, then let you go with a scolding. She didn't want you getting in trouble. And you could've been in a world of trouble."

"I am in a world of trouble," he muttered, grabbing for more fries.

For the first time all day, Shawn wanted to smack the boy. When he was Darryl's age, he lived in a constant state of danger. Someone was always starting some shit, and he was always involved, running around with eyes wide open, on edge, waiting to get shot or arrested. Sure, Aunt Sheila railed at him, read him the riot act and the Bible, but trouble? That wasn't trouble.

What a sweet thing this kid had going. Two living parents, a grandma and uncle who loved him enough to twist the ears on his beautiful stupid head.

"Oh, your mom is gonna have some words with you, but that's not what I'm talking about. That woman could've called the cops on you. You could be in jail right now instead of feeling sorry for yourself at Burger King. Hell, you're the one always talking to me about Black Lives Matter. How you gonna go to a rally for a black kid got shot for doing nothing, then steal a car and ram it into an old lady? I don't have to tell you you could be dead."

Darryl took a loud slurp of his milkshake and his eyes filled with tears. Shawn felt his anger soften into despair. He couldn't think of the last time he'd seen his nephew cry, and he couldn't help it, he remembered stroking his little shoulder as he sobbed for Old Dan and Little Ann.

"I'm not trying to make you feel bad. But you gotta understand. I am *furious* with you. You're a child, ditching school, going on joy rides. But you're plenty old enough to wreck your life and bring your whole family down with you. This is when shit gets permanent. The choices you make are gonna stick, they're gonna follow you."

He listened to his own voice, and it sounded strange to him, heavy and reproachful and slightly false—like he'd rehearsed this speech in front of a mirror. The despair settled into his gut; he'd said all of this before, when Darryl got caught cutting school. That was supposed to be a man-to-man, come-to-Jesus kind of talk, not something trotted out every few months because it changed nothing.

"Do you want to end up like your dad?" he asked, desperation rising to his throat.

He could tell from the stunned look on his nephew's face that he'd tripped right over the line. He didn't mean for it to come out that way.

"Why not?" Darryl said, with sudden force. "He's my dad. I can't be like him? Who am I supposed to be like, then? You?"

Shawn heard the contempt in his nephew's voice and knew it was something he'd held hidden, that now he could never take back. It hurt, as Darryl had meant it to hurt, and Shawn had to push it down deep to keep his calm. "I didn't mean it like that," he said. He looked at Darryl with all the fear and love he had for him. There was so much he almost shook with it. "I don't want you to be like me either. I want your life to be better than both of ours."

The boy put his face in his hands and cried. For all his swagger, his pose of hardened dignity, he was still a child. Shawn reached across the table, light-headed with relief, and set both arms on Darryl's quaking shoulders.

They left Ray's car in the parking lot—Nisha and Ray would pick it up later, she said—and Shawn drove his nephew home, where Aunt Sheila and Dasha were waiting. Darryl was exhausted, and Shawn texted Nisha an update and decided to let her run the interrogation. She was his mother, after all; he was content to sit with the kids until she got home while Aunt Sheila went around the kitchen fixing dinner.

So they were all together, watching *Shark Tank,* when Nisha called him on his cell. Shawn excused himself to give her the full report, and Darryl looked doggedly at the television as his uncle rose from the sofa.

"Hey," said Shawn, picking up. "Everything's fine here. You on your way home?"

"Not quite," said Nisha. "Shawn, they arrested Ray."

THIRTEEN

THURSDAY, AUGUST 29, 2019

Yvonne looked terrible. Her hair was unwashed, her skin waxy, her cheeks sunken and gray. She looked almost worse now that she was out of the coma, a body awakened undead. The room smelled ripe. Human smells, and flowers browning in soiled water. Grace wondered who else had visited, who had bought bouquets in the depressing shop in the hospital lobby. It seemed there should be more of them—she was suddenly aware of the bareness of the room, and knew that if she were unconscious for a week, she'd want to wake up to a jungle, a sign of her many well-wishers, the people in her life who cared about her and wanted her to pull through. That seemed like the only upside to getting shot—it was a way to fulfill the fantasy of viewing your own funeral. How devastating to return from the verge of death and be disappointed.

Grace hadn't visited in two days; she'd felt so sorry for herself, she could hardly move, and now her heart pounded, fearful of an accounting. Even Miriam had managed to come every day and sit with their father. Paul, solemnly dutiful, had spent the whole week on the hospital grounds, leaving only to sleep. Grace wondered how he was coping, tried to picture him alone in their empty house. Did he sleep in his bed? Did he wish Grace were home? He said nothing, and she felt spared by his silence.

It was morning, the start of visiting hours, and Yvonne was waking up again, now from a less perilous sleep. She gazed weakly at her family gathered around her, and Grace found herself staring at the pillow behind her mother's head. She was terrified, suddenly, of being alone with Yvonne, of what they would and wouldn't say.

Miriam spoke first. "Umma," she said. Her voice broke on the word—it was her first time addressing their mother in two years.

Yvonne's mouth opened. Her lips made a parched sound as they parted. She swallowed, and when she spoke, her voice was faint and tremulous. She looked at her prodigal daughter, beautiful and beloved, and said, "You came."

How many times had Grace prayed for this reunion? For two years, their rift had been her primary source of anxiety and grief. It was easy to imagine that their reconciliation would make her life whole, that things would go back to normal, the wound closed up, the scar faint and easily forgotten.

But it was all wrong now. Her mother, whose known totality she'd taken for granted, was a murderer who'd nearly been murdered by some wild avenger. Grace had made a fool of herself before an unsympathetic world. And these three, her own family. These past two years, Grace had seen herself as their cornerstone, the only one caring and brave enough to keep them together; and the whole time, they'd been lying to her, each one of them in on it, protecting the lie. She was the outsider, the ignorant stranger who knew none of the rules.

Yvonne was alive. Fifty-four years old, and she'd beat an attempt on her life. How different things would be if Ava Matthews had been so lucky. Grace was relieved—whoever Yvonne might have been to anyone else, Grace wasn't prepared to lose her mother. And she knew—even Miriam knew—that this was a time for gentleness, for letting Yvonne settle into her recovery and deal with her trauma as the victim of a violent crime. But as she waited for her mother to turn from Miriam and acknowledge her, all she could think about was rushing the hospital bed and screaming.

And then Yvonne looked at her, and what she saw must have told her that everything had changed. The vagueness vanished from her eyes, a gauzy veil lifting. Grace had never seen her mother look so scared, and she felt pity for her for a moment, and a cruel, ecstatic thrill of power.

"Hi, Umma," she said.

Yvonne whispered, "Grace," then closed her eyes. Her eyelids looked as thin and papery as the wings of a fly, and they quivered, shut hard against her waking.

She kept them closed for several minutes, and Grace wasn't sure if she'd drifted off again or if she was only pretending. Paul cleared his throat, a phlegmy old-man sound meant to crowd out the silence. "Your mom's very tired. Let her get some sleep."

He stood and gestured for Grace and Miriam to follow him into the hallway. Yvonne lay perfectly still.

"The detective called me," said Paul, when the door had closed behind them. "They made an arrest."

Grace grabbed his arm. "Who?"

"The girl who was killed . . . Ava Matthews. Her cousin just got out of jail. The police think it was him."

They were silent, and then Miriam scoffed, her face gone a sudden red. "They 'think' it was him? Based on what?"

"Lower your voice," he said in a warning tone.

"I'm sorry, Appa. That just sounds like such lock-up-the-nearest-black-guy bullshit."

She stormed back into the silence of Yvonne's room, leaving Grace with her father, who would answer no more of her questions.

S he wanted to be away from the hospital, away from her family, but she knew she couldn't go far—her mom might wake back up at any hour, and Paul would expect her to be there, as she would want to be there, if things were the way they were supposed to be and not fucked upside down.

She hadn't been to Woori all week—Uncle Joseph had been covering for her—and she found herself fantasizing about the pharmacy, its serene sterility, the steady stream of boring labor. It was only ten minutes from the hospital. She could hide out there for a while. Maybe she could even be useful.

She drove over in a rush and found Uncle Joseph behind the counter, filling a script, while Javi manned the register. They were spread thin—Javi was filling in for her parents, from the looks of it, leaving Uncle Joseph with the tech work—but they seemed to be doing fine without her. Javi was helping out Mrs. Paik, a regular customer with a long, treasured list of ailments. He was a good-looking Guatemalan kid who spoke surprisingly decent Korean, and the customers loved him for it, especially the ajummas.

The bell rang out as she opened the door, and all three of them turned, their expressions turning soft and somber. "Oh, it's Grace. Wait just a minute." Uncle Joseph spoke in his calm, lilting Korean, and the kindness in his voice made Grace want to cry.

Javi rang up Mrs. Paik's purchase and gave Grace an awkward half wave. She and Javi had always gotten along, but she wondered now if he'd seen her turn as an internet racist, if he'd never see her the same way again. She floated a weak smile and then bowed her head at Mrs. Paik, who stared at her a little too long and with too much interest. Mrs. Paik was just a patient, someone Grace advised as needed on her many medications, but she was one of a large group of Korean women who felt free to ask whether Grace had a boyfriend and when she intended on getting married. Maybe it was a mistake to come here—she should've known better than to walk into Hanin, the village marketplace of the north Valley's Koreans.

Uncle Joseph came out from behind the counter and addressed Javi in English. "Javier, I go to lunch, okay?" Grace waited as he left the tech with his marching orders, her expression as neutral as she could manage.

Mrs. Paik came right over and grabbed her hand, pressing it between her bony fingers. "Aigo, you look so skinny," she lamented. "You have to eat well. Be strong for your mother." To Grace's relief, she was gone before Grace had time to respond.

"That busybody," said Uncle Joseph, clapping his hand on Grace's shoulder. "You didn't have to come in."

"I know. I felt like it."

"Have you eaten?"

They walked the fifty feet to the food court, where he told her to sit while he ordered them lunch. Grace had known Uncle Joseph her whole life. He was one of her parents' few close friends, and she'd grown up with his kids, playing at each other's houses, their families taking weekend trips together to Oxnard and San Diego. She remembered him as a younger man—though all adults had seemed unfathomably old back then—carrying Stacey on his shoulders. Now he was in his sixties, his hair thick but gray, his lean frame interrupted by a disproportionate paunch that stood out when he tucked his polo shirts into his slacks.

He was, in many ways, closer to Grace than her real aunts and uncles, who lived in Chicago and Seoul. But their relationship was mostly professional these days, the pharmacy providing enough substance for a bond that had always been warm without any special intimacy. This would be their first lunch together at the Hanin food court, though they both ate here regularly. Grace wondered, with dread and curiosity, if he was about to try and counsel her.

"How is your mother?" he asked, switching to his tentative accented English.

"She's awake now," she said. "I mean she's asleep right now. But she's out of her coma."

"Does this mean she is out of danger?"

"I think so, yeah. I mean she's not going to die."

"That's good. Everyoney is praying for her."

Grace almost smiled. He still said "everyoney," even though he had to know by now it was wrong. It used to drive her and Miriam crazy.

The table buzzer went off, skittering across the laminate— their food was ready. Uncle Joseph got up and returned with a tray crammed with naengmyeon, ddukbokki, kimbap. Food court food she usually ate out of pure convenience, but as she looked at it, her mouth watered. She hadn't been eating well with her mother in the hospital.

She thought of Mrs. Paik, her display of neighborly concern, and looked at Uncle Joseph. "If I ask you something, will you tell me the truth?"

"I will try," he said.

"You knew about my mom, didn't you?"

"What do you mean?"

She whispered, suddenly conscious of every person within earshot. "That she killed that girl."

He took a slow sip of water, swallowed it, and sighed. "Yes."

"Did everyone know?"

"Who is everyoney, Grace?"

"Everyone but me." She heard the petulance in her voice.

"The people . . ." He thought about what he had to say, then switched back to Korean. "The people who knew your parents then, they all knew what happened. It was a terrible tragedy, and your family needed all the support they could get."

She'd binged on articles and videos about Jung-Ja Han, and she remembered now, the Koreans who filled the benches of the court-room, the community showing up for this murderess, giving quotes to whoever asked in her defense. Her church had raised money to pay her legal fees, a move that must have changed her life. She'd started with a public defender, but by the time the case went to trial, she'd hired a silver-tongued black lawyer, who painted her as party to the tragedy. He was a smart man and a fervent speaker, but Grace knew that wasn't why her mother hired him. She paid him to stand in court, his black body forgiving her on behalf of his community. She could see the courtroom full of Koreans, nodding their heads, saying amens. That church must have been Valley Korean United Methodist Church, the church Grace grew up attending. It hadn't occurred to her until now, and the thought made her lose some of her appetite.

Uncle Joseph went to that church. It was how he met her parents. Grace plotted out the timeline—he'd been Paul's employer for most of her life, before he became his partner. He must have hired Paul right after the old store burned down, maybe when others were less eager to help. So he hadn't just known Yvonne's history; he'd been instrumental in its burial.

"Does Stacey know?" she asked.

Uncle Joseph opened his mouth, and she saw him consider lying. "Jesus, everyone but me."

She hadn't thought about Stacey Kim in a long time. Uncle Joseph's daughter was her age, and they'd been friends once, until Stacey grew up ahead of her. One year, Grace gave Stacey a Morning Glory organizer and a sheaf of lovingly selected stickers for her birthday, and she accepted them without excitement, blatantly favoring the Hard Candy lip gloss and nail polish she received from her other party guests. Within two weeks, Stacey was ditching Grace to hang out with a different group of girls, the ones who wore makeup and giggled when the youth group oppas walked by. They were never close again—she hadn't even seen her since Uncle Joseph and Auntie Su-Kyung's divorce—though they were friends on Facebook. Stacey was an interior decorator now, married with a kid, living in Santa Monica. A life that had nothing to do with Grace's, and she had known, probably for years, Yvonne's true name, her shameful history.

"There aren't that many of us, and we're all gossips." Uncle Joseph looked at her then, his mouth opening and closing and opening again. "You know about my family, too, don't you?"

She reddened, caught off guard. Uncle Joseph had been at the center of one of Valley Koreatown's scandals about five years back; she knew all about it, but had never discussed it with him. He and Auntie Su-Kyung had been married twenty-five years when he had an affair with the minister's wife, a woman he fell in love with over a series of Bible studies and choir practices. They left their spouses and married each other, alienating their children and scandalizing the congregation. Grace had more or less stopped going to church by then, but she managed to hear about it, and not from her parents. So that was how it worked, then—you assumed people knew all there was to know, that they talked about your most private failures when you weren't around.

Now that she thought of it, her parents had shut her down when she brought up the rumor at the dinner table. Paul was sharp about it—he nearly snapped at her to mind her own business, saying none of them knew the whole story, that no matter what anyone said, she should know Uncle Joseph was a good man. It had shamed her a little to be scolded by her father. It made sense, looking back, that Paul had strong opinions about gossip when greater sins failed to move him. Their family stability depended on a high level of privacy and decorum; the Parks had secrets to keep. And, of course, they felt grateful to Uncle Joseph.

She nodded, guiltily, and he smiled at her, reaching his chopsticks across the table to take a bite of ddukbokki. It felt strange, talking openly about something they'd both known for so long. She realized she'd never held the affair against him. She didn't like cheaters, as a rule, but she liked Uncle Joseph, and his new wife seemed like a nice woman. She had always assumed, on some level, that there must be a story that would satisfy her morally.

"Everyoney's a sinner, Grace. It's only Jesus who makes us good."

"We're not all murderers," she said.

He winced and sucked in air through his teeth—disapproving, she guessed, of Grace speaking ill of her mother.

"Remember the thief Jesus saved on the cross?"

Grace nodded.

"Jesus forgives all sins as long as we repent them."

"You've repented?"

"Of course."

"But you didn't go back to Stacey and her mom. You married Cho-samonim."

She glanced around the food court, wondering if anyone could hear them. It was an extraordinary conversation, but Uncle Joseph didn't seem in the least bit fazed.

"You can't undo a sin. Your mother knows this better than anyone. You can only pray and try to make things right with God."

She remembered how much she disliked Korean church in the end. The college boys in youth group sharing cigarettes with the pretty high school girls; the preening ajummas who spoke piously of starving children, their arms heavy with competing pieces of Louis Vuitton. They might've protected each other from outsiders, but these church people tore their neighbors down. They talked shit and behaved badly, safe, maybe, in the knowledge that Jesus had paid their accounts.

"So what does repentance even mean?" she asked. "You can just make the world a worse place and then square it up with God? What about the people you hurt? What do they care about your apology to Jesus?"

He shook his head, slowly, sadly, like she was still a child and he hated to disappoint her. "You can't always make things up to people. Sometimes squaring up with God is the only thing you can do."

FOURTEEN

THURSDAY, AUGUST 29, 2019

Ray was being held at Men's Central downtown—a hellhouse, even among jails—while the cops decided what to do with him. He'd spent the night there, and Shawn and Nisha were hoping to get him out before the sun went down again. Not that there was much they could do. So far, Shawn had sat by in supportive silence while Nisha made phone call after phone call from his couch, unwilling to let the kids and Aunt Sheila know unless it was absolutely necessary. She'd been the one to line up an attorney, a hawkish criminal defense lawyer named Fred MacManus, who was ready to go the minute he was summoned. Nisha said he was a big get—a hotshot who made regular appearances as a legal analyst on TV. He cost an obscene amount of money, even working at a discounted rate. But Nisha was ready to sell the house to keep Ray from going back to prison on a trumped-up charge.

Two months out, and he was getting hit with attempted murder and everything else that came with it. Shawn thought of that detective, Maxwell, coming around asking questions, without a scrap of evidence, just hoping he could show up and shake something loose. The stupid motherfucker had gone and arrested Ray.

Unless Ray was the stupid motherfucker. Unless his cousin was foolhardy and vengeful enough to give up his freedom for an old grudge.

He wished he could talk to Ray, but he was only allowed one visitor other than his attorney, and that was Nisha. She went to work—said it was better than staying home worrying—and would see her husband after.

Shawn was home with Monique. It was a Thursday, one of his odd days off, and Jazz was at the hospital. Monique kept him busy, but she was less chatty and energetic than usual. She was too young to understand what was happening, but she sensed something was up. It worried Shawn, how easily kids absorbed the spilled poisons of the grown-up world.

He was prepping her lunch—tuna sandwiches cut into tiny triangles—when his phone rang. He rushed over to answer, not even stopping to wipe his fishy fingers until he read the caller ID. It was just Duncan.

He answered anyway. "What's up?"

"I told you to call me," said Duncan.

"That's right." Duncan had called the night before, then asked Shawn to call back when he was alone. With everything that was happening, he'd plain forgotten.

"Are you still with Nisha?"

"No, she's at work."

"What you doing right now?"

"I got Monique. I'm making her lunch."

Monique looked up at him from the couch, where she was flipping through a book of dinosaurs.

Duncan breezed past Shawn's answer. "Listen, can you come by the bar? We need to talk."

"What, now?"

"No, we needed to talk fucking yesterday."

Shawn looked at Monique, who was watching him, her eyes wide and head tilted, ignoring her dinosaurs completely.

"I got Monique today."

"Bring her."

"To a bar?"

"It's my bar, and it's empty now."

"Maybe you better just tell me over the phone."

"This is more like a face-to-face kind of conversation. How old is the kid again? Five?"

"Three."

"Yeah, whatever, just bring her."

Shawn fed Monique and loaded her up in the car, already feeling a fool for letting Duncan yank him around. But if there was something he had to say about Ray, Shawn knew he needed to hear it.

Duncan's was a dive bar off the freeway, with darts and a jukebox and plenty to drink. He'd been its manager for ten years—back when it was called "Roger's"—and had taken it over when his old boss retired, selling it to Duncan at a good price. It was nothing special, in the grand scheme of things, but the Antelope Valley was starving for bars, and he did good business. Folks were driving home drunk from Duncan's every night of the week.

The only other car in the parking lot was Duncan's, a 2001 Porsche Boxster. Shawn wondered if Ray was supposed to be working. Duncan didn't do much bartending anymore.

He was waiting behind the bar when Shawn walked in with Monique in his arms.

"Hey, Monique," said Duncan. "Remember Uncle Duncan?"

Monique shook her head suspiciously.

"Say hi, Momo," Shawn said, almost smiling. "He's friends with me and Uncle Ray."

"Hi," she said, then hid her face in Shawn's neck.

"I gotta talk to Uncle Duncan for a minute, okay?" He pried her loose and set her down on a barstool, taking the one next to it.

"Here," said Duncan. He presented her with a notepad and a fistful of stick pens, red and black and blue. "You can color or something if you want."

"Thank you, Mr. Duncan," she said. She uncapped a pen and scribbled dutifully.

"What do you want to drink?" Duncan asked.

"I didn't come here to drink," Shawn said. "What's going on? How'd you even hear about Ray?"

Duncan raised his eyebrows. "What, you ain't heard nothing? They picked him up here. Made a whole fucking scene."

Monique's head lifted a bit at the sound of the curse word. Shawn and Jazz made a point of not swearing in front of the kid, but she still recognized the tenor of a bad word.

Shawn could picture it: Ray at work, chatting up customers. Ray led away, head down, in handcuffs.

"I haven't talked to him. Nisha talked to him some, but there wasn't time for telling stories."

"They said he shot Jung-Ja Han. That's what they got him for, yeah?"

Shawn nodded.

"That's what I thought." His mouth contorted and he gripped the wood of the bar like he was in pain. "Shit," he said.

Shawn wondered if he'd been summoned to give Duncan the inside scoop. He wouldn't put it past him, the trifling son of a bitch. "Didn't you have something to tell me?"

Duncan hesitated, then nodded. "I know he didn't do it."

"What do you mean, you 'know'?"

"I mean, I was with him when the bitch got shot."

Shawn felt his chest loosen. The relief was so powerful he slumped in his stool. Ray had an alibi after all. "He was at work?"

"No. I put Marv in charge of the bar. It was a Friday night, cuz. We were out."

Duncan chewed his lip, his face clenched, and it struck Shawn that his cousin could be innocent and still be undone. The reality was Ray was in custody and his best friend was here, talking to

Shawn, instead of shouting his innocence from the rooftops. The alibi had to be dirty.

"You were supposed to be taking care of him," he said, glaring at Duncan.

"What's that supposed to mean?"

"I mean we all trusted you to look out for him, and now what?" He looked at Monique and kept his voice even. "You got him banging again?"

"Hold up." Duncan laughed, a meager sort of laugh. "No, it ain't like that. You know I don't do that shit, man."

"Then what's that mean, you were 'out.'"

"You're not gonna like this." He gave his head a theatrical scratch. "Have you met my girl Cindy?"

It turned out Duncan had a girlfriend of sorts, a twenty-five-year-old hairdresser named Cindy he met on a dating app. Nothing serious, but they hung out sometimes, and last week, she came into the bar with her friend Denise.

"She was this girl Cindy knew from L.A., thinking 'bout moving to P-dale, and she wanted to show her a good time. So I decided, why not have us a little party, right?"

Shawn listened, dreading the rest of the story.

"Ray wasn't working Friday, so I called him up, and the four of us decided to meet up at my place."

"What time?"

"It was early, man. Five, maybe five thirty." At least two hours before the shooting. "We were gonna have a drink and go out, get food somewhere."

If they'd gone to a restaurant, there was a good chance someone would remember seeing Ray. "You went out?"

"No, and see, this is the problem. We stayed in." He shot Shawn a guilty, suggestive look: one raised eyebrow, a wince at the mouth. "Know what I'm saying?"

Shawn felt his jaw go slack. "Ray and this girl Denise . . ."

"It wasn't my fault, alright? We all had a couple drinks, and me and Cindy went to my room for a minute, and when we came out, we heard them in the bathroom."

Shawn thought of Ray sneaking into a bathroom with a girl like a horny high school kid and shook his head in disgust.

"So then what? Ray just went home?"

"We chilled for a bit. Ordered pizza, had another drink. Then Ray went home."

"What time?"

"Not late. Before nine, probably. He was gone by the time I heard about the shooting."

"He couldn't have—"

"What, driven to Northridge drunk, with his dick still wet, and tried to kill someone? I doubt it. Anyway, they said it happened around closing, and that store closes at seven. He was with me at seven, I know that."

"And your girl Cindy and Denise, they were there, too."

"Yeah, if the man wants an alibi, he got an alibi. So you tell me. What do I do?"

Right now, Nisha was at her job while her husband sat in jail, not because she wanted to be there, but because she needed that job to support her family, especially now that they had a lawyer to feed. Shawn thought about Nisha, about the ten years she'd waited for Ray, raising their kids and standing by, patient and lonely and faithful. He knew Ray had strayed before. Nisha told him it had been a problem when the kids were little, and Shawn could tell it was the one thing that made Nisha think about leaving him in the long years he was away. But Ray was a middle-aged man now, probably getting plenty from his wife. Shawn was younger than his cousin, and it had been a long time since he'd been tempted to misbehave in the name of desire. He was settled and content, grateful for Jazz—no ass in the world was worth taking what he had and lighting it on fire.

Two teenage kids, over twenty years of marriage—that's what Ray had pawned for a one-night stand with a young stranger. Shawn mourned the hard-earned loving calm that had finally come to their family. He thought of the strife to come—Nisha heartbroken, the kids in confusion, the lines that would have to be drawn. He wondered if they'd ever all gather at Aunt Sheila's again, and he hated Ray then, for his weakness and evil.

"You got an alibi, you gotta give it to him," he said.

Duncan nodded. He'd needed the permission. "You think Nisha would walk out?"

"She might. Hell, she probably should."

"It was just the one time. Nigga was locked up ten years."

Shawn cast his eyes pointedly toward Monique, who had abandoned her notepad and was now resting her head on the bar, watching them listlessly. Duncan gave no sign of noticing.

"Girl came on to him and he caved. He's only a man, Shawn. Nisha knows that."

Shawn couldn't tell if Duncan was lying. He probably was. This was Ray's best friend, a forty-four-year-old bachelor who still talked about women like he did when he was in high school. It was amazing to Shawn how much he'd looked up to him then. But that was a long time ago now. "Nisha made it through the same drought."

"It's different for men. Come on, Shawn, I gotta explain this to you?"

He knew how hard it had been for Nisha, but he didn't have the energy to lay it all out. Besides, Nisha wouldn't like him telling Duncan about her low days, her weak days, her moments of wretchedness and need.

"You gotta talk to the police," he said instead. "He threw a grenade at his marriage when he slept with that girl, and he'll have to deal with that. But they're trying to get him for attempted murder. That comes first."

"I guess I don't have to tell them every damn thing."

"Don't be stupid. They'll question you. Probably question those girls, too. They'll get the whole story, with time stamps, and it'll be better for Ray if you just come out with it." He thought about Ray, back in a jail cell, getting more and more desperate. "I'll bet he already told them anyway. But if he lied first, they might not believe him. You can get him out."

"I guess the police ain't gonna tell Nisha."

"But Nisha's smart. She'll know Ray's not telling her something, and she'll find it out."

"From you?" Duncan's face twisted with something like distaste, like after all they'd talked about, it was the idea of Shawn betraying Ray that offended him most.

It didn't sit well with Shawn either. Ray was his cousin, his brother. He'd always had Shawn's back, and he was first in line for his loyalty. What good would it do to upend his life, when Ray showed himself perfectly capable of doing that on his own? Shawn thought about his niece and nephew, both parents home at long last at this fragile age. This would devastate them, and of course they'd side with their mom. What if they cut ties with Ray, this father who had, after all, been gone most of their lives? How could Shawn play a part in that?

He wanted to erase what he'd just heard, let Ray and Nisha be Ray and Nisha. She would be happier not knowing, there was no doubt about that. But the idea of keeping it from her made him feel sick.

"I don't know, man, I gotta think about this."

There was a silence, and Monique piped up to break it. "Papa Shawn. Did Uncle Ray do something bad?"

Both men stared at her. It was startling, how much this kid picked up, even if she was sure to lose track of it within a few hours.

"No, sweetie," said Duncan with a panicked smile. "Uncle Ray's just fine."

Shawn was relieved Ray hadn't shot Jung-Ja Han. He didn't want his cousin to go back to prison—not for shooting that woman, not for anything. But Jung-Ja Han was a murderer. She'd taken away their sister. How many times had Shawn fantasized about taking revenge himself? He would've been mad at Ray's stupidity, his impulsive selfishness, but he would've understood. He would've understood that a whole lot better than this.

FIFTEEN

FRIDAY, AUGUST 30, 2019

race sat at her desk reading over the list of instructions Paul had handed off to her. The nurse had explained them to him in her presence, but Grace, her mind a roaring jumble, hadn't been paying close attention. She knew what medications to give and when to give them, but everything else seemed new and terrible. She googled "how to give sponge bath" and found an illustrated how-to guide and listened for stirring in her parents' room.

It was strange being back home. The tidy, quiet house now felt like a haunted place, a place of secret violence. Grace couldn't help thinking the house itself had betrayed her, in league with the rest of them, masquerading all her life as a normal house and not the house of a murderer. Even her room made her uneasy. It looked like a child's room, her bed a daybed lined with stuffed animals, her walls still hung with the posters that had moved her in high school—the cartoon girl group Sailor Moon, the Korean boy band Big Bang. She had a plastic Dragon Ball alarm clock that used to get her out of bed every morning, and it still sat on her desk, though it had long since stopped—God, she thought, was that on the nose. It was hard to believe this room had felt so comfortable so recently. Grace would be anywhere else if she had the choice.

Less than twenty-four hours after Yvonne came out of her coma, her doctor had cleared her to go home. It had taken Grace by surprise—she'd never known anyone who'd been shot and fallen into a coma before, but she would've thought that was serious enough to warrant more time in the hospital. A month, at least. Certainly more than a week.

But last night, they brought Yvonne home from the hospital, not strapped to a stretcher, but buckled into the front seat of Paul's car, without special caution or ceremony. Miriam picked up dinner from the Hanin Market: plastic-wrapped packages of ddukbokki, soondae, and kimbap, with a sweet potato cake from Tous Les Jours for dessert. It was a thoughtful gesture that let her avoid the homecoming for an extra thirty minutes. They'd had a wan celebratory dinner in Paul and Yvonne's bedroom, the first meal they'd all shared in over two years. Just a week ago, Grace would've been thrilled to know such an event was in her near future. But of course, everything was shit now.

Yvonne had gone to bed early, and when Miriam excused herself to go home to Blake, Grace thought about going with her.

But Paul had stopped them both. "I have to go back to the store," he said. "Can you girls take care of Mom tomorrow?"

Grace had to stop herself from rolling her eyes. Paul didn't report to anyone; the store had been fine without him all week. He'd spent most of that week pacing the halls of the hospital, and no one had been blowing up his cell phone, demanding his return to Woori Pharmacy. Paul just didn't want to be the one to attend to his wife, now that he'd have to do more than fret from a different room. Grace had noticed his eyes glaze over as the nurse went over the litany of instructions. Apparently, he didn't see them as his concern.

Grace looked at Miriam, the only one in the family who was neither employed nor gunshot.

Miriam's mouth curled, like this was unexpected, unwanted, and unfair. "I have a lunch meeting tomorrow. Blake set it up for me. It's with this showrunner with a deal at Netflix."

"Okay, so you have lunch plans?" Grace asked in disbelief.

"They're not just 'lunch plans.' It's a work thing. This guy might hire me down the line. It'll look bad if I cancel. For me and Blake."

"You can't say, 'So sorry, but my mom just got out of a coma'?"

"He's never met me, and he's kind of an important guy. He doesn't want to know all about my life."

"Grace," Paul cut in, his voice stern and scolding. "You stay with Mom."

"What? Are you serious? I'm the one who should go back to work."

"Joseph will understand. Miriam doesn't need to explain everything to this showrunner." He pronounced "showrunner" uncertainly; Grace was sure he'd never heard the word before.

Uncle Joseph did understand. "Your mother comes first," he said gently into the phone. "Take as long as you want. I'll be fine here." This goddamn Confucian culture. If Grace quit her job to take care of Yvonne, Uncle Joseph would understand that, too; if Yvonne's condition were permanent, he might even expect it.

Yvonne spent most of the day sleeping. There wasn't much else for her to do; she had to lie down, and the drugs kept her tired. Grace passed the time playing game after game of Candy Crush. She'd bought a book about Ava Matthews—written by that Jules Searcey guy, it turned out—and had it open on her laptop, hidden behind the game. She'd meant to start reading it before Yvonne got out of the hospital; now, she found it impossible to look at with her mother in the next room.

It was a hot weekend, one of the hottest of the summer, and the air-conditioning wasn't strong enough to battle the Valley temperatures, which had been well over 100 degrees all afternoon. Yvonne had been quiet and undemanding; her one request was a bath, and Grace decided it might as well be now.

Yvonne was awake when Grace let herself into her parents' bedroom.

"Did you eat?" she asked Grace reflexively.

"It's after four, Umma. I ate a while ago. Are you hungry?"

Yvonne shook her head.

"Do you want your bath?"

She sat up in bed, wincing. "Help me up," she said.

Grace wasn't sure how best to help a recovering gunshot victim get out of bed, but somehow, she and Yvonne managed to fumble up together. She held her mother's waist, hoisted her side against her own. Even with her plodding, uneven gait, Yvonne was troublingly light, just a brittle frame weighed down by sweaty pajamas.

Grace was accustomed to seeing Yvonne naked—they went to the Korean spa together often enough—but she had to hide her horror as she helped her mother out of her clothes. Yvonne had lost a startling amount of weight, more than Grace would have thought possible, even lying unconscious in a hospital room for a week. Her skin, soft and thin like worn leather, seemed to hang loose on her body. This struck Grace harder, at first, than the actual wounds, covered neatly with gauze and bandages.

"Run some hot water," said Yvonne. The tub was empty—the instructions warned against letting the wounds soak. "Just a little bit. I'm cold."

Grace let the tub fill up two inches while her mother shivered against her. Yvonne sat on the rim and gripped Grace's shoulder as she swung her legs inside, testing the water with her toes. She nodded, and Grace helped lower her into the tub.

Yvonne sighed as she sat down. "This is pathetic."

It was hard to argue with that. She looked small and breakable, crouched naked, spine curved, the outline of her vertebrae showing through her skin. She'd been shot in the front, and the bullet had exited her body beneath her ribs. The wound was dressed, but there was a large bruise all around it, a halo of purple and green. Grace took the mixing bowl she'd grabbed from the kitchen and filled it with hot water.

"Umma," she said. "Lift your head. Let's wash your hair first."

How many times had Yvonne bathed her daughters in this tub? Grace wasn't sure how old she was when she started bathing on her own, but she had vivid memories of being in the tub, both with and without Miriam, their mother—never their father—squatting on the bathroom floor, washing their hair. Even after Grace started showering, Yvonne would force her to submit to ddae miri at least once or twice a year, scrubbing with a coarse cloth until great gray worms of dead skin and dirt emerged from every surface of her body, leaving her pink and raw and clean.

Grace always disliked this painful ritual, even more so when she realized it wasn't something most of the other kids suffered. She remembered the night she put an end to it. She must have been twelve or thirteen, not a child anymore, by her own calculation. Yvonne had walked into the bathroom while Grace was showering—back then, Miriam was the only one in the house who ever locked a door. Yvonne was singing her ddae miri song, a silly little jingle set to a Korean pop song: "Ddae, ddae, ddae, ddae, ddae, ddae, ddae . . ." It had cracked Grace up when she was younger, but that night it grated on her, the cutesy intrusion on her privacy. She snapped at Yvonne, in a way that stunned them both. What she could see of her mother's face through the steamed glass filled Grace with shame.

She lathered Yvonne's hair. It felt thin and fragile between her fingers. Grace noticed the gray roots growing from the top of her bowed head, the cheap dark brown dye job turning purple.

"You can shampoo harder. My head's not injured," said Yvonne. "Here, I'll just do it."

Before Grace could stop her, she brushed her daughter's limp hands out of the way and started working her scalp with unnecessary vigor. It was a sulky move, not typical of Yvonne, and it brought the sting of tears to Grace's eyes. Her mother hated to be helpless, and Grace had no idea how to take care of her.

Yvonne let out a yelp and dropped her arms, then wrapped them tight across her abdomen.

"Umma! Just stay still. You have a hole in your fucking torso."

Grace almost covered her mouth—she never swore in front of her mother, let alone at her, and she saw that it made Yvonne flinch. But she let it stay said. It was undeniably true.

Yvonne stopped resisting, and Grace did her best washing her hair, then her body.

"You used to love when I washed your back," said Yvonne, subdued, as Grace sponged her shoulder blades with soapy water. "Do you remember?"

Grace nodded, then realized her mother couldn't see and made a sound of agreement.

"You liked when I drew shapes. We used to practice the alphabet during bath time."

Grace could feel the gliding touch of her mother's fingers. The tickly zags of *M, W, Z*. The long straight lines of Hangul vowels.

"I have to clean the wounds," she said.

She peeled the dressing free and sucked in her gasp as she stared at the bullet hole. It was a hideous thing, dark and gory, meat colored. The exposed inside of the body, never meant to see the light of day.

She dabbed at it uncertainly, and Yvonne groaned; her back clenched under Grace's hands. Grace could not imagine this kind of pain.

Yvonne's breath was heavy. She hugged her knees as Grace redressed the exit wound.

"Someone told you, didn't they?" She spoke into her knees, so softly Grace wasn't sure she heard right.

"Umma?"

"Appa told me."

Grace was silent. She'd been waiting to have this conversation, but now that it was here, she wanted to punt it to a future Grace, one who was better and wiser and not staring at her mother's naked gunshot back.

"You can barely stand to look at me—you think I haven't noticed? Because of something I did before you were born."

Grace couldn't think of a single thing to say.

"You don't know what it was like back then. Koreans were dying, did you know that? We were getting robbed at gunpoint, murdered for cash and beer. These gangsters, they were like animals. I didn't even want to be there. I begged your father to sell the store. Miriam was only a baby. I was scared something would happen to us."

"But she was just a teenage girl," said Grace. She couldn't bring herself to say the name out loud and hear it hang in the air.

There was silence, and then a sob. "It was a mistake. I wish every day I could undo what happened. But I *can't*. How much do I have to pay for it? For that one mistake? Do I have to lose my daughters? Will that make it right?"

"You're not losing your daughters, Umma." Grace started to cry, overwhelmed with pity and rage and love and disgust. "For one thing, we're both alive."

She went back to the task at hand, the one that was defined and doable, and Yvonne grew still and quiet under Grace's clumsy touch. This was all wrong. Grace rarely fought with her mother. She was the peacekeeper, the easy child, the one who held steady while Miriam claimed the spotlight. But maybe this wasn't a fight at all—because what was negotiable? Where was the resolution? Grace could never accept what her mother had done. It would always be between them.

"Grace, stop crying," said Yvonne, in the stern voice she'd used to shush her when Grace acted petulant as a child.

It had the same effect as when Grace was younger—she cried harder.

"Grace, stop it."

"I'm sorry, I can't help it." She sniffed, inhaling a thick glob of snot. "This is the worst thing that's ever happened to me."

She felt herself turn red. It was a ridiculous thing to say, she knew, when a girl had died, when her friends and family had lived through her murder. Yet it was clear, too, that Yvonne felt victimized by her history, as if the girl's death were something that had happened to her. And didn't Grace have the stronger grievance? She was an innocent. Her mother had sinned and had failed to protect her from the fallout.

Yvonne turned her head to face her and smiled an exhausted, heartbroken smile. "Good. Then I can't have been such a bad mom." She stretched her arms back and rested them on the floor of the tub, exposing her naked front. She nodded at the bandages there with her chin. "Help me with this."

Grace opened the dressing and gazed at the startling wound, the hole blown open beneath her mother's slack, emptied breasts.

Ava Matthews stared out at Grace from her computer screen, and for the first time, Grace forced herself to stare back. The portrait was grainy, black and white, printed in the first pages of *Farewell Waltz: The Life and Death of Ava Matthews*. It looked like a school photo, with nothing but gray haze in the background. The girl wore a fussy dress with puffed sleeves, and her hair was carefully ironed, bangs molded into a thick round fringe that made her look maybe eight years old. She had soft eyes and a full mouth cocked into a wry smile. A face full of humor and innocence. A face Grace hadn't let herself look at before.

It was hard enough to know that her mother had killed. There was a part of her that didn't want to know any more, didn't want to think of this girl as a person, as precious and human as anyone else. But there she was, and Grace found herself wondering about the sound of her voice, her likes and dislikes, her dreams. She scrolled to the next page and started reading.

Ava Matthews had never known her father, and she'd lost her mother when she was eight years old, to a drunk driver. Grace felt this like a fist around her heart. She was twenty-seven, and losing

Yvonne still seemed like an insuperable tragedy. She couldn't imagine how her life might have been if she'd lost her as a child. According to the girl's aunt, who took her in along with her little brother, Ava went blank the year her mom died. She wouldn't talk to her aunt and uncle; she ignored her teachers, got in trouble at school.

It was music that drew her back out. She'd always had a good ear on her. She sang in the children's choir at Trueway Baptist, and because her aunt never let her stop going to church, she kept going to practice, even in her grief. The choir director had a soft spot for her, and she started giving her free piano lessons on the church's old baby grand. Ava had talent, and she played with beauty and passion. Starting her last year of junior high, she participated in a string of youth competitions around L.A., going up against kids who had formal training with professional teachers. Ava didn't even have her own piano, but she won a Chopin competition with a $100 prize, moving the judges with her rendition of the *Farewell Waltz*.

It was the kind of victory that ended Disney movies, the story of a disadvantaged girl beating the odds and delivering the performance of a lifetime. Grace played piano until college, and she remembered those competitions. The hours of practice that went into them, her mother cheering and spurring her on. The cold rooms, the steely judges, the reverberation after the end of each song. Grace never won, though she came close once, with a Bach partita. For an irrational split second, she wondered if she'd ever competed with Ava Matthews, both of them teenagers with froofy hairstyles in modest, uncomfortable dresses, sitting up straight and spreading their fingers. Their nerves as responsive as the singing strings.

But Ava was dead before Grace was even born. The brutal truth crashed over her brief, benevolent fantasy. This wasn't the story of a girl. It was the story of her death.

Grace stopped reading and searched for more information on Ava Matthews. She wanted to know all there was to know, even if it hurt. But there wasn't much more out there, just articles she'd already read and references to *Farewell Waltz*. She saw now that Searcey had even written some of the initial *L.A. Times* coverage—he seemed to be the main authority on the girl's life.

She stared at his picture online. There was, she thought, a gleam of righteous conviction in his eyes. This man had wielded his pen to take her mother to task, but Grace couldn't say he'd been dishonest or even mean. He showed such obvious sorrow over Ava Matthews's death, and Grace felt it with him. Maybe this man wasn't her enemy. Maybe he could help her.

She searched her inbox for his emails—he'd sent seven of them, all of them polite but firm and urgent. He'd given her his phone number.

"Hello?" It was past ten o'clock now, but he picked up after one ring, before she had any real idea of what she might say. "Hello?"

"Hi." She swallowed, hearing the dry sound of her mouth. "I'd like to speak with Jules Searcey."

"This is he."

"This is Grace Park," she said.

"Grace, of course, hi." There was a rush of sound on the other end of the line. Whatever he was doing, he'd dropped it to give her his full attention. "It's good to hear from you. How is your family doing?"

Yvonne was asleep. Grace had bathed and clothed and fed her, and now Paul was home, a warm body to lie next to his wife and call for backup, from Grace or the hospital, should anything go wrong. He was, at least, uncharacteristically tender with Yvonne. Nothing crazy—Grace wasn't sure she'd ever even seen her parents kiss—but his voice was softer, and he touched her shoulders, held her hands, offered to have Grace bring her food and water.

"They're fine," she said, absurdly.

"And how are you?"

The question took her by surprise. The gentleness in his voice. "It's been a hard week."

"I want you to know I was appalled by the behavior of Action

Now," he said. "They have a reputation for harvesting outrage for page views, but I thought this was beyond the pale, even for them. I hope you understand that they don't represent all journalists."

"Thank you." She had to bite her lip to keep from crying.

"Listen, I'd love to talk in person sometime. Do you think you can meet me? Maybe this week? It might be good for you, with everything that's happening. I know it must be overwhelming, to be at the center of this storm. But you should take the chance to tell your side of the story."

There was that line again. *Her side of the story.* What did that even look like? What part of this story belonged to her? "I don't know if I can," she said.

"I understand. But please think about it, okay? You have my number." There was a smile in his voice. If he was disappointed, he hid it well. "Was there something else I could do for you?"

"I started your book," she said, still trying to work out why she had called.

"Thank you. That's—I'm happy to hear that."

"The cousin they arrested—is he the one she lived with? The one whose mom helped raise her?"

He hesitated briefly. "Yes."

She paused. Put as much persuasion into her voice as she could manage. "I want to talk to him."

"That's gonna be tough. I can't even reach him. Only his lawyer."

She chewed on her lip. She was a little relieved, now that she stopped to think about it, that circumstances prevented her from facing her mother's shooter.

But she needed to do something. Ava Matthews might be gone, but she had left family, who carried and cherished her pieces. "She had a brother," she said. "I want to see him."

"What's this all about?"

"I just want to talk to him."

Searcey sighed. "I don't know if that's a good idea, Grace."

She felt the emotion rise in her throat, and she let it creep into her voice. "This is all just so new to me. I didn't know about any of it until someone tried to kill my mom."

"You didn't know about the other shooting?" He sounded surprised.

"Not until last week."

Grace held her breath through another long pause.

"Listen. I'd love to help you, but I can't just give you contact information. It would be unethical."

Grace kept silent. She could hear the wavering in his voice—he wanted to help her, or at least get on her good side. He was gearing up to tell her what he could do.

"If you really want to get in touch, you should talk to your sister."

She held the phone tighter, unsure she'd heard him correctly. "I'm sorry. Who?"

"Your sister. Miriam. She should know how to find them."

SIXTEEN

SATURDAY, AUGUST 31, 2019

She'd shown up that evening on Aunt Sheila's doorstep—like a Jehovah's Witness, his aunt said. Shawn could picture her knocking, supplicant and demanding. Nisha was gone, visiting Ray again. Duncan had gone in with his alibi, but it hadn't been a get-out-of-jail-free card after all, not when Ray had already told a few contradicting stories. Ray was still at Men's Central, his wife, none the wiser, standing strong behind him. Had either of them been home, they might have shut the door in Grace Park's face. Aunt Sheila invited her in for tea.

They were sitting at the table, speaking softly, eyes gleaming, when Shawn came by after work, his arms full of takeout. He'd left Jazz and Monique at home, expecting a solemn night checking in with the kids, conferring quietly with his aunt. And here she'd gone and dropped this bomb on him, in the name of Christian hospitality.

Shawn recognized her immediately. He hadn't watched the video, but it had been sent to him enough times that he'd seen the stills. The Korean girl with the cut lip, sprawled on a sidewalk, shouting. He might've recognized her anyway. She had her mother's round face, the high soft cheekbones and narrow chin that made her look young and unthreatening. The face of an untouchable killer.

Her eyes widened as she took him in. Was there fear there? Did she dare insert herself into his life and then act afraid?

She snapped to standing, as if suddenly aware of her own rudeness.

"Hi," she said. "I'm Grace." Her hand jerked at her side, indecisive, and then she extended it, unsure of whether he'd take it.

He stood there staring at her until she put her hand down, blushing terribly.

"Shawn, honey," said Aunt Sheila. "Do you know who this is?" As if she were a welcome and honored guest, a saint or a marvel.

He set the bags down on the table but remained standing. He was half a head taller than the girl, who looked downward, at a spot on the carpet somewhere around his feet.

"Yeah," he said, looking past her at Aunt Sheila. "You didn't see the video, did you?"

Grace Park closed her eyes and narrowed her shoulders. Like she was powering through this unpleasantness. Wincing and cringing, but ultimately undeterred.

"Video?" asked Aunt Sheila.

"Her face is all over the internet. What's she doing here?"

Grace opened her eyes and looked at him again. "I swear I'm not here to cause trouble. I just want to talk," she said. "I know they arrested your cousin."

"She just found out what happened to Ava." Aunt Sheila spoke softly, tenderly, as if some of that grief might belong to this girl. "She only just heard what her own mama did because somebody tried to kill her."

"Somebody." Shawn almost laughed and addressed Grace for the first time. "You think my cousin shot your mom."

"I—I don't know anything. But I understand he must have been—that you all must have been—very angry with her. I'm not here to like cast—"

"She thinks she can help us, Shawn," Aunt Sheila cut in. She never did have much patience for stuttering nonsense. "She can talk to her parents. Who knows? If they don't press things with the cops, that could take some of the heat off the case."

"My mom is recovering. It's not like anyone died this time." She swallowed the last two words and turned red all over again. "I've already met the detective. He might listen to me. I want to help."

"She was at the Alfonso Curiel rally," said Aunt Sheila, putting an encouraging hand on Grace's arm.

"My sister and I—we're aware that there's a lot of injustice, particularly when it comes to police and like black victims of—of violent crime. If there's anything we can do to make things easier for your family, I want to . . ." She trailed off looking for words and then just nodded. "I want to."

There was a long silence as she waited, throat rolling, for Shawn to say something. His family was in crisis. He needed to talk to his niece and nephew, his aunt. He did not need to deal with this mess of an overgrown child who was nothing and nobody to him.

"He didn't do it," he said firmly. "I know that for a fact."

"Then all the more reason to save him from prison." The words came out fast and barely formed, and she opened her mouth to spill more of them.

He held up a hand to stop her. "Why are you here?"

Her mouth fell slack. She had the wounded look of an eager student cut off by a teacher. "What?"

"I said, why did you come here?"

"Shawn," said Aunt Sheila.

"Don't 'Shawn' me, Auntie. I want to know why she came. Because it wasn't to save Ray from prison."

Grace looked down at her hands, but he could see that her face had changed. There was no pride in it. Her jaw quivered; her nose threatened to run.

"I came to tell you how sorry I am," she said, bowing her head so deep he feared she would get on her knees. "I'm sorry about what I said in the video. It was all brand new to me, and that reporter backed me into a corner. But more than that, I am so sorry that my family caused your family so much pain. I've been reading about your sister, and it sounds like she was such a sweet, talented, smart girl. I keep thinking, she probably wasn't that different from me. I played piano, too. I can't even stand it, thinking about how she'd be alive if it weren't for us."

She was in tears now, and she sat down at the table, where Aunt Sheila patted her gently on the shoulder. Shawn wanted to yank his aunt's hand away. How could she sit there encouraging this bullshit? This girl was nothing like Ava. It didn't matter if they both played piano and loved their families and went to church on Sundays. They could have a thousand things in common, but that didn't make them alike. If Ava were like Grace Park, she would never have been killed.

"I'm not defending her, okay?" the girl went on. "I know what she did. But my mom isn't a monster. She told me yesterday how much she wishes she could take it back. I know she's sorry."

Even Aunt Sheila hardened at that line, her back straightening as she pulled away. "Now wait a minute. I know she didn't send her daughter to apologize on her behalf after all these years," she said.

Grace shook her head. "Oh no, I didn't mean— She doesn't know I'm here."

"Jung-Ja Han has had almost three decades to apologize. Instead, she lied and manipulated her way out of prison, then disappeared without so much as a tearful glance in our direction. No, we aren't fool enough to accept that."

"I understand," said Grace, putting a hand to her heart. "I can only speak for myself, and I am truly, truly sorry."

"You've got nothing to feel guilty about," said Shawn. "You know that. You weren't even born."

She lifted her face toward him. Eyes shining, expectant. Waiting for absolution like it was a wafer he might place upon her tongue.

Of course that's what she was after. The same thing that Searcey was after, more or less, and every nonblack person who found out who he was, and what had happened to him, and looked longingly his way. Ava wasn't there to receive their goodness, so they poured it, sloshing, wherever they could. Aunt Sheila used it, and he couldn't blame her. But he couldn't stomach it anymore. Not since he was a child, getting his head rubbed by every kindhearted motherfucker who warmed his soul from a safe distance at the bonfire of Shawn's tragedy. He was forever a black child who'd been publicly wronged, and so he was an altar for the well-meaning pilgrims, who wanted his grace in exchange for their patronage. At least Ava got to die before they made a production out of the great tragedy of her life.

"You want me to forgive you, don't you? That's why you came."

"I wanted to help," she said, her words so weak he doubted she even convinced herself.

"I didn't watch the video, and I get why you said whatever it is you said. Other than that, I've got no fight with you. You did me no wrong, and I have no reason to forgive you."

He watched her go over his words to find if she'd gotten what she wanted. She hesitated, then spoke again, evidently dissatisfied. "I just wanted to say I was sorry. That's all. This is all so new to me."

"It's not new to me. I've been living without your apology for twenty-eight years, and I've managed. So has Aunt Sheila."

His aunt was quiet, but she nodded, her head heavy. How dare this girl come to their table, pleading about injustice, acting like his sister was a dead body she'd discovered, one they had to help her do something about right now. When they'd buried her a thousand times over. When they'd done their best, the only ways they knew how, to keep her alive.

After she saw the girl to the door, Aunt Sheila claimed exhaustion and went to her bedroom, where Shawn hoped she was napping and not crying into a pillow. He unpacked the takeout—orange chicken and beef with broccoli, fried rice and chow mein—and called the kids out to help set the table.

The door to Darryl's room bust open the second he said their names, and they both came tumbling out.

"Who was that?" asked Dasha, her eyes sparking, concerned. "Where's Grandma? Is she okay?"

Darryl said nothing, but his shoulders were squared and tight, and Shawn could tell both of them had been listening in as hard as their ears would allow.

"Nobody," he said. "Grandma's just tired. Here, let's set the table and eat. Food's gonna get cold."

"Come on, Uncle Shawn. Who was that Asian lady?"

"Did you meet her?" Shawn asked. Something about the idea unnerved him.

"Not really. Grandma made us go to our rooms. But we saw her. And we know something's up. We're not stupid." She looked to her older brother, as if for confirmation. Darryl nodded vaguely. "This is about Dad, isn't it? And that Korean woman. The one they say he shot."

Shawn sat down and closed his eyes. He had to collect himself. Dasha was right—they were not stupid. Their father had been arrested. Even if Shawn tried to protect them, they knew how to read the news. But this was something different. That girl had come with her burden, her blood; she had thought nothing of bringing it here. The kids—his kids—had seen her; she'd forced their paths to collide. It was nothing short of an invasion.

"What did she want?" asked Darryl.

"Don't worry about it," Shawn said, his throat dry. "She's got nothing to do with us."

III

The day of the verdict, Aunt Sheila kept them home from school. She said it was so they could all be together, but Shawn knew there was more to it than that. He heard the nerves in her voice, saw the fear and pleading in her outstretched hand, her soft mother's smile.

At 3:00, they gathered. Uncle Richard and Aunt Sheila, Shawn and Ray, the four of them hip to hip on the sofa, links on the same chain. By 3:15, Aunt Sheila's hand was warm and damp where she gripped Shawn's arm. It felt like the courtroom all over again. His heart thudded and his head throbbed, his body struggling to contain his dread and anger, his screaming hope that maybe this time, things would be different. That the difference might reach back and change everything else.

It had been almost six months since Jung-Ja Han's trial. Aunt Sheila had spent that time in agitation and protest, condemning the judge, the jury, the whole justice system. The decision was an atrocity, the sentence a bad joke, and everyone seemed to know it. The people, the prosecutors. Even the media seemed to be on their side. But just last week, the state appeals court held up the judge's decision. It was unanimous—a united front. Every back turned on Ava and her family. Shawn didn't know one person who thought this was right or even conceivable. Maybe Shawn didn't know one person who mattered.

Aunt Sheila straightened in her seat and Uncle Richard turned up the volume.

The verdict was in.

The reporter's face gave away nothing, but Shawn knew all the same what would come out of the white man's mouth. Whatever hope Shawn had vanished like fog in daylight.

They've all been found not guilty.

It was a clean sweep for the defendants.

The mayor is expected to call for calm throughout the city.

I don't think there's much doubt that there's going to be quite a reaction.

Not necessarily relevant, there were no blacks on the jury. There were twelve on the jury, of course. Ten of them were white, one was Latino or Hispanic, and one was an Asian.

Smoke rose in a pillar like something from the Bible, dark and alive and climbing, becoming one with the gray sky. Shawn felt a pinprick of heat on his forehead, touched it and gazed at his finger. Ash. It was everywhere. Flakes of it landing like snowfall.

He opened his mouth, tasted the burning air. His eyes stung, scalded with smoke and tears.

Ray clucked his tongue. "Damn. Niggas ain't messing around. Not today."

Shawn saw Ava lying on the floor of the liquor store, and for a panicked moment, he thought it was burning with her in it, her body—the body of his sister, buried a year ago in a small grave in a dirty cemetery, where the weeds grew wild—pinned forever to the place he last saw her alive.

"Shawn!"

He was halfway across the street when Ray caught him by the elbow.

"What you think you're doing? Can't you see the place is on fire? What's the matter with you?"

He watched it burn as Ray dragged him away. The sign was blacked out now, almost illegible. Figueroa Liquor Mart a thing of the past. It was what he wanted, he realized now, what had drawn him after Ray into the street, with Aunt Sheila shouting behind them. The store had been closed since the day Jung-Ja Han killed Ava, the family scared, with good reason, that the locals would come looking for vengeance. Word was they'd been trying to sell the place, but no one wanted to buy. It was cursed. Haunted. An evil place that deserved to burn.

But who else had the right to destroy it?

He shook Ray off and ran, half choking on bitterness and acrid air. Home. He'd go home. Home where he had no father, no mother, no sister.

What did Ray know about anything? If it weren't for Ray, they never would've had to go to Figueroa in the first place. They might've never met Jung-Ja Han. If it weren't for Ray and that asshole Frank, Ava would still be alive.

He ran without thinking, just one shoe dropping in front of the other, but when he looked up, Frank's Liquor was right there in front of him. Lights out, doors closed, like it was trying its best to hide. He heard footsteps running toward him, then slowing until Ray stood next to him.

"Frank the Crank. He used to scare the shit out of me," Ray said. "Bet he wouldn't scare me now."

Shawn tried to picture him, came up with a tall, thin man with graying hair, a stern face made sterner with glasses. It was true—he might've cowed them when they were kids, but they were older now, Ray a straight-up banger. But then again, it wasn't a Crip or Blood who killed Ava.

"You think he's in there?" Shawn asked, his voice croaking.

"What?"

He cleared his throat. Spat on the ground. "Frank. You think he's in there?"

"Don't look like it," said Ray. "Why?"

Shawn walked up and tried the door, Ray following behind. It was locked.

The door was glass, and he peered inside. Their old corner store, familiar even shrouded in darkness. His eyes adjusting, he made out rows of snack food and toiletries, a wall of refrigerated drinks.

"It's empty," Ray said. He pulled at the door, rattling it, making a little bell chime at the top. It didn't budge for him any more than it had for Shawn. "Damn," he said. "I was gonna clean him out of magazines."

Shawn looked back toward Figueroa Liquor and found the fire. It wasn't the only one. The air was hazy, the sky getting dark. Night falling, smoke rising. The streets were filling with people. He could see them roaming, hear them shouting from blocks away. It was on now. The streets zapped with energy. He could feel it, and he knew it was something big, surging through the neighborhood, the city. Shawn and Ray buzzing on the same frequency as Aunt Sheila and Uncle Richard at home, as all the people in the world who'd been forced to tune in. *Everyone is a part of this.* The sweat on his skin sang out.

Frank must've heard the trouble coming, closed up shop, and gone home. As if this weren't his problem. As if it were as simple as leaving, waiting out the storm from a different island. He was wrong. He was in this. And he had shit to answer for.

Shawn was getting in. What was a locked door anyway? Just a plea for obedience, asking people like Shawn to be civil and turn around, as if that had ever helped them. As if they didn't know what to do with a little bit of glass.

For a moment, he thought about punching through the door—it seemed like it should be that easy. Then he collected his thoughts and looked around, scanning for something he could use instead of his fists. There were no baseball bats or hammers; no fallen branches either. But there was a broken curb at the edge of the parking lot, a loose piece of concrete sitting right there like a key to a castle in a video game. He walked over, picked it up, Ray watching him with his mouth open.

"Oh, shit," Ray said. "Do you know—"

Shawn threw the concrete block and it broke through the door, leaving a jagged hole big enough for his arm to reach the lock.

He opened the door and entered, Ray behind him, stepping carefully.

"This is some shit." Ray laughed.

"Don't move!"

They snapped their heads toward the voice. It belonged to a Korean man, positioned behind the register like a soldier in the trenches, head and gun rising over the counter. Frank.

He looked older and skinnier than Shawn remembered, his face gaunt in a way that made Shawn think he could be sick. But what did that matter? He had a gun, and he was pointing it right at Ray.

Shawn's mouth flooded with fear and anger. "Or what?" he said, the hardness in his voice surprising him. "You'll shoot us?"

The gun didn't move, but Frank's eyes shifted to Shawn, appraising him. Shawn tried to see himself as this man saw him. He was fourteen now, not as tall as Ray, but much bigger than he'd been a year ago, more a man than a child. He'd been growing by the week—one day, he'd realized he was the same height Ava was, and one day soon he'd be the same age. His face, too, was older, the baby fat fallen away, the happy glow of the old days gone with it. He hardly smiled anymore.

He was a thief. A threat. A thug. Dark skin and danger.

They held still and silent, standing off, until Frank lowered the gun. "You're the brother," he said, staring at Shawn.

Shawn stared back, keeping his face steely, hiding his surprise.

"You're the girl's brother. The one Han Jung-Ja—" He swallowed, unable to finish the sentence. "You kids come here before. I remember."

There was a gentleness in his voice, and a part of Shawn understood that this man felt sorry for him, that he saw his pain and acknowledged it. This part of Shawn understood that Frank had never meant him harm, and that he meant him no harm now. That he was just a man minding his livelihood. But the part of him that blazed understood things differently.

"She died 'cause of you," he said, his voice quiet and dry.

"What?"

He cleared his throat and spoke louder. "I said, she died 'cause of you."

Frank looked from Shawn to Ray with genuine confusion.

Ray picked up a stack of magazines and threw it on the floor. "Why'd you have to be such a hard-ass, huh? Over a motherfucking magazine." He picked up a *Penthouse,* glanced at the cover and threw it down with the rest. "What's this cost? Two dollars?"

Shawn looked at Ray. Two dollars. That's what Ava had in her hand, ready to pay for the milk that cost her her life. She was holding those dirty bills when she died.

"Why you here anyway?" Ray asked. "Any of you?"

The question hung nastily in the dirty air, disappearing into the sound of approaching sirens—fire or police? Frank straightened, standing taller behind the counter, a man defending his pride. "This is my store," he said.

"Yeah? What, you couldn't do this in Korea? This ain't home for you. We don't want you here. You think we're stupid, yeah? You think we pay ten bucks for some potato chips and apples and we don't know you ripping us off."

"Do I look like rich man to you? I work hard, you steal from me, you threaten me. My friend Mike Oh, he get killed. He has family, and he die for hundred dollar in cash register."

Shawn knew the story, or at least the tune. Jung-Ja Han's lawyer trotted it out about a hundred times during the trial. All the Korean liquor store owners killed by shoplifters in South Central in the year before the shooting. Fucked up, yeah, but he'd gotten tired of hearing it. Like some bangers running stickups had anything to do with his sister, shot in cold blood.

His mouth was parched, his tongue noisy. "How about your friend Jung-Ja Han?"

"She is not my friend," he said. "She did wrong. I'm sorry."

But he was behind the counter, staring down two black hooligans on the other side. His eyes gave him away. This motherfucker felt sorry for her, and he deserved whatever he was going to get.

Shawn didn't notice the other boys until the bell rang and they tumbled in. Four of them, older than Ray, their faces vaguely familiar. One of them—the short dude with giant arms—might have been a Crip called Sparky, who shot his neighbor's dog for disrespecting his parents' lawn.

Frank snapped his attention on the newcomers, raising his gun. "Get out!" he shouted.

Sparky looked at his crew, then at Ray and Shawn, giving Ray a nod of recognition. He smiled. "What, you gonna take all of us?"

Frank hesitated, his grip visibly weakening. He blinked once, and Sparky pulled his own gun, pointing it right at the Korean man's head.

"You know I know how to use this," he said. "Now I'm not trying to lose control today, but I gotta defend myself if you don't put that thing down."

Frank didn't move, and Sparky walked toward him, his stride swinging and slow, weighted by the shorts that brushed his calves. Step by step, he closed the gap between them, leading with the gun.

Before anyone could say anything, he had it an inch from Frank's forehead.

"You best get going, old man. This place don't belong to you no more."

Frank's skin turned a sallow yellow. He looked older than he had a minute ago. He closed his eyes and nodded, his thick eyelids trembling, his papery cheeks shiny with tears.

He said nothing as he let Sparky escort him out of the store. Shawn watched him leave, saw him turn back and take one long look, a heartbroken man saying goodbye. He almost felt sorry for him. Then he remembered—Jung-Ja Han had cried, too. For her reputation. For her livelihood. Her sorrow for herself. There were things worth mourning and things that weren't. Frank's Liquor was just another corrupted place.

The boys went to work like they'd done this a thousand times. Sparky took the gun, took the money out of the register. His crew went from aisle to aisle, picking things up so fast it didn't seem possible they were stealing at random. Ray joined in, bumping fists with Sparky, and Shawn looked around, wondering what he wanted.

He didn't want magazines, or batteries, or beer, or cigarettes. He didn't want snacks, or diapers, or lottery tickets. He looked around him at all the junk, this ugly store that meant enough to Frank that he stood his ground to protect it, crouched in the dark with a gun. What did Shawn want with any of it?

What he wanted he couldn't have. Blood unspilled. History undone. So what good would a pack of gum do him?

He coughed. The others were hollering and laughing, and their noise mingled with the fire that knotted the air. He caught a whiff of his T-shirt—soot and smoke. There was only one thing he wanted to do.

He found a fifth of vodka and poured it over the pile of magazines on the floor, the sharp stink of the alcohol cutting through the smell of burning. There were cigarette lighters by the register, but he knew he wanted matches. He found a box of long ones. Thirty-two count. He only needed one.

The paper caught with a satisfying whoosh, the flame springing eager and immediate. He stared at it, mesmerized. It crawled across the pile, glowing and growing, and it seemed to Shawn that he had summoned this thing, not with a match and vodka, but by the sulfurous light of grief and rage that howled out from within him. Now, watching this fire outside himself, he felt nothing but curiosity and awe, like he was witnessing the birth of somebody else's creature. He wanted to see what it would do next.

"Shawn!" Ray's hand came down on his shoulder and yanked him away as the fire crept outward, warming his feet.

Shawn stumbled, pulled out of his reverie, and saw the others rushing past him out of the store. He followed, Ray leading him by the wrist, while the flame climbed up the magazine rack, building as it caught more and more and more.

They stood in the parking lot, all of them watching. Sparky laughed, and his crew laughed after him.

Sparky slapped Ray's back and jutted his chin out at Shawn. "That your little brother?"

"Cousin," Ray said, looking at Shawn like he hardly knew him.

Sparky whistled and laughed some more. "Little cuz is crazy."

It lasted six days. Six days of fire, a judgment poured over the earth. Figueroa Liquor Mart was gone, and Frank's Liquor. Florence Liquor & Grocery, Empire Market, and Jingle Bell Liquor, too. Laundromats were destroyed, the machines jacked for coins. Dry cleaners looted, plenty of people grabbing the chance to take somebody else's clothes. Some places put up signs, like lamb's blood, on their doors. BLACK OWNED, they said, and they were passed over. Sometimes.

Terry's Interiors got the torch, and Rod Davis Firestone, and the African Refugee Center. After a while, fire didn't discriminate. They called in the National Guard. Sixty-three people were dead.

Shawn watched it all happen. When the law didn't come, the lawless spread out. There were bangers everywhere, bold because the police were gone and because they had a truce for once, their priorities shifted away from each other. When they started getting crews together to ride up into Koreatown, Shawn went with them, riding in the back seat of Sparky's grandma's Ford Escort, not even bothering to lie to Aunt Sheila. Koreatown—it was where the Koreans were. Jung-Ja Han's people. The people who believed and supported her, who thought Ava was Han's bad fortune, a thing that had happened to her, like a car crash or a storm. It made sense to him, to take this outcry to Koreatown. They would bring this judgment to them. To her community, her family. To her.

When it was over, everything had changed. Wherever he went, he saw the extent of the ruin, the cooled remnants of days of unchecked wrath. Where there had been buildings, there were now building frames like children's pictures scribbled in pencil, gray and blurred and skeletal, on the verge of disintegration. Roll-up doors defaced by graffiti and ash, the metal warped so they'd never close again. Rubble and trash littered the streets like fallen teeth, like dead skin, the rot of a ravaged body.

The neighborhood looked like a war zone, a place like nowhere he'd ever seen outside of photographs. But he lived in it now. Victim, civilian, soldier, insurgent.

He was different, still changing, the core of him destabilized and re-formed by the fire. He joined up with the Baring Cross Crips, Sparky vouching for him, saying he'd been through it, that he was stone cold for fourteen. Ray and Sparky and four other guys jumped him in at the parking lot of Trueway Baptist the week after the uprising, the church's pink stucco walls charred black, all the way up to the steeple. They formed a circle around him, each of them locking eyes on him and nodding, starting the ritual. Ray came at him first, and they swung at each other like they had a dozen times before, landing a punch each before the other boys moved in in turn. He kept his fists up and gave them his best, and they knocked him down, each of them laying hands on him until he was on the ground. As he lay there taking hits, his muscles singing, the taste of blood in his throat, he gave himself over to the boys and the pain. How great it was, the controlled aggression of family. To know the hurt would never be more than he could stand.

SEVENTEEN

SUNDAY, SEPTEMBER 1, 2019

Grace combed the room for her Bible, going through her drawers, the boxes of books and photos and keepsakes in her closet. She knew she still had it somewhere, the pink leather NIV with the gold-trimmed pages, once among her most prized possessions. When she'd gone to youth group each week, the kids would chant when someone showed up without a Bible: "Naked Christian! Christian naked!"

"It's fine, Gracious," said Miriam. "You know they're over the moon that we're going. Just don't wear a pentagram, and you're golden."

Last night, when Grace got home from Palmdale, Paul caught her slinking to her room, fatigued and defeated. He said to be ready for church in the morning, as if reminding her of something they'd discussed and settled. Yvonne was feeling strong enough, and Miriam had already agreed to come home and go with them. Grace slept poorly, waking up all night from stressful, realistic dreams. When she finally found her way into a deep sleep, Miriam came and woke her, a full hour ahead of schedule.

Miriam sat on the floor, watching Grace tear through the bedroom. She wore an embroidered white blouse and a conservative blue skirt. Her face was fresh, with a light layer of makeup: her skin dewy, her cheeks touched with a virginal blush. She picked idly at the fibers of the faded green carpet, rolling the long flossy threads in her palm, and looked for all the world like she was gathering summer flowers in a field. Grace could hardly stand to look at her.

For half her life, until Miriam went to college, Grace shared her bedroom with her sister. Twin beds two feet apart, their desks conjoined against one wall. They did their homework side by side, gossiped as they fell asleep, snoozed the same alarm clock until Yvonne scolded them from their doorway. It was one of the backdrops that gave color to her broad memories of childhood. She and Miriam tucked in like Snow White's dwarves, like the little girls in *Madeline*.

But they weren't little girls anymore. The room was small and stifling with both of them in it.

Miriam flicked the back of her leg as she walked by. "Will you sit the fuck down?"

"Ow! What the hell, Unni? That hurt."

But she sat down, sullenly, on the floor next to her sister.

"So?" said Miriam. "Are you gonna tell me how it went?"

Grace hesitated, then gave her the short version of her visit with Ava Matthews's family: that she had gone, and that it had not gone well. There was no one else she could talk to, and it felt good to unburden herself. Still, she kept the most embarrassing details behind, privately hoping she might forget them.

Miriam shook her head. "I told you not to go over there."

"You're the one who gave me the address."

"Under duress," she said.

Grace didn't argue the point. She hadn't threatened her sister, but she'd played it big, harping on the betrayal of Miriam's lies by omission.

"Why did you even have it?" she asked.

"I tracked it down. Pretty much right after I found out."

"How?"

Miriam shrugged. "It wasn't that hard. I'm not a journalist or anything, but I can do basic research."

"So why did Jules Searcey, of all people, know you had it?"

Miriam stared at a carpet fiber as she balled it up between her fingers. "I reached out to him. Like you did, apparently. We knew some people in common, and he seemed like my best bet to get in touch with the family. I asked if he'd feel comfortable setting up a meeting. And I think I asked if I had their address right, in case I wanted to send something."

"What, like an Edible Arrangement?"

She closed her hand around the fuzz and raised her middle finger. "Better than just showing up."

"But you never met them?"

"No. Because I respect people's boundaries." Grace started to object, but Miriam laughed in a way that let her off the hook. "Anyway, Searcey never got back to me. What's he like, anyway? Shawn Matthews. I've never even seen a photo of him. He seems to keep a low profile."

Grace tried to picture Shawn Matthews. He was a big man, tall and heavy looking. Not fat, but solid, with tattooed arms and large hands he kept clenching and unclenching, a nervous habit that seemed to be unconscious. He had an ordinary face that was already fuzzy in her memory. Dark skin, shapely lips, thick eyebrows. Black hair cropped close to his head. He wasn't bad looking, but she doubted she would've noticed him in a restaurant or on the street, except that he was black.

And his eyes stood out. She remembered them now, the way they seemed to see right through her.

Paul knocked on the door, scattering her vision. "It's time," he said. "We'll be in the car."

She was too old for youth group now. She and Miriam sat with their parents, for the main service, the one Paul and Yvonne still attended nearly every Sunday. Grace surveyed the congregation, wondering where all her old church friends had gone. Maybe they'd dropped off over the years, as Miriam had when she was in middle school, as Grace had in college. They weren't here, in any case. Small blessings, Grace thought.

She should have been overjoyed. Her mother was healing; her family, too. Technically, she owed it to God to be in church—she'd made about a hundred promises after the shooting, pledging eternal faith and gratitude for Yvonne's deliverance. But as her lips formed around the old hymns, the words of prayer, she found her soul shrinking inside her, seeking refuge from God's light.

Pastor Kwon was up now. Grace had known him since she was a child, and he always said hi to her when she came to church, usually on Easter. Today's sermon was on the Parable of the Lost Sheep, and she was pretty sure Kwon-moksanim looked right at her family as he thundered through it.

She remembered why she'd stopped going to church. One of her college friends, Samaya, lost her brother, a senior in high school. He and his friends had been drinking, and he drowned in a swimming pool, sucked under by the pump. Nik was Hindu, insofar as he was anything, and Grace couldn't stand the idea that he'd died in that pool to wake up in hell. It seemed so arbitrary, all of a sudden— that the shape of your faith could override everything, that the evil might be saved while the innocent were damned.

"The Park family is with us this holy Sunday." Kwon-moksanim's voice yanked her to attention. She turned to Miriam, who had a tight smile pasted on her face. "God has given them many trials, but we prayed for them, and He listened."

There were cries of worship from the congregation. "Ju yo! Amen!"

"They are all here, together, humble before the Lord. It brings the Shepherd joy to see His sheep. Let us welcome them home."

She folded her hands in her lap and looked down at them, wanting to hide. All these people—they knew who she was, who her mother was; what all of them had suffered and done. It was bad enough bearing their curiosity at the pharmacy, where norms of propriety kept most of them in check. This felt like a punishment—like Pastor Kwon had pushed them onstage, to be heckled and egged.

Then she felt a strong hand patting her left shoulder; another one, on her right, giving her a reassuring squeeze. She glanced at her sister, who had turned to the people behind her, bowing her head in polite greeting. Paul shook hands with an old woman, his face serene. And Yvonne sat tall and waved, acknowledging the attention. Her face bright with feeling.

For the first time all morning, Grace dared to look around.

Uncle Joseph smiled at her, from the other side of her dad, and past him, she recognized more familiar faces. There was Mary Oh, her old Sunday school teacher, and Hyojin Kim, who ran the nail salon across the street from Hanin. She saw Jonah Lee's mom, who stopped speaking to him when he came out of the closet; Wayne Kang, who'd bankrupted his family with his gambling. One by one, they caught her eye and held it, their gazes fervent with blessing.

She knew they were nasty people, some of them, small-minded and flawed, sinful but quick to judge. Yet together, under this roof, they were one body, huddled in an embrace. No wonder her parents came here. The kindness in their faces—her heart swelled, the goodwill like oxygen after this excruciating week. Grace had never felt so forgiven.

Miriam made dinner: spaghetti with tomato sauce, one of the only things she was good at, and the best any of them could do without Yvonne commanding the stove. When it was ready, Paul led Yvonne to the kitchen; she was tired of taking her meals in bed and insisted on eating at the table.

They sat together, their family whole. Paul said grace, and they started their meal in shy, reverent silence. Grace could feel her mother looking at her, at Miriam, with so much love that it almost embarrassed her.

"This is good," said Yvonne. "You're a good cook."

"It's just spaghetti and red sauce, Umma. Anyone can make that."

"I don't know how to make it."

Miriam laughed. "Okay, well, I hope you never find out."

"Blake is lucky to have you cooking for him."

Grace eyed Miriam, wondering if she would protest. She knew her sister feared being seen as the stay-at-home partner, the underemployed wife making dinner for her successful man. Anyway, Blake was so finicky about his food, he usually did the cooking.

Miriam just smiled and nodded. Even she seemed willing to give Yvonne her peace. It wouldn't last, Grace understood, but it put her at ease.

"How is Blake?" asked Paul.

"He's good," said Miriam. "He sold a pilot to Hulu a couple weeks ago."

Paul nodded. Grace could see him puzzling out what Miriam had just told him. Pilot. Hulu.

Yvonne smiled, hearing Miriam chatter. "How long have you been with him now?"

"Two years, almost."

Paul and Yvonne had never met Blake. They'd only heard about him through Grace, when Yvonne pushed her for news on her sister. Grace had been vague and mostly complimentary. They knew he was rich, that he owned a house, and that he and Miriam were probably in love. Her minor reservations, she kept to herself. She had always hoped and believed her mom and sister would make up at some point, and she didn't want to gunk up the bridge by talking trash.

"Do you think you'll marry him?" asked Yvonne.

Miriam caught Grace's eye. Grace bit the inside of her lip, but there was no containing it—the smile broke out of her, and then they were both cracking up. Yvonne glanced from Miriam to Grace and back again, looking stunned and confused but full of guarded pleasure.

Miriam laughed so hard she started coughing. She chugged her glass of water and set it down with a sigh. "Oh, Umma, you're such a mom. You can barely move and you're worried I don't have a husband. You haven't even met Blake. He could be anybody."

"You're thirty-one already. I had both of you by the time I was Grace's age," said Yvonne.

It was true, Grace thought. When Yvonne was twenty-seven, she gave birth to her second child. The same year she escaped a prison term and took on a second identity. Grace felt her high mood start to deflate.

"Okay, I'll be a good girl," said Miriam. "Yes, we've talked about marriage. Don't worry, Mom. I'm not stupid. I do know I have to think about this stuff if I want to have kids."

Grace tried to picture them all at a wedding. Miriam in a white gown, Paul walking her down the aisle. Yvonne dabbing her eyes. Grace the maid of honor. Was that in the cards for them? A day of joy and unity?

She sensed it now—the hope and happiness eclipsing the horror; the horror deferring. She wondered if this was how it would be from here on out. Everything in the open, none of it discussed. It was how her parents had lived, after all, for almost thirty years. The girl's death a terrible incident, but just one moment in their shared history, one they avoided in favor of loving each other and building new and better things. And why not? What else were they supposed to do? Dwell on it for eternity? Kill themselves? Grace could feel the horror soften its grip on her heart—it couldn't survive the attrition of everyday life. Miriam was almost normal again, her anger weak and pale beneath the cover of stubbornness, now torn away.

Maybe this was just how the world worked: people forgot awful truths all the time, or at least they forgot to remember. After all, who wanted to think about ugly things?

She remembered Shawn Matthews's face, clearly now: his taut mouth, his unblinking eyes. Not everyone got to forget. She knew that. But Shawn Matthews was right—Grace hadn't done anything. So maybe she could move on. Maybe she would be lucky.

EIGHTEEN

MONDAY, SEPTEMBER 2, 2019

t was dark by the time they got the truck back to Northridge, and Shawn was eager to get on the road. Jazz and Monique were at the Holloway house. The kids had the day off from school, so Aunt Sheila had been feeding everyone since lunchtime; she'd promised to save him a plate. His stomach growled. He hadn't had time to eat anything proper—they were always slammed on Labor Day.

He was steeling himself for the long drive to Palmdale when Manny found him at his locker.

"How was your Extra Labor Day?" asked Manny, grinning as always at his annual joke.

"Extra laborious," said Shawn.

He closed his locker and turned to his boss. Ulises and Marco had left seconds before Manny appeared, and Shawn suspected he'd been waiting to talk to him.

"You in a hurry?" asked Manny. "Come sit with me a minute."

Shawn wanted to get back, but he couldn't put Manny off, not after flaking on his team twice in one week. He followed him to his office, trying to guess what kind of trouble he was in. Manny seemed like his usual self, but then Shawn had never seen what he was like when he was angry or even especially annoyed. There was no way he would fire him, Shawn knew that, but if Manny had stayed late to give him a talking-to, it had to be serious.

The office was cramped and chaotic. He was never sure what Manny did in here, but it was always a disaster, folders and papers piled up all over the place, even on the floor. Only the bookshelves were kept clear, for photos of grandchildren and an enormous tub of protein powder. Manny was going on sixty, with gray old-man eyebrows and cracked leathery skin, but he was still vain about some things. He had a proud, broad chest and the calves he'd cut as a mover, the muscles like baseballs in his short, powerful legs.

He picked a pile of junk off a chair and set it down on the floor. Shawn sat in the cleared seat while Manny took to his swivel chair behind the desk. The vinyl squeaked as Manny made himself comfortable. A lightbulb hummed overhead.

He leaned forward and stretched his neck from side to side. When it cracked, he sighed pleasantly and looked up at Shawn. "I just wanted to see how you were doing. That's all," he said.

Shawn nodded, relieved. "I appreciate that," he said. "I'm alright. I'm sorry I took off like that the other day. And last Saturday, missing work—"

"Don't worry about it." Manny dismissed the apology with a stiff wave. Shawn saw with surprise that his boss was offended. "The shooting at the Korean place—that's your cousin they arrested, isn't it?"

"Yeah," said Shawn. He remembered how Manny had welcomed Ray, how disappointed he'd been when he decided to quit so quickly. He'd taken a chance on Ray, all because he was Shawn's cousin. "He didn't do it. Ray's not—he's not a violent guy. I wouldn't have asked you—"

"I know, I know. Don't worry, I believe you. And I don't know Ray like you do, but he didn't seem like the type to me either. Seems like the cops are just scrambling. They came asking about you, you know that?"

"I heard."

"I told them no way was it you."

Shawn could picture it easily: Detective Maxwell cornering Manny in this tiny office, asking loaded questions, holding up Shawn's criminal past. The thought made him see red. Shawn wasn't greedy. He didn't need wealth, didn't want fame or even attention. He didn't resent that he moved furniture while fools ran the country.

What he wanted now was what he already had: his hard-earned plot of life, tilled daily with diligence and dignity. His family. His home. His job. Before last week, he'd been on steady ground, stable and happy for maybe the first time since he'd lost Ava. There were things he'd sacrificed in the name of that happiness. He'd learned to tamp down his anger; when his mouth watered with bitterness, he'd learned to clamp his teeth together and swallow the bile. He never bothered anyone, and it seemed fair that he be left alone in return. But here he was, all this shit occupying his thoughts, his time, following him to work.

"So Ava Matthews"—Manny hesitated, but only briefly—"she was your sister."

Shawn cast his eyes down and nodded.

"I remember that shooting, man. The trial, too. It was all so . . ." Manny blew out air through his lips, unable to find the word. "I never put that together. Shawn."

Shawn looked up.

"How long we known each other?" asked Manny.

"Seven years."

"That's right. Seven years." He rubbed at his neck and shot Shawn a rueful smile. "You know, you can talk to me."

"I—"

Manny stopped him with a good-natured laugh. "Jesus, you should see your face," he said. "I'm not asking you to cry on my shoulder, okay? Your business is your business, and I respect that. But if there's anything I can do, you tell me. If you need time off, or you need to run home—you do what you have to for your family."

"Thank you." Shawn didn't know what else to say. He felt light-headed with guilt and gratitude.

"Just no more of this 'sorry, boss, it won't happen again, boss' shit," said Manny, gesturing toward the door. "Don't martyr yourself. Your workers' comp won't cover it."

He could tell there was bad news the moment he walked through the door. Aunt Sheila was lying on the couch with a wet cloth on her forehead, her feet propped across Jazz's lap. Nisha was pacing around the kitchen, whispering furiously on the phone. The kids, even Monique, were out of sight. They must have been sent to their rooms.

Shawn rushed over and knelt by the couch. "Auntie," he said. "Are you okay?"

She kept her eyes closed, but she lifted one hand, reaching toward him. He held it, and she squeezed, weakly. Her skin was cold and delicate, and he rubbed his thumb over soft, large veins, remembering with a shock that his aunt was an old woman.

He looked up at Jazz.

"She's okay," she said, with the calm assurance of a professional. "She just needed to lie down."

"What happened?"

Jazz bit her lip and tilted her head toward Aunt Sheila: whatever it was, she thought it'd upset her all over again.

Nisha leaned out of the kitchen and beckoned him over with a silent wave. He rose, letting go of his aunt's hand.

All the food was still out on the counters, uncovered and cooling—the meal had been interrupted. He found he wasn't hungry anymore. Nisha grabbed his arm and buried her face in his shoulder. When she looked up again, her eyes were wide and wet. "Ray confessed," she said.

"What?"

"Keep your voice down," she whispered. "Ma almost fainted when I told her. She hasn't been sleeping, Shawn. She's been a wreck since they arrested him."

Shawn took a deep breath, trying to regain his composure. It seemed like the crises were piling up, back to back to back, out of his control. "What do you mean he confessed? Did you talk to him?"

"I did, just about the minute Fred called." Ray's lawyer—they were on a first-name basis. "I went right over there and made him look at me."

"And?"

She shook her head. "He didn't do it. I know my husband. I would know if he went and shot an old lady and came home to sleep in my bed. He just ain't that good a liar."

Shawn wanted to believe her, but everything she said was full of holes. Did she really know Ray as well as all that? He had to believe that at least some of his lies got past her. She was soft on Ray, sure, but Nisha was no doormat. She put up with Ray because she believed in him fundamentally, even when she shouldn't.

He needed to talk to Ray. Stare him down and ask what the hell was going on. Shawn didn't know everything about Ray, but he knew him well enough to smell his bullshit. He'd know if something wasn't right.

Was it possible? Duncan had an alibi wrapped up and ready for Ray, but Shawn trusted Duncan about as far as he could throw the man. Ray had been acting shady since he started working at the bar, and Shawn wondered again if they had some kind of hustle going.

But a revenge shooting? That was like the old days, the drive-by days, when they were young and reckless, when everything went straight to their heads. Back then, fear was taboo, a sign you were soft, that you might roll on your homies when the heat turned up. Things were different now. Ray had a wife. Kids. He'd just gotten out of prison, and Shawn knew he didn't want to go back. He couldn't afford to abandon fear. And Ray just didn't seem angry enough to shoot Ava's killer after all these years, with nothing to gain but vengeance.

Then again, they hadn't known where to find her—even Shawn had thought he'd moved on, in his way, before she came back on the map. Was it possible that someone told Ray where she was? Challenged him to do what should've been done? Who would've done it, and why would they have gone to Ray instead of Shawn?

"Then why did he confess?"

"People confess to shit they didn't do all the time. You know that, Shawn."

"I know people do that. But we're not talking about people. We're talking about Ray. Why would he confess to something he didn't do?"

She was silent, and he knew she didn't have a ready answer. He felt guilty for badgering her.

"Well, what did he say?" he prompted.

"He wouldn't talk about it. Can you believe that? He just sat there, hanging his head like a guilty dog." She hesitated before speaking again. "Maybe I'm being paranoid, but I wonder if the cops got to him."

Shawn remembered the detective, the way he riffled through his notes, not reading what was in them, as if he knew they would say whatever he needed them to say.

"What do you mean, they got to him?"

"I don't know, they beat it out of him or something. You know they do things like that."

Shawn had seen cops do all kinds of crazy shit when they thought no one important was looking, and they never thought Shawn was anyone important. He'd been in dark rooms with policemen, too many of them to count over the years. Sometimes it was because he did something. Other times it was because they thought he did, or they thought he knew something, or they knew nothing and needed to bring in the nets.

There were a few times when they'd wanted answers he wasn't giv-

ing them, and they got in his face, pushed him around; he could feel
them aching to hit him. One pint-sized son of a bitch shoved his head
against a wall—an accident, he said, the grin still on him. Shawn's
teeth were loose for days, clinging to gums that felt like sponge and
tasted of fresh blood.

"Did he look like they beat him up? Cuts, bruises, anything like
that?"

"Not that I could see, but you know they smarter than that. They
use rubber hoses, or they don't hit where anyone can see."

This was a big case. He felt that; there was no avoiding it. Jung-Ja
Han took people back to the early '90s, when Los Angeles burned—it
was just what they needed after the Alfonso Curiel shit. The cops had
to be under pressure. To find their man, close their case. Deal with it
fast and neat, before spark met powder keg.

But if they beat a confession out of Ray, he'd let everyone know
it, starting with Nisha.

"He would tell you," he said. "You know Ray won't even suffer a
headache in silence."

"Maybe he was afraid they were listening," she offered. "Or maybe
it wasn't a beating. But he looked bad. Like he hadn't slept or eaten
in days. Maybe they starved him, made him so tired and hungry he
just caved. I don't know, Shawn. But I know this stinks."

Shawn nodded. It did stink, and he was afraid to see what was
rotting under this flimsy cover.

Aunt Sheila mumbled something from the living room. They
looked at each other—they'd been quiet, Shawn thought—then went
to the couch.

Jazz excused herself to check on Monique, and Nisha took her
place, massaging Aunt Sheila's skinny legs as she sat down.

"Ma?" she whispered.

Aunt Sheila opened her eyes. "He couldn't have done it," she said,
her voice dry and croaking. "Not my boy."

"We know, Ma," said Nisha. "We'll get this sorted out."

"They must've cornered him. That confession ain't worth the paper it's signed on, if he ever even signed it." She blinked and the tears started coming. They rolled into the deep grooves lining her cheeks.

Nisha bent over her, stroking her hair. "Don't you worry, Ma."

Aunt Sheila turned to Shawn. She whispered, "You think he could've done it, baby?"

Shawn hesitated. "I don't think so."

She studied his face and found the uncertainty he couldn't quite hide. She raised herself on her elbows. "If he did do it, he better not see one more day in prison. He ain't killed no one, and he spent more time in there for his nonsense than that woman ever did for killing my little girl in cold blood. I'm not gonna let her take my boy away, too."

He forgot sometimes that Aunt Sheila's love was unconditional. She was so staunch, so morally unyielding, that he felt himself measured against some version of himself, an unassailable man who made all the right decisions, who'd made them all along. But she held tight to all her principles, and the most important of these was that family came first. It confused her, when this principle came into conflict with the others. She ran back and forth between denial and defense, exhausting herself to keep all the balls in the air.

Aunt Sheila wouldn't entertain the idea that her baby girl could steal a quart of milk. But if she'd been a killer instead of a victim, Aunt Sheila would've worked as hard to keep her free as she did to procure her justice. And she would've believed she was right the whole way through.

He heard the unmistakable sound of the garage door rolling open, and for one bright moment, he thought it was Ray, coming home. Then he saw the door to Darryl's room—it was open, just a few inches, where it had been closed before. He turned to Nisha, who was already looking at him with an expression of naked alarm.

Shawn bolted to the garage. He got there just in time to see Darryl start Ray's car and throw it in reverse. He was too late to stop him from driving away.

NINETEEN

TUESDAY, SEPTEMBER 3, 2019

t felt good to be at work, answering the phone, sorting prescriptions, the day floating by on dozens of small, impersonal interactions. She felt the protection of her ordinary competence, the bright, contained space of the pharmacy. Miriam was at home attending to their mother. Paul and Grace were back at Woori, relieving Uncle Joseph, who'd worked the store every day for over a week.

They didn't speak much, and there was an almost normal quality to their not speaking. They were coworkers in their own spheres, with no need for polite chatter. These days, there was too much to talk about, but it was all too big to touch in the store, in front of Javi and their customers.

The detective came in late in the afternoon, just over an hour before closing. Paul noticed him before she did. She saw her father tense behind the register, alert as a guard dog, his mouth starting to curl. The bell rang as Detective Maxwell swung the door open and sauntered in, already looking around.

"What do you want?" asked Paul, by way of greeting.

"Hello, Mr. Park. I was actually hoping to speak with your daughter." He nodded at Grace with his chin. "How're you doing today?"

"I'm fine," she said, as he approached the counter. "What did you want to talk about?"

"Can I buy you a cup of coffee?"

She looked at Paul, who gave her a warning glare.

"I don't know if—"

"It'll only be a few minutes," he said, cutting her off amiably. "But if you'd rather talk after you close up, I can wait."

She saw Paul glance through the glass doors of the pharmacy, and she knew he was thinking about all the nosy Koreans. Detective Maxwell stood out at Hanin. A white man with the definite air of a detective on business. She could picture him waiting for her in the food court, seated alone at a wobbly Formica table in his tailored suit, flipping through his notes. Scanning the market, which was, after all, adjacent to his crime scene.

Paul grunted. "I can cover. Make it fast." Addressing his daughter, as if she were the one in control.

Maxwell insisted on coffee, which they got from the Korean bakery.

"Tous Les Jours," he said, reading the name on the sign. "French, huh? Like Paris Baguette." He winked, and she smiled back, cautiously.

He chatted with her, asking about her job, where she went to school. He was friendly, almost flirtatious, and she braced herself for whatever it was he wanted from her. They sat down in the food court, and Grace tried not to notice the attention they drew.

"Ray Holloway confessed," said Maxwell.

Grace bolted upright. "That's great."

"It is."

"Is that what you wanted to tell me? You didn't have to come all this way."

He was silent for several seconds, just watching her. She smiled uncomfortably, wondering what he was looking for. Then he leaned across the table, his eyes scanning the room like he was about to share a secret. "Your parents are holding out on me," he said.

"What makes you think that?" She took a sip of her coffee, in large part to hide her face, though she was sure she had nothing to hide. It wasn't bad, actually, with the amount of cream and sugar she put in.

"How long you been working at Worry?"

It took her a second to realize he was talking about Woori. "Two years."

"You ever get patients you just know are looking to score?"

"Once in a while." She wouldn't have thought so before, that there were Korean addicts. But she'd had a handful of suspect customers, a few of them showing up again and again with scripts cribbed from multiple doctors. They couldn't hide their relief when their pills came through, and when Grace asked them questions, they invariably disappeared. "Why?"

"I've been doing my job for over ten years. It's plain as day when someone's trying to get one over on me. I don't care if they're suspects, witnesses, or even victims—they all lie." He sat back and cracked his knuckles. "Your father's worse than most."

"Why would he lie to you?"

"He's been lying to me from the beginning. I know that. He had things to tell me, if he wanted, and he didn't say one word."

"That was before," she protested. Before Grace knew anything. Before it all came out.

"I saw cameras at the store," he said, ignoring her. "Are they functional?"

They had security cameras set up in the pharmacy. Nothing fancy—her parents didn't have the tech savvy. They were mostly there to discourage shoplifting. Grace had never seen the footage.

She remembered the video of Jung-Ja Han killing Ava Matthews. Grainy, blurred, and decisive. She should have thought to ask about the cameras. She would have, if she hadn't been so distracted. Was it possible there was footage of Yvonne's shooting? Paul hadn't mentioned it, and he apparently hadn't turned any recordings over to the police.

"I don't know anything about those." She spoke carefully, wary of a trap. "You'll have to ask my dad."

"I already did." He sighed and ran a hand through his hair. "He said they're just for show. But I don't buy it."

It wasn't the most implausible lie. Koreans were cheap. Woori Pharmacy had once been Woori Optometry; it would've cost almost nothing to get all new signage, but Woori—"our"—was generic enough that they kept the name, cutting the "Optometry" and hanging a green cross in its place. Grace had seen similar moves wherever Koreans owned businesses, and it wouldn't have surprised her to learn that half their security cameras were dead props.

But she had been working when Paul had the cameras installed. She remembered him overseeing the process with care. It was possible that they'd stopped working and hadn't been fixed, but they certainly weren't just for show.

"I'm sorry. I can't help you." She shrugged, straining for nonchalance. "I have to get back to work."

He kept his eyes on her as she rose uncertainly, hoping he wouldn't stop her from leaving.

"I'm trying to nail the guy who tried to murder your mom," he said. "You'll ask your dad about the cameras."

It wasn't a question. He knew he was right, which meant he knew he'd disturbed her.

He got up and shook her hand. "You have my number if you find anything out."

Grace nodded. She had his number. "Thank you for the coffee."

Paul waited for the drive home to ask about Maxwell's visit. He kept his hands on the steering wheel and watched the road, as good a reason as any to avoid looking at Grace.

"What did he want?" he asked.

She hesitated. Paul did not like to be challenged. He didn't answer questions just because they were asked. If he snapped at Grace for suggesting he mixed up a couple of prices, he might bite her head off for asking why he'd lied to the police.

"Dad, did you tell Detective Maxwell the cameras were just for show?"

He said nothing, but she saw the tension in his jaw.

They drove in silence, and Grace knew Paul would be happy to never speak of the subject again. He focused on the road and sped enough that Grace noticed, as if all would be well once they touched down at home.

"Why would you tell him that? It's such an easy lie to figure out."

"What did you say to him?"

"I didn't say anything. I had a feeling you lied to him, and I didn't want to get you in trouble."

He nodded. "Good. Let me handle the police."

"But what the hell, Dad? Are you withholding evidence? When Mom is the victim?"

"You want answers."

She almost laughed. "Of course I do. Someone shot my mom. There's a man in jail for it. I want to know if he's the guy, and if he is the guy, I want him to stay in jail."

"Do you think that's what she wants?"

Grace didn't know what her mother wanted. For most of her life, she'd assumed she and Yvonne wanted the same things. Her mother was happy when Grace was happy. She shared in her daughter's successes and worried about her shortcomings. She wanted Grace to like her job and maybe get a nice boyfriend. She wanted their family to be together and well.

"Isn't it?" she asked.

"Your mom doesn't care if this man goes to jail. She just wants things to go back to the way they were before."

"That's impossible," said Grace. "You know that."

"It is if we stay in the news. If there's a long trial. If we have to testify. You don't know what it was like."

"I have some idea," she said, her face going red just thinking about her own viral infamy.

"You're too young to remember, but it destroyed your mom. We lost the store. We had to move. And then she almost never left the house. If it weren't for you and Miriam, she might have killed herself."

He said it matter-of-factly, and Grace believed him. It seemed fitting, in a way, that Yvonne had lived for them, against her own will.

"I'm not letting her go through that again."

"But we need the police to help us." She thought of Shawn Matthews, so sure of his cousin's innocence. "What if it wasn't the guy they arrested? What if the shooter's still out there? He tried to kill her once. Why wouldn't he come back?"

She felt the panic climb up her throat as she spoke. Paul wouldn't even look at her.

"Dad? Do you not care?"

He veered to the side of the road and parked the car, his whole body emanating fury. She'd ignited his temper at last.

"I can protect my own family," he said. "No one is hurting your mother ever again."

"Okay, Appa, okay," she said. She stopped herself from asking how.

"It's the police who put a target on her in the first place," he said.

"What're you talking about?"

"Do you know how many people were killed in South Central back then? It was like a battlefield. Every day, somebody shot. I knew people who were killed."

"I know, Dad. I've heard all this before."

"The LAPD chose our story. They called a big press conference. Made speeches about justice. They promised to get your mother charged with first-degree murder. Do you think they did that every time a black teenager was killed?"

"But she was——"

"I know what she was. It was a tragedy. But that's not why they picked this case."

"Why then?"

"Because it was less than two weeks after the Rodney King beating, and they were getting hammered on the news. Every day, they played that video of four police officers beating an unarmed black man. Every day for two weeks. Then your mom shot that girl."

Grace saw the logic in what he was saying. She'd seen the King video. The cops were out of control, and she had no doubt that they'd pull a trick like that. They had to be dying to change the subject. "They got to act like they cared about black people."

"They wanted to be heroes, so they made your mom their villain."

Paul was talking fast, and Grace saw how gratified he was that she was following, that she was agreeing with him.

She shook her head, remembering the Figueroa Liquor Mart footage. "They didn't make Mom shoot an innocent girl."

Paul pretended not to hear her. "When our store burned down, they did nothing. And it wasn't just our store—they let all of our neighbors down. So many Koreans lost everything. Some of them, I know they blamed us. But it was the police who made us the villains, and then they abandoned us. They let us take the fall. All the rioting in South Central and Koreatown, and they were nowhere."

"But that was almost thirty years ago. They're trying to help us now."

Paul shook his head, and Grace saw that nothing she could say would push him off this hill he'd guarded all these years. "They're not on our side. They won't protect us."

She was the only one in the house with a laptop. Yvonne rarely used a computer, and when Paul needed to send an email or print a document, he used the old desktop. The one they kept in a corner of the living room.

Grace hadn't used this computer since high school, when it was sort of new, before she got her own laptop for college. It was a miracle that it still worked, though she supposed her parents didn't push its abilities.

She waited until they went to bed, then waited a couple hours more, until she could hear Paul's long, quiet snores whispering down the hall.

She got out of bed and crept out into the living room. It felt wrong to sneak around in her parents' house, though she did know exactly how to get to that computer without making a sound. She'd never really betrayed her parents' trust growing up, not to meet a boy or steal booze, but she had made a habit of using the computer after they fell asleep, mostly to read manga and watch YouTube videos with headphones on. Once, she'd watched porn just to see what it was like. She closed out and deleted the browser history within minutes, so scared and ashamed that she couldn't even begin to enjoy it.

What she was doing now was much worse—she didn't know what Paul would do if he found out. She booted the computer, horrified by its noisy, whirring respiration. If her parents woke up, she'd have to lie to them, tell them her laptop had died and hope they weren't savvy enough to call her on it.

The hard drive was mostly uncluttered. Her parents didn't keep much on there. Mostly practical things, like tax documents, and the occasional photo downloaded from an email.

She found the videos in a folder labeled SECURITY, left unprotected, in plain sight. She might have laughed at Paul on another day, but right now his naivete only made her feel guilty. They were arranged by date, ending with August 23, the day of the shooting. She scanned the clips, starting from just before closing time.

The shooting had happened deep enough in the parking lot that it didn't register with the camera. Or, now that Grace thought about it, any of the other cameras the Hanin Market tenants might have had up. She wondered if the shooter had known how to avoid them.

She saw Javi leaving for the day, then Yvonne stepping out to buy groceries. She watched herself meeting her mother and closing up, the door shutting behind her at 7:37 P.M. The store went dark after that—a pharmacist had to lock up, by law, and only she and Uncle Joseph had keys. But there was another clip, more than fifteen minutes later. After the shooting.

At 7:55, Paul walked into the store. Grace tried to remember when he showed up at Hanin, whether he'd taken her purse and left her alone before driving them to the hospital. She couldn't picture it, but he must have—he was in there, looking directly at the camera. He balled his fists and approached, getting closer and closer, until he stood on a stepstool and filled the screen. Grace paused and studied his face. Alone in the empty pharmacy, he let his emotions show in a way Grace wasn't sure she'd ever seen before. He looked pale and haunted and murderous, and she understood with awful clarity why he'd been stonewalling the police.

The idiot thought he was going to solve this.

He was planning to study the feed and find the man who shot his wife. Whatever he found—even if it was nothing—he couldn't turn the recordings over now. Not without ceding his ground and letting the detective know that he'd withheld evidence.

There was a full week of clips, plus a handful of older ones Paul must have saved from automatic deletion. She started with these, sifting through, trying to identify what it was that made them stand out to Paul. She saw herself behind the counter, sometimes Uncle Joseph; Javi and their other tech, Tae-Hee, who worked when Javi was off. They all tagged in and out, as they did day to day—but Yvonne was in every clip, working the register.

Grace watched the customers approaching the counter, picking up their medications, shopping for supplements and lottery tickets. It looked like business as usual, and it took a few clips before Grace saw what caught Paul's attention. She paused on a black man, not inside Woori but walking by in the corridor outside, eyeing the store.

She rewound and watched again. His interest seemed passing, she decided, like he was reading the words on the window just to have something to read. But that's what she was looking for—people who stood out, who could be casing the store; people who might be stopping to get a good, long look at Yvonne.

There was one in every clip—not just black people, who were rare in Hanin, but passersby who slowed down to peer through the window. Grace watched the flow of people passing the pharmacy. It was steady and familiar; she recognized a lot of the faces. Mrs. Oh, who worked the jjajangmyeon place in the food court. Rogelio, the young cashier who always flirted a little when she bought her groceries, asking after her parents, the burgeoning drug trade. She scanned them, wondering if they had anything to tell her.

She sat up and rewound a clip from August 1. A black man walked slowly along the window, peering in with intense focus, as if trying to memorize the layout or to puzzle something out. His line of sight reached Yvonne, who was busy at the register, and lingered.

She paused the video and tried to zoom in. When that failed, she stretched the window as far as it would go. The image was pixelated but not unintelligible. She could see his smooth, rounded face; the awkward way he held his shoulders. He wasn't a man at all, certainly not Ray Holloway, who was middle-aged. This was just a teenage boy, plump in the cheeks, with his hands in his pockets, wearing clothes that were too big for him by half.

She stared and stared, a bad feeling in her chest, growing tighter and denser like a coiling length of chain. There was something here that wouldn't let her look away. She followed the lines of his face, the soft mouth, the straight nose; paused on his eyes, squinted under boyishly bushy brows. She knew it with a certainty that rang like an alarm: she had seen this face before.

TWENTY

TUESDAY, SEPTEMBER 3, 2019

Shawn sent Jazz home and spent the night waiting up with Nisha. At midnight, she ordered Dasha to go to bed, and Shawn convinced Aunt Sheila to take a sleeping pill, to save them another reason to worry. They slept in snatches, sitting in the living room, waiting for a phone call, listening for the doorbell, the garage. But Darryl didn't call, and he didn't come home.

When morning came, they had nothing to show for their vigil but a wretched, anguished exhaustion. Nisha had to go to work—it was that or sacrifice her job to this crisis, admit defeat in its face and put in for a long leave of absence.

Shawn had coffee waiting for her when she came out of her room, showered and dressed for work. She took it gratefully, and he hoped it would be enough to perk her up for the drive to LAX. The bags under her eyes were almost as black as her lashes.

"I know it's easier said than done, but try not to worry yourself all day," he said. "He wasn't kidnapped. He thinks he knows what he's doing, so he's probably not in danger. He'll come back home when he figures out what a fool he is. Probably today."

"What if he doesn't?"

"Then it'll be tomorrow." Shawn could hear the hollowness in his own words.

Nisha didn't bother to challenge him again. He was clear out of reassurances, and she must've known it. "What do we do, Shawn? Would it be crazy to call the police?"

"We can't call the police. Not when we don't know why he took off."

She bit her lip. She didn't want to think about why Darryl was gone. She'd been shutting down the why all night, the few times Shawn tried to bring it up. They'd find Darryl first, ask the other questions later. But whatever he was up to, even if it was nothing, he was a black boy running around away from home. Cops needed to be about a thousand miles away.

"I'll look for him," he said. "I'll try his friends again."

Shawn hardly used Facebook. He hadn't grown up with it, and he had no particular desire to spend his free time mining his real life for items of interest to present to people he went to school or church with, for their entertainment or their judgment. His life was too public as it was. The one thing he found social media good for was keeping tabs on the kids. Dasha and Darryl were active users, and he liked that he could see who they were friends with, what they were up to, without having to drag it out of them.

They'd spent hours last night messaging every friend of Darryl's they knew by name from Nisha's account, asking if anyone knew anything and leaving both of their phone numbers. No one called back, and most didn't even bother responding. Probably thought Darryl's mom was being paranoid, freaking out because he stayed out one night. The last night of a long weekend, too. Shawn hoped he was with friends, groaning with embarrassment over their shoulders.

"Try Brianna again," said Nisha. "She might have enough sense to tell us if she knows something."

Until not too long ago, Brianna Lacey was Darryl's girlfriend. She was the first girlfriend Darryl had ever had, and for the six months or so they were together, they were all but inseparable. Shawn had met her several times and was disappointed when the two kids broke up, just a few weeks before Ray came home. Nisha was right. Brianna was a good girl. Soft-hearted and quick to worry. If she only knew how scared they were, she'd do anything in her power to help.

It was almost seven when Nisha left, and Shawn tried to sort out what had to be done in her absence. He had the day off from moving, one small mercy, but with Aunt Sheila unwell, Ray arrested, and Jazz and Nisha at work, he was the one adult left to keep watch over the besieged family fort. He dropped Dasha off at school and went home to change clothes and pick up Monique before Jazz had to leave for the hospital.

He took her back to the Holloway house, where he played with her as well as he could while keeping an eye on the door, the phone, the computer. She was wide-awake and punishingly hyper, and he was grateful when Aunt Sheila got out of bed and offered to entertain her while he caught a couple hours of solid sleep.

He woke up to a call from Nisha.

"Brianna came through," she said. "Says she was asleep when we messaged. I just got off the phone with her."

"She know where he is?"

"She says no, and I believe her. She wouldn't call just to lie to me."

"Did she say anything else?"

"She said she was happy to help, so I asked if you could talk to her. You think you can meet her today after school?"

"I shouldn't just call her?"

"Well, I was thinking maybe you should go over there anyway, see if Darryl's hanging around."

She'd already called the school earlier, and they weren't surprised to learn he wasn't in class. Shawn doubted Darryl was just chilling on campus, but Nisha was right—it was worth checking out, and Shawn knew she'd go herself if she weren't seventy miles away.

"You could maybe drop into the principal's office, too. I said we had a family emergency, but it could help to go in person. I don't want him getting kicked out of school after all this."

"I'm on it. I can pick Dasha up, too, as long as I'm gonna be there."

"Thank you." Her voice was heavy with relief. "We don't deserve you, Shawn."

"Don't say that. We're family," he said. "And we all deserve a whole lot better than this mess."

The principal was gone or busy—either way, she wasn't there for Shawn to plead with on his dumb-ass nephew's behalf. He made his case with the receptionist instead, an elderly Latina woman who lit up when she saw Monique. He told her just enough about Ray's arrest to trigger her fascination and sympathy, and she promised to tell the principal Shawn had come by. She gave Monique a cream soda Dum Dum when they left.

He felt a little guilty, parading the child around. Aunt Sheila had been happy to watch her, but she wanted to follow Shawn, and he had a feeling he could use her help. Sweet-talking school administrators, keeping suspicious eyes off his back—it was almost always better to be seen as a black dad than just a black man, but maybe especially at a high school.

Brianna agreed to meet him on campus after classes let out. By the time he made it to the front gate, she was already there, standing next to Dasha in front of a row of buses. The two girls were waiting for him, but they weren't watching. They were turned toward each other, their heads close, their faces grave. He could see their lips moving, and he didn't have to read them to know they were whispering about Darryl.

Monique ran, making a beeline for Dasha. Both girls looked up and put on big smiles for the little one.

"Monique!" cried Brianna, crouching down so her face was level with the child's. "You're so big now. Do you remember me? Brianna." She said her name brightly, pointing at her own chest.

Monique nodded shyly and let herself be hugged.

"Hey, Dasha," said Shawn, squeezing his niece's shoulder. "Do you think you can show Momo around for a bit?"

"What for?" she asked, looking at him sideways.

"I need to talk to Brianna."

"So? I can talk to Brianna, too."

Brianna glanced between them with an uncertain smile and held Monique's hand as she stood back up.

"Just give us a few minutes, Dasha," he said, hearing the stern edge in his voice. He remembered the empty lot across the street, where Darryl used to hang out with his friends, trying to catch tadpoles in ditch water. "Show Momo the tadpoles."

She glared at him for a full fifteen seconds. It shocked him— he'd never seen that look on her face before. She knew what he was doing—that's what her eyes said—and she thought it was stupid, which meant it *was* stupid. Dasha wasn't Monique. She was too old to protect by sending her off out of earshot. Still, he couldn't have her with him, not if there was any chance her presence would keep Brianna from talking.

"Come with me, Momo," Dasha said, giving in at last. Monique obeyed, happy to follow the older girl anywhere.

"Such a cutie," said Brianna, as they watched the girls walk away.

They stood without speaking, and Shawn could feel Brianna growing antsy. She was a lovely girl, with a heart-shaped cinnamon-brown face and a spray of tiny freckles like a Band-Aid over the bridge of her nose. Hoops and studs glinted from several piercings on her ears, and a small silver crucifix hung around her neck. She wore short, tight-fitting clothes, but the impression she gave was utterly innocent. Sweetness and good manners, with the natural exuberance of youth. Its restlessness, too, its discomfort with silence. Her fingers twisted the frayed hem of her cutoffs.

"I'm sorry about Darryl's dad," she said at last. "And everything else that's going on with your family."

He nodded. She didn't ask what was happening, though he knew she must have been curious.

"Have you heard from Darryl?" he asked. "Since yesterday?"

"I don't know where he is," said Brianna apologetically.

She cast her eyes down, and Shawn could tell she was debating whether to sell out her ex-boyfriend to his concerned uncle. He said nothing, not wanting to sharpen her sense of duty to Darryl. He watched the gate instead, the kids waiting for pickup, for the buses to board, backpacks sagging from their shoulders. It was another hot desert afternoon, and he could see the impatience on their unknowing faces, glowing with sweat and youth. They couldn't stand still— they tapped the asphalt with their feet, they cracked their knuckles and twirled their hair. Half of them had their phones out, looking down at their screens, then up at their surroundings, to check if things had changed to their liking. This was where Darryl and Dasha belonged, in the safety of confined spaces, with gates to keep them from leaping unbridled toward every excitement. The dangers of shining things in dark places.

He felt Brianna fidget while she waited for him to say something else. When he turned back to look at her, he knew she would tell him what he needed to know.

"To be honest, I haven't been able to keep track of him for a while now," she said.

"Because you broke up," he prodded.

She shook her head. "No. I mean yeah, we broke up, but it's *why* we broke up. He started acting weird, and I wasn't having it." She looked around at all the kids who might overhear them. "Can we walk?"

They walked to the football field, which Shawn knew from watching Darryl run track. There was football practice going on, but the bleachers were mostly empty. Brianna chose a spot in the shade, and Shawn sat next to her. He picked up right where she left off.

"What do you mean, he was 'acting weird'?" he asked. "Like when he was cutting school?"

Brianna shrugged. "Yeah, cutting school, acting tough. He never used to be like that. You know him. He's a teddy bear. But all of a sudden he's swaggering all over the place, talking about how his dad and uncle were OGs, that they went to prison and all that."

She cast her eyes up at him shyly, as if she'd forgotten for a second that Shawn was Darryl's uncle.

"Anyway, he started disappearing on me. I'd call him or text him and he'd ignore me, sometimes for days, and when he popped up again, he'd pretend like nothing happened. It was like he had a secret life or something, and it got old fast."

"That's why you broke up with him?"

She started to say something, then stopped herself. When she spoke again, her face was hidden from him, cradled in one hand, and her words came from that vulnerable place.

"I didn't break up with him. Not in my mind," she said. "I gave him an ultimatum. I said if he ghosted on me again, it was over. And he ghosted on me. Whatever bullshit he had going was more important."

Shawn wanted to tell her it wasn't true. He'd seen Darryl after the breakup, shuffling around, listening to maudlin love songs and snapping at Dasha. He and Nisha had even joked about it—the kid was so sad, it broke their hearts, but it was sweet, too, how typical he was, a teenage boy dumped for the first time, moping around like a kicked dog, the earphone cord like a tail between his legs.

But this girl would know he had no idea what he was talking about. He and Nisha had seen what was easy, the straightforward boy they wanted to see. What had they missed?

"What was he doing? You gotta know."

"I don't *know* anything," she said.

"But?" he prompted.

She touched her necklace, pulled the pendant forward for Shawn to see. It was a crucifix, but rounded and abstract, like a silver balloon animal.

"He put this in my locker a couple weeks ago. It would've been our eighth monthiversary."

"It's pretty," he said, unsure where this was going.

"It's from Tiffany's. It was in the blue box and everything. This cost one seventy-five. I looked it up. With tax that's like two hundred. Where'd Darryl get two hundred dollars for something like this?"

Shawn stared at it. Imagined Darryl walking into a jewelry store and picking out this precious, dainty pendant for the girl he wanted to win back. Nisha hadn't mentioned it, and he had a feeling Nisha didn't know about the gift. That in itself made the whole thing suspect. Darryl would've asked his mother for help, under normal circumstances.

"Do you have ideas?"

"Nowhere good, not if you don't know." She lowered her voice. "It's gotta be drugs or something, right?"

The way she said it, like someone who only knew crime from TV, grabbed Shawn by the heart. Just months ago, Darryl was on that side of things, rubbernecking across the divider like any other dumb teen. Did he really throw himself in the action, after all the warnings from his mother, from Shawn and Aunt Sheila?

Shawn said nothing, and Brianna filled the silence. "And he's been hanging out with Quant and them, and like, why? They aren't friends. Quant's like thirty-five years old."

Shawn blinked. "Quant?"

"My cousin. You know him, actually. He used to live in your neighborhood."

The name came to him, clear and out of the blue. "Quantavius Fox?"

Shawn remembered him. He was younger than Shawn by at least five years. A little homie when Shawn was in his twenties, at the peak of his game and his reputation. Quant was a tall, chubby kid, always nursing the patchy beginnings of a beard. He used to tag his initials on anything he could find, like a child who'd just learned to write his own name. Sprayed QF onto trees and abandoned cars. Scratched it onto street signs and toilet seats.

Shawn might have forgotten all about him, except Duncan liked to keep Shawn posted on all the old neighborhood folk, especially the ones who moved to the Antelope Valley. A few years back, Duncan had mentioned that Quantavius Fox was running a transplant crew, a ragged set of Crips relocated from South Central to Palmdale and Lancaster. Shawn had thought it sounded pathetic—a bunch of guys in their thirties and forties, soft-bellied and reminiscing about the old days. It hadn't crossed his mind that they might be recruiting.

Brianna smiled. "You remember him. He'd be glad."

He thought of doughy-faced Quant filling Darryl up with bullshit, telling stories of guns and glory, the old days buffed up with lies and exaggeration. For the first time in years, Shawn played it cool when he felt dangerous. As if it meant nothing, he asked her, "How do I find him?"

Shawn had hoped to surprise the man, but Brianna said Quant wouldn't like it if he just showed up at his house, and she didn't volunteer an address. Quant didn't have an office, and Shawn didn't have the time to stake out the gangster's favorite haunts and hope he'd turn up. So he dropped the kids off and waited while Brianna called her cousin and arranged a meeting—Quant was hungry, and he said Shawn could come see him at the Chipotle on Mall Ring Road.

Shawn watched him from the parking lot. Quant was seated on the concrete patio, chomping down a burrito. He didn't look like he was waiting for anyone.

Time had been kind to Quantavius Fox. Shawn wouldn't have recognized him if he hadn't known to look. He'd been a big kid and was now a big man, but any fat he'd had on him had long since turned to muscle. He had a broad nose that had been broken and healed on a slant, looking more roguish than busted. The beard had grown in, and he kept it long but trimmed neat, like a hedge bush. It had to take some measure of skill to keep it clean while eating a burrito.

He wiped his hands on a napkin and stood up when he spotted Shawn. He was taller than Shawn remembered, too, at least six foot three. There was strength in his arm as he patted Shawn on the back.

He was a man now, not young anymore, but younger than Shawn, who felt his age reflected in Quant's eyes, studying him with vague curiosity.

"Shawn Matthews," he said, drawing it out. "What's up, man? It's been a minute."

He spoke with a familiarity the two of them had never shared. Shawn recognized this for what it was: an assertion of power.

"It's been more than a minute," said Shawn. "Last I saw you, you were boosting spray cans to tag gas stations."

He was out of practice, but it came naturally, this game of dominance. He supposed the detective had given him a good spar.

"Shoot, that was a long time ago." Quant grinned, as if the young Quant who followed Shawn around didn't exist anymore. As if that young Shawn didn't exist anymore either. He sat back down, and Shawn joined him. "Is it true you move couches now?"

His tone was sly, and Shawn had to stop himself from reacting. "Yeah," he said. "It's a job."

Quant stared at him and nodded. He took a big bite out of his burrito and chewed, still staring and nodding.

Shawn wasn't unfamiliar with feelings of inadequacy. He was a middle-aged man with a job that provoked no envy, too old and tired to start something new, his once promising future mostly behind him, left unclaimed. There was a time when he assumed he'd go to college—that Ava would go, and he would follow. Study science or literature. Become a teacher or a doctor. His girlfriend had the education, the good job, and he understood why some of her friends and family didn't trust him straightaway. He knew he wasn't inspiring anyone with his unlikely success story; he wasn't one of these ex-cons who opened restaurants or wrote poetry or went to law school.

But he'd been proud of his life, the one he'd made for himself after prison, working hard and hurting nobody. He would've thought he could stand tall in front of a grown-ass man still playing gangster, trying to look down on him across a fast-food burrito.

Instead, he felt like a fucking fool. He'd played by the rules, the same rules that had put him in prison longer than his own sister's murderer, for getting caught with drugs, for shooting at rival gang members in a firefight. He'd sucked it up, done his time, and come out with discipline, resolved to lead a quiet, law-abiding life. And for what? Ray was in prison, and Shawn knew it could've been him in there, too. His innocence didn't protect him. He couldn't choose his way to a life without trouble.

He looked at Quant, this man who oozed confidence and aggression, tattoos gleaming on every inch of his thick, brawny arms. Shawn remembered Uncle Richard—quietly kind, careful with his words, measured in his emotions. The only father Shawn had ever known, but how little he'd admired him, after Ava died. He found other men to look up to, men who wanted to leave their mark on the world, whatever that mark might look like. So why did it surprise him that Darryl would look at Shawn and turn elsewhere?

He'd been naive. He knew what he got up to when he was his nephew's age, all in spite of Aunt Sheila's interferences, her long list of precautions. It was enough to make him wonder why anyone bothered—kids were gonna be kids, and no matter what you did, some would get in trouble; some would get arrested; some would die.

He knew the answer, of course. You bothered because you had no choice. There was no love without the bothering.

Shawn set his arms on the table and leaned closer to Quant. "I'm looking for my nephew, Darryl," he said. "You know where he is?"

"He missing?" the big man asked, his mouth still full.

"He left home yesterday and we can't get in touch with him."

Quant swallowed his food. "That don't sound like he's missing. He's probably just chilling somewhere."

"Got any idea where?"

Quant pretended to think about it, then shrugged. "He'll turn up. I wouldn't worry about D. He's a smart kid."

It was what people said about Shawn when he was a teenager. As if being smart could keep him out of trouble. It had, in a way— Shawn had avoided the stupidest shit and the longest sentences; he'd managed not to rob a bank and get hit with federal time; he was also alive. But prisons were full of smart black kids. Graveyards, too.

"How would you know that?"

"D's my boy."

Shawn clenched his fist under the table. "What's that supposed to mean? You got him banging?"

"Banging." Quant chuckled. "I know what you're thinking, old man. It ain't like that up here. No one's going to war over territory. We're not shooting it out at the Antelope Valley Mall. But you know how it is. It's a tough world for a nigga. You know these white folks in Palmdale don't like us. Their sheriffs neither. We gotta stick together. Me and D, we're friends."

Shawn recognized the tune. He'd sung it himself plenty of times before.

"And what do you do when you hang out? You and your sixteen-year-old friend."

He shrugged again and picked up his burrito. "You don't gotta worry. I'm looking after him."

Shawn stood, and before Quant realized what was happening, he grabbed him by the collar and punched him in the solar plexus. Quant gasped, and Shawn threw him on the ground, the half-eaten burrito landing beside him.

Shawn was panting, and he didn't bother to hide it. It had been years since he last struck a man, and no amount of exercise could make up for age, or keep dormant belligerence ready and trained for a sudden fight. But he had connected, and he had caught the younger man by surprise. The adrenaline felt good—alarmingly good, the first taste of sweet fruit long forbidden. It charged through him, replenishing his body with the illusion of power and youth. His knuckles ached, and it all came back to him: the beatdowns he'd given, the fights he'd won. He'd let himself forget how much he enjoyed it, the intoxication of dominance. No one gave him the last word anymore, and he had to be okay with it, this constant swallowing of pride. Well, he was taking the last word now. He'd think later about what it might cost him.

TWENTY-ONE

WEDNESDAY, SEPTEMBER 4, 2019

He'd offered to meet her in the Valley, but she was glad she decided to make the drive out. It had taken her a full hour, even with light traffic on the 405, and at the end of it, she was in a brand-new place. Venice was on the opposite side of L.A., and it felt like an entirely different city from where she lived. The streets were full of skinny white people with cool sunglasses and well-groomed dogs, who seemed completely accustomed to being out and about on a weekday afternoon. They struck her as downright exotic. None of them seemed to notice her, and she was grateful for that. She'd worn an old faded Dodgers cap, a shield against her internet fame.

Jules Searcey was waiting for her on the back patio of a café, one that specialized in green tea. He'd converted a table into a cluttered desk, covering it with his computer and papers, his phone and chargers. She recognized his red Moleskine from the bar.

He stood up and rushed over to shake her hand. "Thank you for coming all this way," he said. "Would you like to order something? It's on me."

She got green tea soft serve in a waffle cone. It was almost two and she hadn't eaten, and she felt she deserved to have ice cream for lunch.

They sat down, and she answered Searcey's bland little questions—

how was the drive? how do you like Abbot Kinney? have you been to the boardwalk?—letting him put her at ease while she finished her soft serve. When he finally brought up Yvonne, she didn't resist.

"She's still weak," she said. "But I know you don't recover from a gunshot wound overnight. I think she's doing about as well as can be expected."

"And how are you managing? You mentioned you didn't know about your mom's role in the Ava Matthews shooting." He peered at her through his wire-rimmed glasses, and she thought his sympathy was genuine. She realized she wanted this man to like her.

"It's been a lot, honestly," she said. "But we're doing better than I would've imagined a week ago."

"That's good to hear."

He smiled at her, and she took a steadying breath. He seemed to sense that she was gearing up to speak and waited quietly, sipping his tea.

"I want to help Ray Holloway," she said. "I don't think he did it."

He blinked and let out a soft, surprised laugh. "That's not what I was expecting to hear. So you believe Duncan Green."

She searched her memory for the name. "Who?"

"The guy who started this whole Twitter campaign." He pulled something up on his phone and showed her the screen.

It was a tweet from a man named Duncan Green, @duncangreen machine: I took this picture in Palmdale on 8/23 at 7:35PM. The man is my friend #RayHolloway, who's been arrested for shooting #JungJaHan in Northridge at 7:45PM on the same night. I told @LAPDHQ, but they won't listen. RT if you think #RayHolloway should go free.

The picture showed a middle-aged black man who looked like Ray Holloway, with a young black woman seated deep in his lap. They were both grinning, their eyes shiny with alcohol.

"I didn't know about this," said Grace, staring at the screen. The tweet had been shared more than forty-five thousand times.

"The story's been trending all day. A lot of people are skeptical, of course. Green is Ray Holloway's best friend from childhood. He has good reason to want to protect him."

"Do you think he's lying?"

Searcey shrugged. "He could be. I don't know him."

"But you know Ray Holloway. Do you think he's guilty?"

"I don't know Ray that well either. I haven't actually seen him since 2007 or so. And he did confess to the shooting. I know that's not absolute or anything, but it's not unconvincing."

She'd thought so, too, until she saw the video from the store. It came to her, late last night—she'd seen that boy at Sheila Holloway's house. He was in the living room with a younger girl, probably his sister. They were watching TV when Sheila opened the door for Grace, and they both stared at her openly until Sheila told them to go do their homework. They were her grandkids, she told Grace. Which made the boy Ray's son, or Shawn's.

Grace was thrown by Duncan Green's tweet. It was the kind of thing she always felt was too wild, like when that black woman committed suicide in jail, and people on Facebook swore up and down that she'd been murdered. Grace had always believed, without really thinking, that the world was fair and reasonable. There were systems and structures to keep society alive and safely regulated, and it didn't make sense for her to mistrust them when she understood them so little in the first place.

But this time, she knew. The system had failed. The agitators, the conspiracy theorists—they were right.

The clip didn't prove anything, but it explained a whole lot. Why Ray Holloway was in Palmdale during the shooting. Why he chose to confess anyway. The boy had taken the time to drive to Northridge, just for that one look through Woori's window. He'd found Yvonne and come back to hurt her. Grace would bet the store on it.

"People make false confessions all the time." She'd read about this somewhere around four in the morning, when the security footage wouldn't let her sleep. "Shouldn't the police know better than to just take their word for it?" She set her teeth, thinking of Detective Maxwell. She'd grown up watching men like him on TV, and even when she was wary of him, she'd assumed he was truth seeking and competent. Every day, there were rotten cops in the news, and still she had been bamboozled. "I mean they're supposed to protect people, right? How can they be so bad at their jobs?"

"They protect people from other people. Question is who are 'people' and who are 'other people'?" He blinked and took his glasses off, cleaned the lenses with the hem of his shirt.

She thought of her mother, a criminal and a victim; the bullet fired and the bullet taken, the arc that joined them a shelter, one that had protected Grace all her life. She thought of Ava Matthews and then of Alfonso Curiel, both of them teenagers, dead for nothing. How many more had died between them?

But her mother was not a trained officer of the law. She was just a person, someone who'd never even learned to fire a gun. And the police had offered her up, to draw attention from their own mistakes. They would do it again if they had the chance.

"It's been twenty-seven years since the riots, right?" she asked.

Searcey nodded. "And the Watts Rebellion was twenty-seven years before that."

She nodded back—though she wasn't quite sure what he was talking about—and continued her thought. "And the same things keep happening. Like every week, there's some new police shooting. Rodney King—I mean I know what happened to him was terrible, but . . ."

She paused, and Searcey picked up the thread. "Rodney King only blew up because George Holliday got him on video. You have to assume there was police brutality that never made it to the public, but they showed that one video on every news channel across the country for a full year. Even dead kids don't get that kind of coverage anymore. There are too many videos. They bleed together. People get desensitized. I'd bet the Rodney King beating wouldn't even break a few thousand views on YouTube now. He was a felon resisting arrest, and he survived."

"Alfonso Curiel isn't on the news anymore."

"He would be, if Trevor Warren had been indicted. If there was a trial coming. But there isn't. As far as most journalists are concerned? The story's pretty much over."

Grace thought of Alfonso Curiel's mother, pointing at the camera. *Remember his name.* "Now Ray Holloway is the story," she said.

"The good news, if you can call it that? It's all part of the same story. Even if the news cycle has moved on, people remember Alfonso Curiel when they see Ray Holloway. Especially here, in SoCal."

"Ray Holloway should be free," she said. "The police got it all wrong. I *know* it."

Searcey stared at her with renewed interest. "You witnessed the shooting," he said. "You're one of the only people who could make that happen. Did you remember something? Did you see anything that would help Ray?"

She could turn the clip over to Searcey or even Detective Maxwell. It was probably the right thing to do. But what would it accomplish? If Duncan Green's picture wasn't exonerating, the video wouldn't be either. And Ray Holloway wouldn't want it getting out. Her parents either—they just wanted to move on, and Grace had had just about enough of the spotlight.

"You said you could get in touch with his lawyer, didn't you?"

F red MacManus looked like he could be on TV. And he had been, from the looks of it—there was a framed photo of him with Rachel Maddow on one of his hundred bookshelves. He was a good-looking man, tall and trim in a sharp blue suit with a skinny gray necktie. He was black, which had surprised her. Not because he was a lawyer, Grace reasoned, but because his name sounded Irish.

"Please have a seat, Miss Park," he said, gesturing toward a plush leather chair in front of his desk. "I'm sorry I kept you waiting. It's been hectic here, what with this new social media campaign. I just got done talking to KPCC."

She sat and noticed a framed picture of two college-age boys, one of them clearly graduating, with a colorful sash draped over his gown.

"That's my son's college graduation. UCLA, like me." He settled into his massive desk chair with a slight smile. "He's the smart one. The pretty one's at Stanford."

Grace's mouth fell slightly open—she hadn't put together that the two boys were his children. "Did you have them when you were twelve?"

His smile widened. "You know what they say. Black don't crack."

She laughed. She hadn't heard that before.

"I was glad to hear from you," he said, his expression still light and amiable.

She'd called from her car, already on her way over to his office in Century City. His assistant had fussed over her while she waited, offering her water and coffee and cookies, promising he'd be with her the second he was free.

"I want to help your client," she said. "Ray Holloway. I don't think he did anything."

If MacManus was surprised, he didn't show it. "I don't think he did either." He waited for her to continue.

"We aren't interested in pressing charges," she said. "My family, I mean." She wondered if that mattered, if they had the power to wish this all away.

He must've seen the stupid hope in her face. "That's not how it works, unfortunately. Ray is a convicted felon on parole, and he confessed to a violent felony. The state can't drop the case on your say-so."

"What if I had proof?"

His desk chair creaked, though she didn't notice him shifting. "What kind of proof?" His voice was even, but there was a hungry, attentive glint in his eyes.

What would happen if she gave MacManus the video? Would he show it to his client? Or would he just hand it over to the police and the prosecutors and send them after the boy Ray Holloway had gone to jail to protect?

She took her time, wanting to feel him out without showing her whole hand. "What if, just hypothetically, I had proof that someone else was involved, but your client didn't want you to use it?"

The "just hypothetically" didn't do much, it turned out. His eyes lit up like she'd flashed him a map to the Holy Grail. "You have proof that someone else was involved?"

"I didn't say that."

The lawyer fell back in his chair. He looked frustrated. Grace wondered if he suspected his client was holding back on him. He certainly didn't seem to know what she knew.

And she wouldn't tell him. All at once, she felt in league with Ray Holloway, and the idea suffused her with a sense of warmth and well-being—what she was seeking, she realized, when she'd visited Shawn Matthews. Here was a man who'd only just gotten out of prison, sacrificing his freedom for the sake of his family. It was like something out of a folktale, beautiful and noble and rare. A father's love, proven under fire. She would protect it; she would keep his secret.

"You said you wanted to help him," said MacManus.

"I do," she said. "I witnessed the shooting, and I don't think he did it. That has to count for something, doesn't it?"

He thought about that and leaned forward again. "We're talking hypothetically, right? If you or your mother were to remember something about the shooting, something you didn't already tell the police—that could change things. I think the prosecution would have a much harder time if they knew you'd testify he wasn't the shooter. In fact, I could see them giving up if they knew you'd get up and say that."

Her heart beat hard as she pictured the man free, the boy free, tearfully reunited because of her intervention. She knew what Mac-Manus was asking, in his plausibly deniable way. The price was cheap for what she'd be getting.

"My mom won't testify. I'm positive about that. And I'll tell them I saw the shooter and that he wasn't Ray Holloway."

He searched her eyes and nodded once, satisfied. "Has the DA's office contacted you yet?"

"No," she said. "I've only talked to the detective."

"They will. In fact, I'll tell them they need to talk to you."

TWENTY-TWO

THURSDAY, SEPTEMBER 5, 2019

The phone buzzed on Shawn's pillow, where he'd been keeping it by his ear every night since Jung-Ja Han was shot. He slept so lightly these days it might have been overkill, but he didn't want to miss the wrong phone call. Darryl's photo popped up on the screen, and Shawn slipped out of bed into the dark hallway to answer.

Darryl's voice, creaking and nervous: "Hey, Uncle Shawn."

So the little punk was alive. He crouched down on the carpet and rested his head on the wall. He had to close his eyes to steady himself.

"Darryl," he said. "Jesus Christ."

"I'm sorry."

"Where are you? Where you calling from?"

"If I tell you, will you come and not tell Mom?"

"Just tell me where you are."

Darryl hesitated but gave in anyway. He needed help. "I'm at Mc-Adam Park. In the playground."

He remembered watching Darryl swinging on the monkey bars, butt and knees dusty from horsing around in the dirt. The broad smile when he made it across and jumped off, landing on his feet. Big teeth gleaming, bright eyes seeking out Shawn. Asking, *Did you see that?*

"Don't move. I'll be there in ten," Shawn said.

The light went on as he put on his pants. Jazz sat up in bed, haloed in soft dusty lamplight. Her eyes were clear and wide. She'd been awake, then, probably since the phone rang.

"Are you going out now? It's past two in the morning."

Shawn realized he hadn't checked the time. These past days had pried him away from his routine, demanding his readiness and attention. He'd been on constant standby, like Jazz on the exhausting nights she took call, when she went to bed in her scrubs, prepared to rush to the hospital to deal with a stranger's crisis. But this call had lasted over forty-eight hours, and Darryl was his own flesh and blood. He was running on love and adrenaline, and he was supposed to be up for work in four hours.

"Sorry, Jazz," he said. "Go back to sleep. I won't be long."

She didn't move, just stayed propped up on her elbows, looking at him. "Was that Darryl?" she asked.

He thought about lying. He might have, if he thought there was a chance she'd believe it. "Yeah."

"Oh, that's great, baby." Her whole body seemed to sigh with relief. "He's okay, then?"

Shawn didn't know how to answer her. He turned to put his socks on and spoke into his knees. "He's found."

Jazz was quiet for a minute, turning this over. "But whatever made him go off like that, it's right there with him."

Shawn started getting up to leave, but she stopped him with a hand on his elbow. He sat back on the bed, took her hand and kissed it. "I gotta go, Jazz."

"I'm worried about you," she said. "I don't want you to get into something you can't handle."

He thought of Detective Maxwell. Of Quant, the big gangster glaring at him from the ground. There was his job, too. He was grateful to Manny—it looked like Shawn might take advantage of his kindness after all—but he hated that he couldn't just show up to work. He could feel his waning commitment to the structures and requirements of this peaceful life.

Jazz continued, her voice reasonable and gentle. "You can't be the one to solve his problems. You know it as well as I do. You call the wrong person, visit the wrong place, they'll throw you back in prison before Monique can even say goodbye."

He knew she was right, and yet knowing it changed nothing.

"He's like my own child, Jazz. What choice do I have?"

Darryl hadn't run far. McAdam Park was on Thirtieth between Q and R, a couple miles up from his house and only a mile from Shawn's. It was nowhere for Darryl to hide, if that's where he'd been hiding. Someone was bound to run into him. He and his friends liked to skateboard there—Shawn knew this because he'd bumped into them once when he was with Monique. It was a family hangout, dense with their memories. Warm, idle afternoons. Picnics and baseball games. Shawn saw them now like a reel of home movies, fuzzy and sweet. The sunshine, the desert wind, his arms holding wholesome, bright-skinned children.

But it was a different place at night. The lights were out, leaving it plunged in darkness, all the color hidden away. It was quiet but not silent, and the sounds that emerged were restless and furtive and human. Shawn felt eyes on him as he walked past the baseball diamond. When he looked, he saw two men draped across a bench. One of them bobbed his head at Shawn as he passed. There was a time when Shawn would've stopped, seen if there was anything he could sell them, if they had money to buy. It shamed him to remember and to think of Darryl running the same kind of game.

He saw Darryl right away, sitting hunched on a low swing, silhouetted against the night. He knew his shape, his adolescent posture, ever changing but somehow always Darryl, slouched and self-conscious. He got up when he saw Shawn approach, grabbing at a chain. It rattled against the swing set's frame. A thin, scraping, metallic sound.

It was a cool night, and Shawn felt the chill through his clothes, like the bone-wan desert moonlight was seeping in and coating his skin to leach the heat away. Darryl was wearing jeans and a hoodie, zipped all the way up to his chin. It was his favorite hoodie, green fleece with white lining, and Shawn saw that it was worn from washing. Darryl had a backpack with him, laid down at his feet, but Shawn guessed he hadn't packed anything proper. How pathetic he was, this nephew of his. Just a child run off from home.

Shawn hugged him, and Darryl let him, waiting a full two seconds before slinking back into his swing. The boy needed a shower after two days stewing in his own teenage stink.

"You smell foul," said Shawn. He lowered himself into the other swing. It creaked under his weight.

Darryl laughed weakly.

"Where the hell have you been?"

"Here, there," he said. "Just driving around."

"You been sleeping in your dad's car?"

"Sleeping? I ain't been sleeping, Uncle Shawn."

The boy had to be exaggerating. It had been more than two days, and Shawn knew the dramatic tendencies of teens—he'd had them, too. Then again, his teen years were legitimately dramatic, and so, now, were Darryl's. And whether he'd slept at all or not, his face showed the strains of insomnia, his eyes sunken, the skin of his cheeks plum purple in the dark.

"I drove up to Lompoc yesterday."

"You know your dad ain't at Lompoc, don't you?"

"Yeah, I know. Just wanted to go up there. I never drove to visit him when he was in prison. Not one time."

"You didn't even have your license. Still don't."

"I had my permit." He was wallowing now.

"Why aren't you home? You know what this is doing to your mom?"

"I can't go home."

"What'd you call me for?" He shook his head, hitting on the answer. "You're out of gas. And money. Is that it?"

Darryl kicked the sand at his feet and nodded.

"So what, you think I'm gonna hand you over a few hundred bucks, no questions asked, and then you'll head on over to Mexico? Send a postcard?"

"I just—" His voice caught as he tried to stop himself from crying. "It'd be better for everyone if I was just gone."

"Stop that," said Shawn. "No matter what you did, that's not true."

Darryl looked at him, stunned, like it hadn't occurred to him that his uncle could see through him. There was something so pure in this, it made Shawn want to hold him.

"Did you shoot Jung-Ja Han?" he asked instead.

Darryl averted his eyes, and Shawn took him by the arm and made him look at him. The boy nodded, and his face dissolved in an aching sob.

"Oh, Darryl." Shawn rested his forehead against his nephew's.

He'd known for days, he realized, ever since Ray's confession, but it still struck him like a kick in the chest. How much time had he spent worrying about Darryl, about his attendance, his friends, the million ways things could go wrong? To have it go wrong like this—it broke Shawn's heart.

"Why?" he asked.

"I had to do something."

"About what?"

"About Auntie Ava."

Her name rang out between them. "You didn't even know her."

"That's not the point," said Darryl, raising his voice. "She was my blood."

He spoke with force, but it struck Shawn as puffed up and hollow. A tribal platitude from a teenage gangster. Words to shout out a window in a drive-by. Darryl didn't love Ava. He didn't shoot anyone just for her sake.

"She was my big sister," said Shawn, looking away from his nephew and at the eternal black sky. "When she died, everything I knew fell in on itself. I used to dream about finding that woman, making her look at me. Humiliating her. Killing her. Are you gonna sit there and tell me you wanted that more than I did?"

Darryl fell silent, the arrogant front laid flat with a single blow. Minutes passed while Shawn waited for him to say something. To explain himself and absolve them both.

When he finally spoke, his voice was quiet, his words nearly chewed up by the wind. "But you never knew where to find her," he said. "I did."

Shawn thought of all the dead ends he'd run into over the years. He'd never stopped looking, and he was sure he would've heard if she'd resurfaced, even for a minute. What could Darryl have caught that he'd missed? He swallowed the knot in his throat and asked, "How?"

Darryl rocked himself back and forth, staring at his foot in the sand. "I've known for over a year. It was right after you moved out. You got a letter. From someone named Miyeon Han."

Shawn searched his memory for the letter, the name. Han—he knew that name, but he'd never heard of a Miyeon. "I never—"

"I found it. I never gave it to you."

He pressed his lips together and waited for his nephew to go on.

"She said she was Jung-Ja Han's daughter. She said she was sorry for Auntie Ava's death and that if you ever wanted to talk about it, you could find her. She put down her email and phone number and asked you to get in touch. There was something about Rwanda and reconciliation. She thought it wasn't right that her mom had started a new life where you couldn't even confront her, and she offered to talk to her for you. But she also said what her mom was up to. That she was living in Granada Hills and ran a pharmacy in the Hanin Market in Northridge."

Shawn dug his feet into the sand. Darryl was talking fast now; it was all Shawn could do to make sense of the words without falling out of the swing. He remembered Grace Park, messy and confused and pleading. It seemed unlikely she'd known her mother's secret over a year ago. Yet Darryl had known. He'd held all the pieces in his hands.

"Why didn't you tell me?"

"Because I didn't want you to know," he said. "I remember how you were, when you got out of prison. And I heard how you were before, too. Always mad, or like you just didn't give a fuck. But you were happy with us, I know it. And then you met Auntie Jazz, and you were happy with her, too. I didn't want to ruin it."

Shawn couldn't believe what he was hearing. What if he hadn't met Jazz? Would he have been home to get that letter? He pictured the envelope, seeing the name Han above his, the instant premonition it would have carried. He had wondered and wondered—where she was, what she was doing—and over a year ago, someone had tried to tell him.

"You thought I'd kill her," he said.

"I didn't know what you'd do. I just knew it was dynamite."

Darryl was right—it was dynamite, and it had exploded. Had Darryl pushed Shawn out of the way only to catch the blast himself? If there was a sorrier outcome, Shawn couldn't imagine it now.

"And *you* didn't trust *me* to deal with it? Darryl, you shot her."

"I wasn't planning to do anything," he protested. "Not when I read that letter. I just tore it up and tossed it so you wouldn't see. But I couldn't unread it, and I kept thinking about what it said. Turns out there's only one pharmacy in that market. I knew exactly where she was."

"So why now?"

"I just wanted to make things right. Everything's so upside down, you know?" He wiped his nose and continued, his voice quivering with passion. "I just kept thinking, nah, it can't just be like that. I thought in this family, at least, we could have some justice."

Shawn shook his head. "Give me a break, Darryl. You didn't shoot her for the struggle."

The boy's eyes blazed at him, brightened with tears. He believed his own bullshit. Had probably spent days bulking up his defenses.

"You been messing with Quant Fox's crew."

Darryl didn't answer.

"I saw him yesterday." Shawn made a fist and ran his thumb over the knuckles, which were still raw from the punch. "I know you been hanging out with him."

"He's my friend," said Darryl.

"You want to be a gangster, is that it? That seem cool to you?"

He looked right at him, flashing defiance. "Quant says you were banging when you were Dasha's age."

"That's right. I was fourteen. Are you fourteen?"

He said nothing.

"Yeah, you should know better. And you know what? My sister was murdered. My parents were gone and dead."

"My dad was in prison for ten years," Darryl cut in. "For some stupid failed robbery where no one even got hurt. And all y'all, even you—you just acted like this was okay, like he fucked up so he deserved what he got."

"And Quant Fox showed you the light. He gave you some Malcolm X pep talk and you just ate it out of his hand."

"He talked to me. He told me shit no one else would tell me. About my dad. About Auntie Ava. About you, too."

"So you shot Jung-Ja Han to prove yourself. To get in with the Baring Cross Crips of Palmdale or whatever crew Quant's got going on, is that it? Please tell me this was your first time."

"What do you mean?"

"I mean is there anyone else you've shot I should know about?"

"No, of course not!" The indignation of a boy who hadn't admitted to attempted murder. "It was a mistake. I can't stop thinking about it. I'm not cut out for this shit, Uncle Shawn."

"I wish you'd figured that out before you went and shot someone."

He sniffled loudly and wiped his nose again. "How did you do it?" he asked.

"What?"

"Quant said you used to run around burning shit, getting in fights, shooting at people. How did you shoot people and get on with your life?"

Shawn thought about it. He'd never been one of the psychos, the ones who savored violence and sought it out. But he'd shot at some people over the years and hit at least one boy he knew of, getting him in the leg. He didn't lose much sleep over it, truth be told, though he was glad he hadn't gotten the boy worse.

"It was part of the life, back then," he said. "We went to war, and we shot at rival soldiers. It was simple as that."

"I don't believe you."

"Maybe simple's not the word for it. But these were bangers. They knew the rules, just like I did. They weren't old Korean women in Northridge."

"Weren't bangers that killed Auntie Ava," Darryl spat. "I don't understand you, Uncle Shawn. How can you act like it's worse to shoot her than another banger? Someone like you. Or like me?"

Shawn couldn't answer him, and Darryl pushed through his silence.

"After all this time, you buy into that bullshit. You of all people. That black lives don't matter. That when you shoot at us, it don't count. 'Cause we ain't perfect. 'Cause we deserve it. But Jung-Ja Han don't?"

"It's not about me buying into anything," Shawn snapped. "It don't matter what I believe. What I believe won't keep you out of prison.

Haven't you noticed? I don't run the police. Judges don't listen to me.
If they think black lives don't matter, then black lives *don't* matter.
People can fuss all they want about how things should be, but I'm
talking about your fucking neck, you stupid child." He thought of
Darryl in prison, becoming a man in that hard soil, away from light,
away from family. It made him want to throw up. Then he remem-
bered the gun—if that gun led back to Darryl, the boy was doomed.
He asked, fearing the answer: "Did Quant give you the gun?"

Darryl shook his head, but Shawn had to be sure.

"I'm serious. Does he know? Does anyone?"

"I told you, no. I knew I fucked up as soon as it happened. I didn't
tell anyone."

"Then what's this I heard about Baring Cross taking credit? Were
you talking big before you did it?"

His mouth was open, and his bottom lip twitched. "Where'd you
hear that?"

"The detective, Darryl. Way he told it, everyone's saying it's BC."

"That's 'cause it's Jung-Ja Han. Everyone knows who she is, that
she's an old enemy. I bet as soon as word got out she was shot, someone started spreading it was our house that did it. But I swear to
God, Uncle Shawn. I didn't tell anyone."

Shawn was grateful, at least, for that small relief. "Then where did
you get the gun?"

"I found it," he said, not elaborating.

"What do you mean, you found it? Where?"

Darryl looked down at his feet. "It was in Dad's car. Under his
seat."

Shawn felt his lip curl. He took a deep, heaving breath, his nostrils
flared. Five minutes out of jail, with a parole officer on his back, Ray
had gotten himself a gun. And stashed it, like an idiot, where his
kid could find it.

"Where is it now?"

"I hid it. In the house. But it's gone now."

He hushed up, and Shawn understood. The cops found it when they searched the house. They hadn't held Ray on nothing after all.

"Dad's in jail 'cause of me," said Darryl. "He confessed. Because of me."

Shawn nodded, watching as his nephew dropped his head into his hands. Darryl looked up at him, eyes red over the tips of his fingers.

"Tell me, Uncle Shawn. What do I do now?"

TWENTY-THREE

FRIDAY, SEPTEMBER 6, 2019

Yvonne was fine, and then she wasn't. She went to bed early, citing a headache, waving off Grace's suggestion that she call the doctor. It was nothing, she said, she'd only exhausted herself taking a walk; she'd been overconfident in her recovery. Grace believed her. Yvonne had been doing so well.

Grace woke to her father shouting her name in the stone dark dead of the night. Sightless, she rushed across the house, the black hallway, not yet free of the webby hold of her dreams. Her feet were cold. Everything else felt unreal.

In shaded lamplight, Yvonne burned and shivered; her heartbeat filled the room. Her hair clung to the wet pillowcase. Her fevered skin radiated corrupt warmth. It was the pale parchment yellow of her chattering teeth.

Grace held her mother's hand while Paul called for help. She spoke frantically at Yvonne, squeezed her bony fingers. Weakly, slowly, Yvonne squeezed back. Her eyelids trembled and her lips parted in the shape of Grace's name. No words came out. Only breath. Shallow and ragged and fast.

She was unconscious by the time the ambulance came, and Grace watched as the EMTs strapped her to a stretcher and loaded her in.

Grace couldn't believe this was happening again. The second time in less than two weeks.

They tailed the ambulance in silence, Paul driving while Grace wavered between terror and disbelief, her eyes following the red flash of the siren light.

Yvonne was already being rushed to surgery when they made it into the waiting room. It was ridiculous that they were back here. Grace wanted to shout at someone—this was a mistake, a bad joke. A surgery for a fever! That was dream logic. She longed for the relief of waking up with tears in her eyes and a sob in her throat, every other thing forgotten.

When the sun rose, Yvonne was dead. The gunshot wound in her colon had become infected, and her body had gone into sepsis—that's what the doctor said, carefully, after her condolence, to admit no fault, to offer no true apology. Grace went off on her, and neither Paul nor Miriam tried to hold her back.

She wasn't even sure what she was arguing. The words flowed out of her without thought, and she kept them coming, committing herself to the moment, the problem, the person to hold responsible. When she was finished, she knew they'd have to discuss arrangements, that she'd have to sit down and let someone else take control. When this scene ended, she'd have to face the immovable fact that her mother was dead, that there was no mistake they could fix that would bring her back.

The coroner would come to take her away—her death was a homicide, so she would have to be cut open. Without speaking, they decided to stay with her until it was time. Grace felt sick at heart and utterly stunned. The shooting had not prepared her. She thought they had made it, that they were home safe.

It still seemed like Yvonne might get up, that she might only be sleeping a very deep sleep. The alternative made no sense at all. It was wrong and impossible, world bending, like a black hole: her mother's body, there under a sheet not two feet away; her mother's oppressive, irretrievable absence.

Paul sat close to his wife, his head lowered near hers. His eyes were shut tight, and he was mumbling, his Korean indecipherable, clogged with tears. She'd never seen him this emotional before—it added to her feeling that none of this could be real. She watched as he searched for Yvonne's hand under the sheet, as he found it there, steadily lifeless, and pulled back away.

Miriam rested her head on Grace's shoulder, and Grace felt her sleeve dampen with her sister's tears.

"I know this is kind of fucked up, but I was feeling lighter, these last weeks, than I had in two years," said Miriam. "I wasn't happy she was shot, but in a way, it felt like this huge weight was lifted. Like she was taking her punishment, and we could finally move on. As a family."

Grace stared at the lump of Yvonne's body—the cadaver. These last two weeks had been torture for Grace. For the first time in her life, her mother had shifted on her, become someone she didn't understand, someone she'd been, underneath, all along. It shook her all the way through, made her question everything about who she was, where she came from, the lies that made her life possible, that had made her. She had thought, for a moment, that she'd learned how to live with her new reality, that she had engineered a way to keep going, to pay her account and slide back into the way things were before. She'd been wrong. She wasn't even close to finding her answers—she needed her mother to help her, to explain herself, to give Grace the things she needed, whatever they might have been.

Miriam droned on, her words buzzing against Grace's shoulder. "This was supposed to be the beginning of something. You found out what happened, and we were all going to work through this together. Learn and grow. Maybe become better people."

Yvonne was done giving now. The conversation was over. Her silence was her final word.

"But I'm thankful we had this last reprieve. That she didn't die thinking I hated her."

Miriam might as well have torn her heart out. Grace could hardly move for the bitterness and regret that coursed through her body, filling her nose and mouth so it was difficult to breathe. It was true: after two years of stubborn estrangement, Miriam had come back just in time for a reconciliation, at what turned out to be her mother's deathbed. Yvonne died with the comfort of her firstborn's return. There was no question about it. Miriam was the one bright spot in her final days on earth. It was so unfair, Grace had to stop herself from scratching her sister in the face. She shrugged her shoulder instead, making Miriam remove her head.

Her mother was shot, and what did Grace do? She spurned her, she railed at her, she wished she'd been born to a different family. For twenty-seven years, she'd thought the world of her mother; for two weeks, as Yvonne lay dying, Grace abandoned her in her heart, and they both knew it.

Never had she been so completely alone. She hated her sister. For being blithe Miriam, the one things worked out for, who took the good in stride, like it was her due. Yes, she had lost her mother, too, but she'd lost her on her own terms somehow. Tragically. Beautifully.

A crack had torn open the earth, and Miriam was on the other side of the chasm. The only side with a path back to safety.

Grace started to pray—she'd fallen into the habit since the shooting, of asking for things, for comfort and peace, for her pain to be taken away. But what good had it done? Her mother was dead. Wherever she was now, she was there forever.

She felt hollow and nauseated, her stomach dropping inside her, the sensation before a long fall. It brought her no comfort to imagine Yvonne drifting into the afterlife. She hoped, in earnest, there was nothing there. Heaven required a hell, and heaven was for the repentant.

She opened her eyes, dizzy and despairing. She would never have a mother again.

TWENTY-FOUR

FRIDAY, SEPTEMBER 6, 2019

Shawn never thought he'd be sorry that Jung-Ja Han was dead. But when the news came—a phone call from Nisha, who'd heard from Ray's lawyer—it brought him physical pain, a twist in his stomach so tight it was momentarily incapacitating. The blows kept on coming, and this was the hardest one yet. Just like that, his nephew's crime had turned to homicide. Darryl was a killer, and Ray would now face murder charges. If he was found guilty, he might never see another day outside.

Just yesterday, they had all been so hopeful. Ray's lawyer had told Nisha that Grace Park was ready to testify to Ray's innocence. Nisha had said nothing about Duncan's photo, the girl in her husband's lap; all she wanted, at least for now, was to bring Ray home. Shawn feared what would happen if charges were dropped against Ray, but the way Nisha told it, it sounded like the prosecutors were convinced of Ray's guilt, and it was just a matter of whether they thought the charges would stick. Shawn let himself fantasize about having all his loved ones back home. It wasn't so crazy, was it? It was only what he'd had ten days ago.

Shawn woke up to the news. Nisha called him at five in the morning, and he drove over, still in his sleeping clothes. The whole house was alive, the air of it hot and thrumming. Aunt Sheila and Nisha had been crying, their eyes wet, red, and bulging. He knew if the kids weren't in the house, they'd be in full mourning. They'd lost Ray—that's what it felt like. Like they'd gathered up his ransom, just to have it raised at the last minute to a price they could never pay.

Dasha sat with her mother and grandmother, the three of them a somber command center, mobilizing every resource they had. Nisha and Aunt Sheila made phone calls—the lawyer, Brother Vincent, Jules Searcey—while Dasha typed furiously on her phone. This little girl had an online audience now, a legion of strangers following the fate of her father.

Only Darryl stayed hidden, cloistered in his room.

Shawn hadn't told anyone—not Nisha, not Jazz—and it made him dizzy that he'd even thought about it, how close he'd come to involving more people. He left the women and let himself into Darryl's room and locked the door.

The boy was in bed, lying with his back to Shawn, his body rolled toward the wall. His posture was rigid, and Shawn could tell he was awake and alert, and that he hoped to hang on to the pretense of sleep.

Shawn sat down on his nephew's bed. "You heard, then," he said.

Darryl was silent, but his body contracted, a spasm jerking through him that Shawn felt through the mattress. The covers were bunched up under where Shawn was sitting, and Darryl yanked them as hard as he could, to gather them over his arms.

"You asked me what you should do," Shawn said, his mouth dry. "I didn't know what to tell you, but I do now."

Darryl stayed still, and Shawn knew he was listening. Shawn laid a hand on the boy's trembling shoulder.

"You do *nothing,* you hear me? And just as important, you *say* nothing. You stay away from Quant Fox and your other wannabe banger friends. They got nothing on you unless you give it to them, and if you give it to them, you better know they gonna use it. They'll get busted one day, and they'll squirm and rack their brains for a trade." He paused and took a breath, unsure how far he should push the boy. But this was too important for the soft touch. "You killed someone, Darryl. And not just anyone. Someone who got the media whipped up, which means the police got whipped up, too. None of these fools gonna keep their mouth shut knowing they have that trump card. Not out of love for you."

Darryl sat up suddenly, flinging Shawn's hand away. He flipped away from the wall and faced his uncle. His eyes were bleary, his skin without luster. While he slept, everything had changed, and now he looked like he might never sleep again.

"I know that," he said, his voice a fierce whisper. "But Dad—"

"He knows, and he's made his own decisions. He's taking his chances, and he could beat the charge."

"What if he doesn't?"

"Then he'll go to prison. It's better him than you."

"But he didn't do anything." He pounded his chest, hard. "I did."

There was a rich irony in this that tickled Shawn in a wicked place. No matter the sentence, that judge had said, Jung-Ja Han would suffer. She would carry the weight of Ava's death for the rest of her life—wasn't that punishment enough? Shawn had known guilt, and he had known prison. Darryl would live with his guilt, and that would have to do for everybody else.

"What's done is done," said Shawn, catching Darryl's fist before the boy hurt himself. "Your debt to society—as far as I'm concerned, that's been paid. You owe your family now."

Men's Central was a hateful place. It was one of the ten worst jails in America, and God knew there was tough competition. Shawn had spent sixty days here, more than a decade ago. He still remembered them—dangerous, soul-grinding days, difficult for even a young man. He didn't want to think about Ray in there, a middle-aged man fresh from freedom and family, back to sharing a stinking toilet and a rusted-out bunk bed in an overcrowded cell.

He hadn't scheduled a visit, and it took him an hour and a half to get through the hurdles of the walk-in, just before the six o'clock cutoff. It depressed him, the insult and hassle just to see his cousin, the questions and the searches; he'd hoped he'd never have to submit to them again. Last time he saw Ray, they were at Shawn's home, sharing booze and memories, fearing exactly this: that one of them would lose his freedom, end up back in a place like this, vulnerable and alone.

Now they were at arm's length, a grimy window between them, flanked by other visitors, other inmates, in two rows of hard stools and metal partitions; guards, alert and grim-faced, ready to step forward and keep them in line.

Ray's months of freedom had been good to him—the open air, his mother's cooking. Shawn saw that now that it was stripped back away. Already, his cousin looked like the man who'd stumbled out of Lompoc, thin and ashen, on the verge of old age.

He picked up the phone. "About time," he said.

Shawn blinked. With all that had happened, with the craziness of the shooting, Ray's arrest, Darryl's disappearance; with a toddler at home and a full-time job; it hadn't occurred to him that he was taking too long to visit. But a week and a half felt a lot longer in here, misery thickened by monotony. He wasn't going to argue with Ray. "How're they treating you?"

Ray shrugged. "You know how it is. They don't have to treat me any way for it to be hell. And they treating me all kinds of ways."

Shawn nodded.

"How's everything at home?"

"How do you think? It's a mess," said Shawn. "Everyone misses you."

"At least it's nothing new. Y'all should be used to having me gone by now."

He studied Ray, his upbeat bravado, knowing it for what it was. "You seem calm for a man who just became a murderer."

Ray rolled his eyes and sighed, screwing his mouth up into a wry smile. "Don't tell me. Nisha sent you," he said. "Are you here to tell me I didn't do it?"

Shawn spoke quietly into the receiver. "I know you didn't do it."

Ray laughed. A dry, husky, exhausted laugh. "You don't know shit. I did it. I shot that bitch and now she's dead. Ding. Dong."

"When you confessed, you didn't know it was murder."

He shrugged. "I'm not sorry about it. What, you gonna tell me to renege? Nisha been trying that."

"I know it wasn't you, Ray. I talked to him."

"Who?"

Shawn shook his head and pointed at his phone. He didn't know if anyone would bother recording this conversation, but he wasn't about to take any chances. He held Ray's stare until the understanding came.

Ray's whole body seemed to deflate. Slumping, relieved. He lowered his phone to his chest and leaned in closer, resting his head on the dirty glass. He looked like a penitent, worn out from confession. When he came back up, he was smiling, a light dancing in his eyes.

"It was me," he said again. But this time, his face told the truth. Shawn sat back. Now they were talking.

"I was already fucked when they found the gun," said Ray. "Even if they don't get me for the shooting, I go back to prison just for having it. And if they match the gun to the shooting—well, you know."

The gun would match, and someone would have to own it. Ray knew that as well as Shawn did.

"What possessed you to get a gun?" Shawn couldn't quite keep the accusation out of his tone. If Darryl hadn't found a gun just lying around, he might never have gone through with this reckless, ruinous plan.

"Every motherfucker has a gun in this country. What're they

afraid of? Anyone got a grudge against me got a gun. I gotta protect myself and my family."

Shawn thought of Darryl, his weak gangster posturing. "No one was trying to get at you. And I love you, Ray, but you know getting that gun didn't protect your family."

Ray's nostrils flared, and Shawn knew he'd touched the raw guilt just under the surface of his cousin's new story about himself. There was no sense digging in further. He switched the subject. "You know there's a whole bunch of people saying you're innocent? You'd love it, Ray. You're all over the internet. Dasha's been showing me. You got fans."

Ray brightened. "Yeah? What do they say about me?"

"A lot of them say you couldn't have done it. You know Reddit?"

Ray shook his head.

"It's like a big message board. There's pages and pages on there about you and about Jung-Ja Han. It's nuts. I don't know where these people find the time. Anyway, lot of folks think you're innocent, and they have all kinds of theories about why you confessed."

"Like what?"

"Most of them think you were forced. A few people think you're covering for someone. My name's come up a couple of times." He smiled at Ray. Darryl was safe, at least from the internet sleuths. A sixteen-year-old with a clean record wouldn't be easy to find.

"They think you killed her?"

"I don't think they really care who killed her. They just think it's wrong you're going down for it. Far as they're concerned, it could've been anyone pulling the trigger. Me. The Crips. The angel of death. Even if you did shoot her, a lot of these people think you were justified. 'No jury would convict.'"

Ray nodded solemnly. "That's what my lawyer's hoping, too, but we'll see."

"Any word on Jung-Ja Han's daughter?"

"I'm the one in jail. I should be asking you."

No one could reach Grace Park. She'd avoided calls from the pros-
ecutor, from Ray's lawyer. Aunt Sheila sent her an email, a long, heart-
felt letter that offered condolences for the death of the woman who'd
murdered her child. Grace ignored this, too. What a surprise—she
couldn't even deliver the thin amends she had promised.

She was in mourning, Shawn knew, and it had only been hours.
Jung-Ja Han was her mother, even if she was something different to
everyone else. Still, Shawn didn't owe it to anyone to be generous on
her account. Jung-Ja Han dying, now, twenty-eight years after she
killed Ava—it felt like a sick joke, a final fuck you.

"Anyway, I'm not counting on her or any kind of miracle." Ray bit
down on his lip and sighed. "I was out for what, two months? Wish
I'd have known. I would've done things different. Spent more time
with the kids."

Shawn didn't say anything.

"Or maybe not. It was hard for me, Shawn. I missed so much being away so long. I love those kids, but they barely know me. And
seeing them after all that time, every day, and every day them not
knowing me—it was too much for me to handle."

"You needed time. Everyone understood that."

"I didn't have time. I made damn sure of that, too."

Shawn kept quiet. In more ways than one, all this was Ray's fault.
If he'd been smarter when he got out, instead of running wild and
leaving a gun out for his kid to find. If he'd just been there when
Darryl was growing up, a boring dad his kids could get sick of. Then
maybe Darryl wouldn't have tried so hard to plug in and share the
family traumas, the family mistakes. But those mistakes were old
and irreversible, and Shawn had made his share of them.

"You were there, though." Ray's voice quivered between sarcasm
and gratitude. "Don't think I don't know that."

Shawn rested the side of his fist on the window. He wanted to hug his cousin, to let him know how much he loved those kids and that he'd be there for them, but that he'd never replace Ray or dishonor his sacrifice. "And now you're here," he said instead, and bumped his fist against the glass.

Ray bumped his own fist on his side, matching it up with Shawn's. He laughed, and tears spilled out of his eyes.

Yesterday, they buried her mother. In an unfamiliar chapel on the side of a Burbank graveyard, Grace sat in the first pew, mouthing hymns, letting the sermon run her by. Pastor Kwon officiated the funeral, and Miriam spoke for the family—a brief, formal eulogy delivered in her tentative Korean. Grace had declined to give her own speech. She couldn't begin to think what she was supposed to say.

The chapel was crowded, nearly every pew full of mourners. She stood beside her father and sister at the open casket, her mother's eerie, waxy, refurbished body visible from the corner of her eye, and she greeted each of them as they filed by. Aunts and uncles and cousins flown in from Las Vegas and Chicago. People from church, from the market; countless others Grace had never seen before. They came at her with kind words and gazes, grasping at her with hugs and handshakes.

They watched her, and they would remember, Grace thought, that she didn't cry at her own mother's funeral. Maybe she was unnatural, but she seemed to be fresh out of tears. It felt like she'd been hollowed, and that drop by drop, cup by cup, she was filling back up with bile.

What was this sham? Practical strangers, paying their two-penny respects, murmuring about God and peace. Her mother had been murdered. Didn't they know that? This was no time for shallow sympathies and useless platitudes. That boy—that killer. He would have to answer.

Grace felt a hand on her wrist and snapped her head back to glare at her sister. Miriam was watching her, open worry on her face. "Hey," she said. "Don't wander off, okay?"

They were in a sea of people, clumping on an enormous lawn in front of Los Angeles City Hall, a hot, howling wind making them sticky and restless. Grace remembered the last time she was downtown, at the memorial in front of the federal courthouse, which glinted across the street, behind LAPD Headquarters. It was only a few months ago, but it felt like a different lifetime, a different incarnation of Grace.

"Look at this turnout," said Miriam.

There were clusters of people in matching T-shirts, like old Koreans on bus tours. Signs floated across the crowd, homemade, crude, exuberant. JUSTICE 4 ALFONSO. FREE RAY HOLLOWAY. HANDS UP DON'T SHOOT. AMERIKKKA ALWAYS WAS AMERIKKKA TO ME. Children held their own signs as they rode on fathers' shoulders, clung to mothers' thighs. It felt almost festive. Drumbeats and chanting, car horns honking as drivers rolled by. Grace caught the unmistakable smell of bacon-wrapped hot dogs, grease and grilled onion and blistering meat.

"I guess people really hated Mom," she said.

"There's more to it than that," said Miriam, without much conviction. "People think Ray Holloway is innocent, and to see him indicted right after Trevor Warren got off—it just looks like justice gone haywire."

"Is that what you think?"

"I understand why people are angry. Trevor Warren is a murderer." Miriam's face twisted, and Grace could tell there was more that she feared to say.

"But?"

"Someone killed Umma." Her eyes misted in an instant. She glanced around and lowered her voice, leaning closer to Grace. "And I don't know why people are so eager to get Ray Holloway off. Why are they so sure he's innocent? He's a convicted felon. He had a motive and a gun that matched. This isn't the fucking Central Park Five."

Grace must have been staring at her, because Miriam turned red and looked away. "You're the one who wanted to come here," Miriam mumbled.

The indictment had been announced just as Yvonne went into the ground. Grace saw the news on her phone in the bathroom of the restaurant in Glendale, where she'd escaped the Korean barbecue lunch with her mother's mourners. It stunned her, the text from MacManus popping up on her lock screen like all the others she'd ignored. She'd meant to contact him, but the days had fallen away from her, her will to act sluggish, unmotivated by any real feeling.

The truth was she didn't give a shit that Ray Holloway was in prison, not when her mother was dead and he was protecting her murderer. She wasn't here to see him free. She was here for the boy. He had to be here.

"He is innocent." She took a slow breath and looked at Miriam. It was time to tell her. "He's covering for someone. I think it's his son."

She showed her sister the video, uploaded onto her phone. Miriam watched it twice, her mouth slack, before gripping her arm. "Are you sure?"

"I saw him. At Sheila Holloway's house. He was watching me. And you can see him here, how seriously he's watching her."

Miriam played it again, pausing on the boy's face. Five seconds, he stood there, his eyes intent on Yvonne. Five seconds, it took him to recognize her; Grace had watched this clip a hundred times, looking for that moment. Wondering if she could see him decide to kill her mother.

"He knew where to find her," Grace said. "You can see it. He walked right up to the window, knowing she would be there."

Miriam's eyes widened as she looked up from the phone.

"Unni. Did you tell them? Did you let them know where to find Mom?" Grace spoke as calmly and earnestly as she could. "Please, Unni, don't lie to me. I'll know."

Miriam swallowed, and when she finally answered, her voice came out cracked. "I sent a letter," she said. "Not to Ray Holloway or his son. To Shawn Matthews. But that's all. It was over a year ago. And he never got in touch."

"Did you mention the pharmacy?"

"I can't remember." Her face was pale, and Grace understood that Miriam had already been thinking about the letter, that she'd turned it over and over in her head since somebody found Yvonne. "I know I didn't give up her new name. But I might have said what she was doing. Where she was working." She shook out her hands, like that might help her expel some of her guilt. "God, was it my fault?"

It hadn't been enough for Miriam to cut Yvonne out of her life. She had to offer her up, sacrifice her safety for Miriam's peace of mind. If this was what she'd done—and Grace was almost certain that it was—it was unforgivable.

Yet Grace couldn't afford to give up her sister. She couldn't lose her, and she didn't want to. She would have to find a way to live with what she couldn't forgive. She looked at Miriam, the fear and anguish on her face as she waited for Grace to answer. Grace let her wait, then gave her what she wanted. "You're not the one who killed her," she said.

The crowd gathered and swelled. Shawn felt the energy boiling off them, riding the Santa Anas as the sun started to settle. The devil winds had come in, and he could see them rippling through clothing, making eyes narrow and hair stand on end. It had been years since the last time Aunt Sheila coaxed him into a public appearance, and he had to admit—there was something breathtaking about it, seeing the people turn out, riled up on behalf of his loved ones.

When the indictment came down, Aunt Sheila called in the cavalry. The rally was already on the books, but she'd been to too many small, quiet protests, her and Brother Vincent and a handful of activists, shaking their fists at every new expression of the same old crushing themes. Not this time, not with her baby facing trial. She spent all day on the phone, goading friends and allies, giving statements to any media outlet that would listen. Dasha had done her part, too, getting the word out to Ray's supporters on Twitter. There was no question the whole family had to be here. Shawn didn't fight it, and neither did Darryl.

Aunt Sheila stood in front with Brother Vincent, who spoke boomingly into a standing microphone, the crowd muttering or cheering every time he took a pause.

"Another day, another message," he preached. "I've known Ray Holloway since he was a child. Why? Because in 1991, his cousin Ava Matthews was taken from us, by Jung-Ja Han. She was guilty—her guilt was on video—and if there were justice, she would still be in prison today. But justice was not served, and regretfully, she was struck down, a free woman. I wish her peace with her God."

Shawn wanted to look at Darryl, standing next to him, flanked on the other side by his mother and sister. But he knew every phone was a camera here, that any glance would be recorded, available for dissection. He found Jazz instead, standing at the front of the crowd with Duncan and Tramell. Monique was smiling wide, holding her hand. Such a good child, sweet and oblivious.

"And let me say, loud and clear," Brother Vincent went on, "that I do not condone revenge or violence. Where blood is spilled, I call for justice. But to arrest and try a man in spite of a proven alibi—a man whose relation to a murdered girl made him a suspect—where is the justice in this?"

The crowd roared. They raised their fists and waved their signs, shouting "Free the man!" "No justice, no peace!"

They simmered down again, to let Brother Vincent speak. Into the pause flew a volley of incoherent jeers, screamed from across the street. Brother Vincent ignored them and took up the mic, but Shawn followed the voices. They belonged to a small gathering on the sidewalk in front of LAPD Headquarters, on the other side of First Street. There were about thirty people clustered in front of the building. A few women stood among them, one with her torso wrapped in an American flag bandanna top, posing for a photo. But most were men, their stances defiant, coiled for conflict. Three middle-aged cop types held a banner, white text on billowing blue cloth, declaring BLUE LIVES MATTER. A younger set wore red hats with black polo shirts, like overgrown prep school kids. They hoisted backpacks and American flags and screamed at the crowd.

Their taunts were lost to the noise of the larger congregation, but the people on Shawn's side had taken notice. He could see their concentration breaking, the anger rising as their heads turned to take stock of the counterprotest.

He watched as first two men, then a dozen, made their way across the street. He was too far to see their faces, but he recognized the resolve in their footsteps, their hard, ready posture. They marched past the police cars lining First, right up to the counterprotesters, who puffed up as they approached, like they'd been waiting for them. They were arguing—Shawn couldn't hear a thing, but he knew exactly what was happening. So when the first punch was thrown—one of the preppy men hitting a protester—Shawn understood that a counterpunch would follow. Within seconds, they were on the ground, and more men were entering the fray. Whether they meant to join or break up the fight didn't matter—the violence snared them; they were part of it now.

A siren rang out; police officers in riot gear moved to contain the fight, to find this spark of anarchy and snuff it out. Protesters shouted and pushed back against the cops. Brother Vincent was still speaking, but the crowd drifted off the lawn, some of them filling the sidewalk, then crossing the street. Shawn wasn't even sure if they knew what they were doing. They seemed to sway and act as one body, extending an arm to meet a threat, running on instinct.

There he was, standing next to Shawn Matthews, his head turned, eyes fixed on something to his left. It had to be hard for him, Grace thought, to listen to all this talk about Ray Holloway, knowing he could put an end to his father's troubles with a handful of words.

"That's him," she said to Miriam. "Do you see?"

Miriam squinted, trying to make sense of his face. They were still a ways away, the crowd thickening as they moved closer to the front of the lawn.

"I can't tell," she said.

Grace scanned the row of people in front of her, looking for an opening in the wall of bodies. "Let's go around," she said. "You'll see when we get closer."

"What are you planning to do, Grace? You can't just rush him. Someone will recognize you. You'll be trending on Twitter within five minutes."

Grace tugged on the bill of her baseball cap, grateful for all the noise. No one was paying them any attention.

The crowd seemed to be shifting, shuffling to the right. Grace took Miriam by the hand, and they followed the flow. It took them closer to the front, the knots of people loosening, opening a crooked path for them to slip through. Something was happening—there were sirens and shouts coming from across the street.

Then she heard her mother's old name, and her eyes snapped back to the stage.

The pastor was done speaking, and Sheila Holloway had swapped in. She looked small and weary, her head drooping toward the mic. Grace had to strain her ears to make sense of the old woman's words.

"I have forgiven Jung-Ja Han," said Ava Matthews's aunt, raising her eyes now to meet the stirring crowd. "I don't excuse what she did, and I can't ever forget, but I forgive her. I hope she is with God, where my Ava went to rest almost thirty years ago. My heart breaks for her family. Because I know what it is to lose someone you love."

Grace felt heat come over her body like a sudden rash.

"But if she can hear me—if God can hear me—if all you people can hear me—I am begging you, don't let them take my baby away. I know my Ray, and I know he did not do this thing. To put him away for it, when Jung-Ja Han was never put away—how many times must an old woman have her heart torn out? How many, before the angels intervene?"

The boy was listening, and Grace could see the guilt and sorrow scrawled across his face. He looked ready to sob or throw up. If Grace had any doubt left, it vanished now.

Miriam put a hand on her shoulder, turning her. "Gracious," she said. "You're shaking."

She noticed the tremble in her shoulders, her arms, her whole body quaking like a thing possessed. She touched her face and felt the wetness on her cheeks. It was the first time she'd cried since her mother died, and she hadn't even felt the release.

Aunt Sheila wept, her grief poured open for this reckless company, for her long-dead niece, her wayward son. She was, Shawn figured, the best person he knew, the most virtuous and giving, a selfless soul who'd anchored him in ruthless seas and saved him a dozen times over. She had suffered enough to make anyone mean, but she took the bitter roots of her heartache and made a healing salve for people she would never know.

And what had it brought her? More grief. More pain.

There was a full-on brawl on the other side of the street. Shawn thought the cops would end it, but if anything, it looked like their presence added fuel to the fire. They were outnumbered, and they must've unleashed pepper spray, or worse. Shawn heard screaming and then a rising chant of "Fuck the police!"

He felt the anger spark in his own chest, the anger that had lodged in him when he was thirteen, a permanent, unruly companion that filled the hole in his life torn out by his sister's killer. Over the years he'd fed and loved it, then tamed and silenced it. He gave up the easy outlets of his youth, those days of open hostility, on the outside of civil society. He'd done it because he was tired, and because he'd been taught, despite it all, to expect rewards for hard work and good, clean living. And it was true, too, that he'd reaped them, at least for a little while. A steady job, a stable home, a loving, beloved family, safe from trouble. Well, he didn't have that anymore, and the anger was still there, had been there all along, Shawn never once able or even wanting to let it go. Because why should he let it go? It was his, the proof of all he'd lost; that he hadn't forgotten, that even when he played along, he saw the world clearly.

There was a burst of applause, and Aunt Sheila stepped back, Nisha receiving her with a hug. It was finally time to get out of this spotlight. He had a powerful yearning to hold Monique, his unknowing little girl.

And then he saw her, that yellow-white moon-shaped face, half hidden under a Dodgers cap. While the crowd drifted to her right, she pressed forward. Her eyes were locked on Darryl.

He turned to his nephew and saw that he'd already seen her. "Stay with your mom," said Shawn. "I'll deal with her."

The way he stepped in front of her, so that his body blocked her line of sight, Grace knew that Shawn knew what the boy had done. Their eyes met and she let him come, neither of them looking away.

"I'm sorry about your mom," he said, when she was close enough to hear. He could see she was crying, and he felt the sting of her grief despite himself. There was another woman behind her—it looked like she was trying to calm her down, hold her back. This had to be the other daughter, the one who'd made a scene in the courtroom, a toddler mewling for her mother. Who over a quarter century later had sent him that letter.

"I'm sorry about your sister," Miriam murmured, casting her eyes down.

"Mr. Matthews," said Grace, "I need to talk to your nephew."

He stayed rooted, resisting the urge to turn around and look at Darryl. "His father's in jail, you realize," he said. "I don't think this is a good time."

She stood close to him and spoke so no one else would hear. "He killed our mother," she said, trying to keep her voice from breaking. "I have proof. If you don't let me talk to him, I promise you I'll use it."

He stood still, hiding the chill that went bolting through him. "What're you talking about?"

"Video," she said.

"You're lying," he said, though he knew she wasn't. It clicked now, why she'd been so eager to speak up for Ray. She had good reason to believe in his innocence.

"She's not lying," said Miriam. "I've seen it, too."

The air turned heavy with the smell of smoke—across the street, a charcoal plume rose up and spread on the draping wind. Someone had started a fire.

"What is it you want?" Shawn asked, leveling his gaze at Grace. "You came to me just two weeks ago, offering to help, and now you're here threatening us."

"I'm not threatening you, I just—"

"You came here instead of taking whatever you have to the police. There must be something you want from us. Tell me what it is." He leaned closer to her, his voice quivering, soft and desperate. "Do you want me to beg? Is that it? Do you want me to get on my knees and ask for your mercy?"

He lowered himself onto one knee and stared at the ground. He didn't want her seeing the fury in his eyes.

She remembered the way he'd denied her before, withholding his forgiveness, turning her away. Was that what she'd wanted? To make him cough it up, now that she had the power? Now that she'd finally been wronged? "No," she said. "Please. Get up. This isn't—"

"Grace." Miriam touched her arm, and Grace looked where she was looking. Ray Holloway's son was coming up behind Shawn.

Grace stared, her mouth falling open. This was him—the one who'd found Yvonne, who'd pulled the trigger and taken her life while Grace watched, unable to stop him. She smelled fire, and it seemed like her mind had fried. When she'd found the video, her mother had been alive, and she'd thought of her assailant as a misguided child, acting out in response to his family's trauma. She'd learned to pity him, and while Yvonne recovered, Grace forgave him—it was easy to be generous, when she thought her mother was paying for death with pain. But he wasn't an episode in Yvonne's life; he was the end of her story. He was a murderer now, same as her, the mark of Cain on them both. Grace had wanted to face him, to see him and tell him what he was. But now here he was in the flesh, and she couldn't find the words.

He bent down and touched the kneeling man's back. "Uncle Shawn," he said.

Somewhere, a car alarm had gone off, red and screeching. It mingled with the terrible sound of Darryl's voice. Shawn whipped his head up and glared at his nephew. "Get back to your mom."

"Why are you doing this, Uncle Shawn?" His face was bright with shame.

Shawn stood. He wanted to cover Darryl, to hide him and make these women forget he was here. "I said, get back."

"I'm going. I came to get you." He glanced nervously at Grace. "They're starting fires now. Grandma says we need to get out of here."

The goddamned fool, he had to come see the daughters. Shawn

could almost smell it on him, the guilt in his sweat. Shawn wanted to grab his nephew and run. All around them, people were on the move, animated by panic and excitement. Rushing forward or outward, making their way across the street. Some darted back, families holding their children close as they climbed up Grand Park, headed for the trains, for a tidy escape. But Shawn knew they weren't done here. The blood and knowledge kept them all pinned in place. They might never be done.

"What's your name?" asked Miriam, directly addressing the boy.

Shawn started to stop him, but Darryl didn't give him time.

"Darryl," he said.

"Darryl, do you know who we are?"

He swallowed, his mouth dry and loud. "You're Jung-Ja Han"— voice cracking—"Yvonne Park's daughters, Miriam and Grace." He nodded at each of them as he said their names.

Miriam nodded. "One thing that's haunted me since I found out about my mom—she wrote a letter to the judge, and she got your aunt's name wrong. 'Anna Matthews,' she called her. And she said she felt sorry for her mother."

Grace's face felt like it was burning, whipped by the scorching wind. This was the first she'd heard of this letter, and she already wanted to forget it.

"This was ten months after the murder, and she hadn't bothered to learn Ava's name. Or that your mother had died." She glanced sorrowfully at Shawn. "I love my mom, but I know she wasn't a good person. I don't think she ever accepted responsibility for what she'd done." She turned back to Darryl, her eyes glistening, and Shawn saw the boy hanging on to her words like they might hold his key to salvation. "You're not like her, are you? You know exactly what you've done."

He shuddered, and Shawn grabbed his shoulder. If he could have picked him up and thrown him to safety, he would've done it without a second thought. Darryl jerked his shoulder away and stepped closer to the women.

"Don't say anything, Darryl," said Shawn. He looked around. They were surrounded by people, most of them too distracted to pay attention to the conflict unfolding as they blitzed by, driven by the noise and commotion, the sizzling air. But there were cameras, and Darryl looked ready to make a scene. "Can't we talk another time?" he asked the sisters. "When there aren't a thousand people who might be listening?"

Grace cleared her throat and found her voice again. "How old are you?" she asked Darryl.

"Sixteen," he answered.

"So you never knew your aunt, did you?"

Darryl said nothing. His Adam's apple wobbled in his throat.

"She's just an idea to you. Our mom—" She bit down on her lip to steady herself enough to speak again. "I know my mom did horrible things. But she was my *mom*. You have a mom. You know what that means. That's what you took away from me."

"I know," he whispered. His lips kept moving, but the words didn't follow, his face crumpling around the things he couldn't say. "I'm sorry."

He stood there, bent forward, his back heaving like he might be breaking out of his body.

Grace hated him. This fragile, pathetic, sobbing boy who'd had strength enough to shoot to kill. Sixteen years old. The age his aunt had been when she died. When a weak, frightened, angry woman, a woman who'd never aimed a gun before, had landed the shot of her lifetime.

Yvonne outlived Ava Matthews by twenty-eight years. A whole generation, tainted with fear and regret. There had been beautiful things, too, love and family, Grace's whole life in the shelter of her unknowing. Yvonne had never atoned, and she had never paid her debt to society. Her escape had meant a stable home for her daughters, with two parents, without the burden of her guilt to warp their childhood. Yvonne did everything right, when it came to them. Grace couldn't have imagined a better mother.

And she had died, in the end, needing Grace's understanding. A resolution. A forgiveness that Grace could never give her because it wasn't hers to give.

She reached both arms out toward the weeping boy. She found his hands and took them in her own. They were warm and wet, and she felt the life pulsing through the meat of his palms. She wrapped her fingers around his and waited for something to happen, for some indication of how she was meant to go on.

Shawn moved toward her, afraid she was planning to hurt Darryl. Her eyes shimmered with a hard, wild light. But then her face softened, and she closed her eyes and bowed her head. They stood there, locked together, in the shape of a prayer.

A man's voice cracked through the air. "The fuck, isn't that that girl?" Grace froze. She knew without looking that he was talking about her.

Another voice came after. "And that's Ray Holloway's family. I saw them standing up there, when his mom was speaking."

There were people stopping now, stilled by the recognition, the promise of close-up drama. Within seconds, it seemed, they became a small crowd.

Miriam maneuvered herself in front of Grace, blocking her body from all the hungry, staring eyes, the cameras lifted with them. "This isn't a show," she said, waving them away.

"Pretty bold of her to come," someone said, projecting loudly for Grace to hear. "Racist trash."

More voices chimed in, jeering and full of disgust.

Grace felt light-headed, overwhelmed. Everything had piled up on her, and here was a host of strangers, flinging insults, craning their necks to see past Miriam. She blinked, her eyes dry and stinging, and saw a palm tree on fire against a darkening sky. She blinked, and it was still there, a waking vision.

Shawn stared at the tree, a pillar of bright flame like a beam sent down from a rip in the evening sky. It was in front of the LAPD building—in the melee, someone had set it on fire, and the fire was climbing fast, up the long, thin trunk. And here, across the street, the fire was catching. He looked at the circle building around them, agitated and vibrant, stoked by the electric atmosphere, by their own passion, feeding off and reinforcing the passion of their neighbors. Their faces blended together in the quickening dark, but they were young and old, black and white and brown and yellow, a raw hunk of the city, brought together by this one annoying, frustrating woman. They were angry, and she made it easy for them—the racist daughter of a racist killer, a focal point for their fervor.

He remembered those six days of violence, fire and havoc wherever he looked, stumbling bodies and stunned, bleeding faces. He watched his city go up in flames, and under the sadness and rage, the exhilaration of rampage, he recognized the sparkle of hope. Rebirth—that was the promise of destruction. The olive branch, the rainbow, the good men spared to rebuild the earth.

But where was the new city? And who were the good men?

Los Angeles, this was supposed to be it. The end of the frontier, land of sunshine, promised land. Last stop for the immigrant, the refugee, the fugitive, the pioneer. It was Shawn's home, where his mother and sister had lived and died. But he had left, and so had most of the people he knew. Chased out, priced out, native children living in exile. And he saw the fear and rancor here, in the ones who'd stayed. This city of good feeling, of tolerance and progress and loving thy neighbor, was also a city that shunned and starved and killed its own. No wonder, was it, that it huffed and heaved, ready to blow. Because the city was human, and humans could only take so much.

A woman pushed forward from the crowd and spat, the saliva

separating somewhere between the two sisters. She was a white woman, young and zealous, recording the action on her phone. "You're everything that's wrong with this country," she shouted.

Miriam laughed, her expression openly contemptuous. "Go fuck yourself, you dumb white twat."

The woman stepped toward Miriam, and the crowd closed in behind her. Miriam tensed up, her fists balling, as if she could repel the villagers who wanted a piece of her sister. Grace stood behind her with a dreamlike look on her face, and she was still holding one of Darryl's hands. The boy cowered beside her, but he had nowhere to hide. Shawn had to do something.

He walked in front of the sisters and stared down the crowd.

"Back off." The power in his voice surprised him.

They fell silent, and he could read their confusion as they tried to make sense of him, a black man, cousin of Ray Holloway, brother of Ava Matthews, coming to defend the daughters of Jung-Ja Han. But what good would it do, for this mob to unleash their outrage on them? It would bring trouble to Darryl, and it would accomplish nothing else. These useless people. City Hall was right there, the police and the courts. They were standing in the heart of the system, hefting their stones for two girls who were grieving their mother.

"This here is a sideshow," he shouted, calling over the noise. "A way for you to feel good while you keep on doing nothing. If you want to do something, leave us be and do *something*."

He flung his arm out toward the erupting riot, the streets and the sinful city. The bedlam had spread, fast and contagious. Sirens and car alarms rang, and the air smoldered, hot and sooty and pungent, crackling with wrathful energy. Shawn stood, facing the mob, until he felt their focus drifting off the women, off his nephew. He wasn't sure if they'd heard him or if their attention had just shifted, drawn by the babel around them. Everywhere, now, people clapped and stomped, chanted and shouted; they ran and they raged and they fought. One by one, and then all at once, the posse dispersed, disappearing into the greater crowd. He didn't care where they went, as long as it was far away from Darryl.

Grace watched in awe as they stalked away, these people who had clamored for her blood. It felt like a miracle, the impossible parting of a hostile sea. Shawn stood where he was, his back to Grace, his silhouette dark against the glowing chaos; he seemed like a prophet of old, tall and noble as the fire and brimstone came down.

Then, he folded forward, his shoulders shaking. He turned, and she saw that he was coughing.

He staggered toward her, breathing into his shirt, and she felt a tickle in her own throat. Her mouth opened, and she caught a deep, singeing swallow of the acrid air.

He peered over his collar and found Darryl—the boy was safe, for now. Grace was still holding his hand, but she let it go as Shawn came closer. She laced her fingers in front of her face and started hacking into them. Her eyes met Shawn's, and then Miriam laughed.

It was a loud, barking laugh, vicious and mirthful. They looked at her, both of them wondering if she'd lost her mind.

"Come on," said Miriam. "Are you seeing this? The fucking flag is on fire."

They saw it then, the California flag—it must have caught a spark from one of the palm trees, three of them now, blazing in front of the police headquarters—the American flag thrashing just a few yards away. On the ground below, men brawled on a lawn that glittered with glass. A car had crashed into a streetlight, and a boy danced on its hood. He was short and slim, a teenager, or maybe a few years older. He stood in the light and rolled his hips to a song they couldn't hear.

Soon, they understood, they would have to figure out what came next—what to say, what to do, how to live with what they knew. Until then, they shared this torched landscape. The fever, the fire. The dancing boy spinning and spinning, now leaping through the air.

AUTHOR'S NOTE

On March 16, 1991, fifteen-year-old Latasha Harlins walked into Empire Liquor Market and Deli to buy a bottle of orange juice. When she went to pay for the juice, the store owner, a woman named Soon Ja Du, accused her of stealing and reached across the counter to grab the girl and her backpack. Latasha fought back, hitting Du four times before turning around to leave. Du retrieved a gun and shot Latasha in the back of the head. The girl died with two dollars in her left hand. The whole thing was caught on video, and Du was convicted of voluntary manslaughter. She received no jail time.

Your House Will Pay is a work of fiction, but as should be apparent to anyone familiar with these facts, it is based on the murder of Latasha Harlins. For the purposes of my novel, I fictionalized this history, populating it with my own characters while staying as faithful as possible to the events as they occurred. Only one of these characters is modeled on a real-life counterpart: Sheila Holloway was inspired by Denise Harlins, Latasha's aunt, who passed away this past December. Denise became an activist after Latasha's death, seeking justice for her niece and for other victims of violence. She worked tirelessly to keep Latasha's memory alive.

If you would like to learn more about Latasha and this pivotal moment in L.A. history, read *The Contested Murder of Latasha Harlins: Justice, Gender, and the Origins of the LA Riots* by Brenda Stevenson.

ACKNOWLEDGMENTS

A huge thank-you to my agent, Ethan Bassoff, who has always believed in me and who read more bad drafts of the first third of this
novel than even the worst wretch deserves. Another huge thank-you
to my editor Zachary Wagman and the rest of the Ecco team: Cait-
lin Mulrooney-Lyski, Meghan Deans, Miriam Parker, Dominique
Lear, and Daniel Halpern. To Maria Massie, who handles my foreign
rights, and to my UK editor Angus Cargill and the folks at Faber &
Faber, thank you for taking this American story abroad.

I relied on many people in researching this book, and I owe them
all my thanks. I am extremely grateful to Peter Woods, who vol-
unteered his help when all I had were a few pages and an idea back
in November 2014. I've fully abused that offer in the intervening
years—talking to him about the L.A. of the early nineties helped
give shape to my story and characters, and when I had a manuscript
to show, he was one of my first readers. Mike Sonksen, Gary Phil-
lips, and Nina Revoyr all gave me guidance in this book's beginning
stages. Nina's *Southland* is the novel that made this novel feel possible.

My friend and neighbor Caroline Yao answered endless texts about
gunshot wounds and the inner workings of hospitals. My friend John
Lee, who runs his family pharmacy, helped me figure out Grace's job
and the Park family business. Grace was an optometrist for several
drafts, and my friend Janice Kim provided the necessary background
for that scrapped career. Yakeen Qawasmeh and Arturo Meza helped

me understand life in Palmdale. John Lee (a different John Lee), who covered both the Latasha Harlins murder and the L.A. Uprising as a reporter for the *L.A. Times,* gave me a wealth of context. Michael Freedman and Bruce Riordan answered my questions about legal matters, and Bruce was kind enough to read my book for procedural inaccuracies and implausibilities.

Stefanie Parker, Jorge Camacho, Alma Magaña, and Jamin An took time out of their busy lives to read their novelist friend's manuscript. Stef and Jorge provided detailed notes and thoughtful questions. (Thanks, too, to Royal Reff and the rest of Stef's group chat.) Nwamaka Ejebe and Ava Baker also gave valuable advice.

Along with my agent, Ethan (poor man), my friends Elizabeth Little and Sarah LaBrie combed through this book in the last stretch, lending fresh eyes to sentences I'd read way too many times to see clearly. Charles Finch also provided some input at that stage.

I am deeply grateful to Sarah Weinman, who has championed my work since the beginning of my career. Also to Ivy Pochoda, Amelia Gray, Ben Loory, Jade Chang, Naomi Hirahara, Kim Fay, J. Ryan Stradal, Yumi Sakugawa, and MariNaomi—it would've been miserable slogging through this book without their consistent encouragement and company.

Thank you to my parents and to Peter, Andrew, and Celestine. Pets and good boys to my assistants, Duke and Milo.

And to my husband, Matt, thank you for your tireless support— your love, your patience, your uncomplicated faith in my abilities. Thank you for reading this book over and over and over again, and for listening to me rant and ramble and obsess about it these past five years. I think I would've done the same for you, but I'm glad that I don't have to prove it.